Also by Olivia McMahon:

Poetry
Domestic Verses (Koo Press)

LOVE AS A FOREIGN LANGUAGE

Olivia McMahon

For Brian

My thanks to Bill Kirton who read an early version and made helpful suggestions, to Magi Gibson and Esther Woolfson for pertinent comment, to Lindsey Fraser for her encouragement, to Tadg Farrington for keeping me on track, to Roisin Farrington for her fine judgment and to my many students over the years, turned here into a motley fictitious band.

Chapter 1

'So am I in love or in lust?' Tess, sitting in a sea of Sunday newspapers, reached for the bottle of wine. *Crisis in the Middle East, Threat of Famine in Africa, Job Losses in The Construction Industry* - the headlines jumped out at her and all she could think of was that article she'd read about love and lust. Why were women always trying to build love stories out of sexual relationships, the writer, one Belinda Chimey, wanted to know. Why could they never see romance for the lust that it was?

According to Belinda Chimey Tess was fabricating a love story out of her relationship with Fergus. She was being stupidly romantic not to see that what there was between them was lust, pure and simple.

'Lust is rarely pure and never simple, with apologies to Oscar Wilde' she proclaimed as she raised her glass. What did the words mean anyway - 'love' and 'lust'? She got to her feet, crossed over to the bookcase and staggered to the table with Volume 1 of the Oxford English Dictionary.

A small brown book, that had been hidden in behind, fell to the floor. She stared at it lying there, quietly giving off a sheen of dust. She had recognised it immediately: *English Without Tears*. Like a ghost suddenly in the room. She bent down to pick it up, forced herself to open it. The torn first page of Lesson 1, almost completely coming away from its spine, clinging on by only a few centimetres, crumpled, grey with the dirt of a Paris street, the paper a pale yellow now round the edges.

My tailor is rich. My tailor is not rich. Our doctor is good. Our doctor is not good. Your flowers are beautiful. Your flowers are not beautiful.

They'd emerged from the bookshop into the warm June sun and were standing on the kerb, shaded by a plane tree high above their heads, its leaves still a young tender green.

'My tailor eez reesh ....' he had started to read out, laughing down at the open book and raising his arm as if in warning - *Attention!* I am about to deny that affirmation.

English Without Tears. She closed the book carefully, shutting in the memory of more than thirty years ago, ran her fingers over the rough cover and put it down. She opened the dictionary and turned the pages, training the magnifying glass onto the tiny print.

love –1: *that disposition or state of feeling with regard to a person which manifests itself in solicitude for the welfare of the object and usually also in delight in his/her presence and desire for his/her approval; warm affection, attachment.*

And then coming in at number 6: *the animal instinct between the sexes and its gratification.*

lust on the other hand was: *desire, appetite, relish or inclination for something, especially sexual.*

Well, was it love or lust then that she felt for Fergus? Surely it was a mixture of the two, it was only people like Belinda Chimey who could keep words apart like that. Who was this Belinda Chimey, anyway? Who did she think she was to be so opinionated? Using words like *love* and *lust* and *romance* and *sexual relationships* like labels you'd stick on jam jars.

And sneering at people for creating stories. People needed to tell themselves stories. That's the only way you could get through life, by telling yourself stories. Stories were what helped you to make sense of things. Making it into a story made it all right, or mostly all right, most of the time.

So what story was she telling herself about her relationship with Fergus? Fergus with his sculpted face, and dark eyes looking at her as they sat opposite each other on the bus that last time in London. The story of two people who lived apart but who were passionate about each other, was that it? Like a piece of music in two part harmony, coming together, parting, then coming together again? Yes, that sounded okay. She was happy with that. As long as they really were passionate about each other. And sure of each other. Looking back at him on the bus that day she had been sure.

But she'd always been sure, right from the beginning, even when he'd been just the occasional blessing, like a sunny day in Aberdeen - the clandestine lover. The excitement in those early days of phoning from a public phone in the town.

'Fergus, I think it's going to be possible in two weeks' time, Saturday night and most of Sunday.'

'Fergus, I've got a conference in Brighton, lasting the whole week. I could stay with you and travel down each day.'

Or a phone call from him at work.

'Tess, I've just found out we're going to be doing a series of concerts in Scotland starting in September.'

Only why this silence now? Why hadn't he phoned? His own phone was broken and he refused to have a mobile so she couldn't ring him. But he could use a public phone, couldn't he? If he was really passionate about her she should be uppermost in his thoughts, he shouldn't be keeping her waiting like this.

'I feel like a teenager, hanging round the phone, waiting for it to ring,' her daughter, Annie - in her late twenties - had said to her last year, annoyed with herself for having got herself into that position of dependence. How about a woman approaching sixty waiting beside the phone? she had almost said but hadn't. Annie would have been shocked at her vulnerability – at *her* age! Annie was like her father, strong, self sufficient, knowing her own mind.

'I hate green, it's a horrible yukkie colour' Annie had announced one day when she was ten. And Bob had agreed. He hated green too. There was nothing to be said for green as a colour.

'But there are so many different shades of green,' Tess had tried to argue, envying them their certainty.

The phone rang. At last. She knocked over her glass as she jumped up to answer it. But no, it was Colonel Forbes from Finochty House up the road - the large Victorian mansion with the pretensions of a miniature Balmoral. What was he doing phoning Tess in her humble cottage? Only Tess of course was educated and an incomer, not quite 'one of them' but not 'one of the others' either. Did Tess play bridge by any chance? Very late notice but could she possibly help them out this evening? They were unexpectedly one player short.

She could see Colonel Forbes bent over the phone in his well-worn, baggy tweed suit, his face pink with the effort of making contact. No, she didn't play bridge and she wasn't free this evening anyway. She couldn't even be bothered to sound sorry. She couldn't imagine anything more boring and depressing than spending the evening in the company of Colonel Forbes and his wife. What a pity. It would have been a chance for her to meet Doctor Mackay and his wife, Brenda. Did she know Brenda? A charming lady, a solicitor working for *G. C. Reedie* (or did he say Greedie?) in town. And then the Van Meers, the nice Dutch people working in oil. She'd met them already, surely. And had Tess been to the Highland Games at Braemar this year? The queen had been there for a short while. She had passed just a few yards from where they were sitting - looking lovely.

She poured herself another glass of the wine and went out with it into the overgrown garden. It had been a lovely sunny day with hardly any wind and the air was still warm. Later there was going to be a sunset like a bag of over-ripe plums hurled at the sky.

This is all there is, this moment standing here. And I am happy.

Trotsky was lying at the foot of the laurel tree, his paws stretched out in front of him, watching intently as sparrows flitted in and out. She slipped off her shoes and walked towards him, feeling her bare soles brushing against the soft grass. Trotsky raised his head in expectation, began to purr loudly, his eyes closed in seeming ecstasy as she stroked him. What a pity she couldn't be in love with a cat.

A skein of geese were passing overhead, high in the sky, their busy cackle just audible. The first flock of the winter, arriving from Iceland.

This is all there is, this moment standing here, looking up at the geese. And I am happy.

Just audible above the clamour of the geese the sound of the phone ringing. She quickly drained her glass and rushed inside to answer it. It was her daughter, Annie.

'How are you, Mum?'

'Fine, dear.'

She woke the next morning with a headache, having finished off the bottle of Cote de Blaye watching two Bunuel films on video, one after the other, and not getting to bed till midnight. Kirsty had arrived in at eleven. Kirsty, more than a year ago now, wanting to escape from a lover she'd grown cold on, had taken refuge in Tess's cottage. The persistent lover had since left Aberdeen but Kirsty had stayed on and Tess was glad of her company – most of the time. But not now, going on about how difficult her mum was getting, just when Catherine Deneuve was gliding into the brothel in *Belle du Jour*.

'I don't know what I'm going to do about her. I'm worried sick she's going senile. She brought out this Madeira cake she'd baked which looked fantastic - an amazing shiny golden brown but the reason it looked so good was because she'd put salt in it instead of sugar - four ounces of salt. I'm starving. Would you like some toast? What's happened to the marmite? Is that Catherine Deneuve? What's she doing?'

The deer had got into the garden during the night she could see, as she stood at the kitchen window, waiting for the kettle to boil. Devastation among the Michaelmas Daisies. What she needed was a seven foot fence to keep them out. Where was Kirsty? It was time she was up. Tess poured water into the pot.

'Hurry up Kirsty or we'll be late,' she called up the stairs as she came to the end of her third mug of tea.

It would be another twenty minutes at least before Kirsty was ready. She'd time to put on her wellingtons and follow the path she'd made through the bracken from behind the cottage to the top of the hill. There was a large granite stone there that she often sat on to look out across at the dark wavy line of hills that ended in the knobbly top of Bennachie. There was an iron age fort on Bennachie and some days she'd sit imagining what it could have been like there more than 2000 years ago. If she stared for long enough warriors began to appear on the broken walls, their hair blowing frantically in the wind.

But this morning all she could think of was Fergus. It was nice being like two tunes in counterpoint, going their separate ways for a time, like streams running down a mountainside. But she needed to feel the inevitability of their coming together again in the end. She needed to feel sure that he was there for her, that she was at the centre of his world. Why hadn't he phoned? Had he started on a different tune with someone else?

The analogy with music became suddenly disagreeable. She jumped to her feet. She'd better be going down.

Chapter 2

Kirsty had better be ready if they were to arrive at the
Institute by nine. Kirsty was always particularly slow on a
Monday morning, loathe to get out of bed and face another
week of teaching French. Kirsty had wanted to be in films,
she'd never planned to stay in Aberdeen and end up teaching.

Tess, on the other hand, loved her job teaching English.
Or rather, she loved English, she loved language. She wasn't
so sure about the teaching, wasn't sure that what she did
could be called teaching, but language for her was elusive,
enriching, challenging, empowering. *English Without Tears* -
that day a passer by had picked the book up from the middle
of the road where it had landed and pushed it into her hands.
He'd seemed to think that it was important for Tess to have it.
The irony of the title had been acute at the time but English,
yes, over the years it had indeed been without tears, a source
of pleasure.

The hem of her skirt was soaking, she noticed, as she
stood by the car waiting for Kirsty to emerge from the house.
She started trying to squeeze the water out of it. What on
earth was Kirsty doing? It was almost half past eight. They
should have left ten minutes ago.

'Sorry, sorry.' Kirsty appeared at last, her shoulder length
blonde hair lifting slightly in the breeze, the collar of an
impeccably ironed white blouse sitting neatly underneath a
sleekly cut navy jacket, a short tight skirt turning into slim
smooth brown legs, strappy black shoes. Kirsty was what was
called petite. Tess, reasonably slim but several inches taller,
always felt oversized beside her. Of course Kirsty worked
hard on herself. She'd spent Saturday afternoon waxing her
legs, pulling out hairs from knee to ankle while Tess had
spent the time pulling out weeds and staring round at what
one kind friend had called her semi-wild garden. She hadn't
even got round to cleaning her finger nails properly she
noticed as she put the key into the ignition.

She caught sight of herself in the mirror. Grey green eyes
staring back at her. She should definitely have spent

yesterday evening henna-ing her hair instead of watching films and waiting for a phone call. It fell straight, curving in nicely at the jaw line, distracting attention – she hoped – from the cluster of little lines appearing either side of the mouth. But the roots in the mirror were definitely showing more grey than reddish brown. The trouble with henna on grey hair was that it tended to turn it orange so she'd soon be ending up with bright orange hair.

But at least with bright orange hair there was no risk of her becoming a member of the grey and beige brigade. There seemed to be an unwritten law some circles that, after the age of fifty, perhaps earlier, you had grey or white hair and you dressed entirely in different shades of beige - for example a light beige anorak with dark beige trousers and matching beige tights and shoes, or alternatively a dark beige anorak, light beige trousers and brown tights and brown shoes.

They set off down the bumpy track lined with beach trees already losing their leaves. A hen pheasant scuttled across the road in front of them.

'I'm supposed to be seeing Laurent at nine.' Tess glanced down at her watch. They'd just make it. But maybe Laurent wouldn't turn up. She'd arrive in her room to find a message on the answer machine. 'Tess, I am very sorry. I 'ave an important meeting zees morrning and I will not be able to assist your English lesson.'

Oh well, she'd have done her best and that would mean two hours of freedom before the new student at eleven. The other teachers at the Aberdeen Language Institute taught mainly small classes of about a dozen and the likelihood of all their students cancelling on the same day would have been pretty small. But Tess, because of her age and experience she assumed, did one-to-one teaching - or training as they called it - mostly to highly intelligent and motivated Frenchmen working in the oil industry and they were always cancelling.

'I won't be there this evening. I'll be at Stephen's,' said Kirsty as they turned out into the main road, recently converted into a dual carriageway and busy with cars flashing past on their way into the city. 'His wife's at a conference down in London. She's away till Thursday. So.'

So, indeed. Last time what-was-her-name was away, Kirsty told her she and Stephen had spent most of the time in his house in the bath with soap suds up to their chins, sipping pink champagne. If Fergus would only phone so she could fix up to go down to London next weekend she'd turn up with a bottle of pink champagne.

'Fergus, let's sit in the bath with soapsuds up to our chins,' she'd say. Or maybe she wouldn't. All right for Kirsty in her early thirties.

'While you're with Stephen, Kirsty, you could try and talk him into getting more students for the Institute.' Stephen was responsible for running the Institute. 'He could go off round France advertising the wonderful courses we offer and you could go with him. We badly need more students signing up for intensive courses, like that batch of teachers that came over last Easter for a whole fortnight.'

They had been a nightmare but the money had been good. Kirsty's job was much more secure than hers. There was no shortage of people in Aberdeen wanting to learn French whereas Tess's student numbers were dwindling. Only six of them now including the new student starting today. And then the three hours on a Wednesday afternoon at the university. Just about enough to live on. Only just. Not enough to go paying someone to put up seven foot fences for her to keep the deer out.

Maybe what she should be doing was running lucrative courses from her cottage. No, that was ridiculous, Kineldie was much too small, even if she did up the outhouses. Unless she limited it to one-to-one courses - plentiful opportunities there if what one was in pursuit of was lust: *Pillow talk* as a variety of English for Special Purposes.

'That's not a bad idea,' said Kirsty. Was she reading her thoughts? 'It would be fantastic to be in France with Stephen, advertising Aberdeen as the best place in Britain to learn English. Much better for the French to come here than to the south coast of England with all those drunken louts, and cafes selling nothing but hamburgers and chips, and shops always telling you they're closed.'

Kirsty seemed blind to the fact that Aberdeen was a bit like that too but then she was prejudiced. Kirsty was an Aberdonian by birth and proud of it.

'And look at this beautiful countryside.' There Tess had to agree. Five miles from the centre of Aberdeen and still open fields and forest and hardly a house. 'And all the castles we have, full of ghosts. And then the whisky distilleries.'

'Oops!' A white car coming towards them on the last roundabout into the city, just a tad faster than Tess had bargained for. She accelerated away from it and glanced across at Kirsty but Kirsty had got out her handbag mirror and was checking her lipstick in it. Yet again Tess had forgotten to put any lipstick on. Not much point anyway as always, within an hour of putting it on, it disappeared without trace. Some one had once said to her 'Tess, other women have make up. You have bone structure.' But now that she was the age she was … and she'd had plenty of time this morning. She could have made an effort to brighten her face up. Just a touch of lipstick, not too much. She'd tried once years ago putting lipstick on the way Kirsty did and Annie had told her she looked as if she'd been eating cherry jam with a wooden spoon. Maybe at the traffic lights coming up there'd be time.

'I hate Monday mornings, three classes one after the other,' said Kirsty, rolling up her lipstick and getting out her comb.

The traffic lights were green. No lipstick today. She negotiated the roundabout by the River Dee - the tide was in - and came back on her tracks to outside the large nineteenth century house that was the Language Institute. Only one minute after nine. Not bad.

10

Chapter 3

She'd forgotten the car clock was five minutes slow. She was late. She thought of Mr Micawber, only with her it was time. Five minutes before nine o'clock, result happiness. Five minutes after nine o'clock, result misery, humiliation, chaos. But why? Why couldn't she just walk up the stairs with dignity and sail along the corridor to her room as befitted an older woman, instead of scrabbling like this, pulling her hat off as she went and unbuttoning her coat?

At the top of the stairs she met Maggie, looking as always elegant and immaculate enough for a wedding photo - bright pink jacket, cream blouse, skilfully knotted silk scarf.

'Hi,' panted Tess, tripping over her coat that she'd now managed to take off. And a moment later a breathless Good Morning to Laurent.

Name: Laurent Dupont
Age: 29
Nationality: French
Profession: oil engineer
+++: youth, intelligence, good humour, nice smile
---: spots, frizzy hair, skinny
Interests: cinema, fishing, girls (?)
Clothes: dark green shirt, nice tie with tulips on it
Lesson Plan: non-existent
What done last time: can't remember

He was already installed at his table, eager and expectant, pen in hand, clean sheet of paper in front of him. What was she going to do with him to fill it and the hour? She looked across at her desk with the mess of Friday afternoon still strewn over it.

'So!' she began, gathering up a half written letter and an eyebrow tweezers and stuffing them into a drawer and transferring the half drunk mug of coffee, already with a scum forming on it, to the windowsill. If you said 'So' briskly enough it gave the impression you knew what you were doing, or so she hoped.

He had on again this morning his very pretty tie - rows of little red tulips on a dark blue background - and his neat dark green short-sleeved shirt.

'So,' she repeated, 'if you *cast your mind back* to last week .... '

She used the phrase deliberately. Laurent, though his English was good, was probably unfamiliar with the word *cast* which was commonly used only in expressions like this. Otherwise it was rare but it would be relevant for him whenever he gave a presentation. A useful phrase to start the lesson off with, something for him to note down at the top of his blank sheet.

But no, he knew the word. He did? Yes, he used it in fishing. Oh yes, fishing. He'd gone fishing at the weekend and caught "*two troot.*"

'Trout,' she corrected. 'It's pronounced *trout* not *troot*. French people make the mistake of pronouncing it as *troot* because in French *ou* is pronounced as *oo*. He looked at her and hesitated.

'Well, the men I am fishing with pronounce it *troot.* '

Ah, yes, of course, this was Scotland. Well, the thing was that words in English which had *ou* in them like *house* and *out* and *trout* in Scots were pronounced with a pure vowel *oo*.

'But in Standard Southern English pronunciation,' she continued, the sound begins as an *a* with wide open mouth and then it changes to *oo* with loosely rounded lips. Watch me: *aaaoo, aaaoo.* Maybe this wasn't the most flattering of images. She closed her mouth.

'You try,' she said. Mouth a little on the small side, thin lips but neat teeth and a clean tongue. Pillow talk, yes. But would she really want to find herself in bed with Laurent? Would he want to find himself in bed with her? No, the idea was ludicrous. She looked at her watch. Fergus should be up by now and on his way to buy milk for his breakfast. Maybe he'd try to phone her from the public phone on the corner.

'Yes, very good. With a pronunciation like that you could pass for an Englishman. During the Second World War, - I've been told,' she added, 'they caught spies by creeping up behind them and jabbing them in the back. If they said *aaaoo* they were English. If they said *aieeee* they were French. If they said *aaaachhhhh* they were German.' Or even Scottish? How many instances had there been in the war of Scots being arrested on suspicion of being German spies?

'Anyway, if you cast your mind back, last week I explained different ways of talking about the future in English and the differences between them. Today we will start by revising this. First the use of the present tense for planned future activities. For example: *At the weekend I am flying to London.'*

Why did she have to choose that as an example? She looked across at Laurent but he was looking out of the window at the sky.

'Aberdeen is in the back of be'ind but you 'ave wonderful skies here,' he said. It was true. For a moment they admired in silence the creamy pink clouds - whipped whites of egg mixed up with a smear of raspberry jam. The sea streaked with pewter. A fifteen mile ribbon of golden sand and away in the distance the smoke of the power station just outside Peterhead.

'What are you doing this evening?' she asked, turning round. He looked surprised. 'Just to practice using the present tense for planned future actions,' she said quickly. 'For example: you could say *This evening I am going to the cinema with my girl friend*'. (Did he have a girl friend?). Or *This evening I am going to the gym.*

'I am repairing the door in my flat. It is doing a noise.'

'*Making* a noise. In English you *make* a noise. Your door - it is creaking? It is squeaking? Open that door and tell me what noise it is making.'

The doors in the Language Institute were old and panelled and made of pitch pine and all in need of oiling. Outside, as he opened the door, she caught a glimpse of Pete on his way to the coffee room.

'Yes, that's right, Laurent. It creaks when you open it. Would you like a cup of coffee?'.

No, if she didn't mind he'd rather leave now and get to his office and start his day. (Wasn't his English lesson the start to his day?). He slipped on his jacket and said goodbye politely. Or was it with relief?

Pete was standing in the coffee room in his flowery tie and bottle green corduroys talking to Franck who was from Stuttgart and taught German. Pete, who, like Tess, taught English as a Foreign Language, was explaining his philosophy of language learning, the importance of involving learners personally, getting them to talk about their feelings and experiences.

'But the grammar,' Franck kept saying, 'in German language is very important the grammar.'

It was the first time Tess had seen Franck in the coffee room and the first time she'd heard more than a few words out of him, though he'd been teaching at the Institute for nearly two years now. He usually just came in, gave his classes and then disappeared. Kirsty called him Mr Gutbye because that is the only thing she'd ever heard him say.

'How was your weekend, Tess?' Pete asked, meaning, what was Kirsty doing at the weekend, did she go out on Saturday evening, and who did she go with? Pete's wife had left him nearly two years ago and everybody had felt very sorry for him. But a few months ago, all the feelings he had previously lavished on his wife and that had been dammed up since her departure suddenly found a new outlet. Pete fell madly, passionately, foolishly in love with Kirsty. Whenever she was around he would just stand there gazing at her - which was why Kirsty tried to be around as little as possible when Pete was there.

'It was okay,' she said. 'Kirsty and I just stayed in all Saturday, gardening, watching videos, doing this and that.' There now, it would be nice for him to hear that.

'How about you?'

Pete had bought himself a computer and had spent the weekend installing it or trying to. It was hard to imagine a computer in Pete's little fisherman's cottage in Footdee among the Oriental rugs and the harpsichord painted dark green that he'd made himself, and the pillar box red wooden floorboards.

'I'm wondering if Kirsty would be able to help me with it.'

Oh yes? Kirsty, it was true, was amazingly expert in such matters but would she want to spend an evening with Pete gazing at her as she booted and re-booted his hard disc or whatever?

'I'd better be getting back. I still haven't thought out what I'm going to be doing with my class at the university for the next ten Wednesday afternoons,' said Tess, sensing Pete was about to embark on a detailed description of why he hadn't managed to get the computer working himself. Besides she'd better check her face out before the new student at eleven.

Back in her room she looked along the shelves of books for titles concerned with teaching writing skills - *Study Writing*; *Report and Essay Writing*; *Academic Writing Skills*; *Good Writing Practice*; *The Written Word*. She found a comb and lipstick in the bottom of her handbag, picked up the mirror she usually kept face down on the bookshelf, propped it up against *The Written Word* and looked at herself. Was that another wrinkle? She remembered her first sighting of a wrinkle just after Annie was born, looking in the bathroom mirror one morning with the sun streaming in. A faint black line between her eyebrows. How did that get there? She'd dampened a finger and tried to rub it out.

She looked to see which department of the oil company the new student who was due at eleven was in. The Exploration Department. A geophysicist - employed to tell the drillers where to drill for oil. Down, down under the sea, kilometres into the earth's crust, down through the seventy million year old Cretaceous, through the Jurassic to the 180 million year old Triassic the drillers drilled until they found what the geophysicists and geologists had hopefully predicted they would find - an oil field. A lot of the time they drilled and drilled and found nothing. Not even a trickle of oil. Maybe it was just a hundred metres away but in which direction?

It wasn't yet eleven. She'd try phoning Fergus in case they'd fixed the phone. Still the 'number unobtainable' sound. She imagined him there by the window, looking out on the people crossing the square, practising his cello, the phone perched on the wonky bookcase in the corner. Not thinking of her.

But where was the new student? It was now ten past eleven. She rang his secretary. Oh, hadn't Thierry let her know? There had been an important meeting at ten thirty he'd been obliged to attend.

'Is he free tomorrow at eleven? Tess enquired, trying to sound not too concerned. She happened to have a slot then - a cancellation. She could just fit him in. She felt like an expensive hairdresser whose business was going down the tubes trying to give the impression they were run off their feet. Yes, eleven tomorrow should be all right. She picked up a pen, turned the page of her green page-a-day desk diary to Tuesday and wrote in *Thierry 11-12* on a sheet otherwise blank except for *Dominique 9 - 10*.

She got out the Personal Details form she always gave to new students and put it under her desk diary so that it would be to hand in the morning. She looked out of the window. The sky was no longer a creamy raspberry, it had turned grey and the sea was completely blotted out. But it wasn't raining. She'd have a cup of coffee, read the newspaper and then go back to the cottage and attack the garden.

As she got into her car she noticed the vacant space where Stephen's car had been. He and Kirsty were already speeding towards bliss. Bliss. That was a nicer word than lust. Did Pete suspect anything? Pete would be much better for Kirsty than Stephen. Maybe Tess should help Pete to win Kirsty, tell him not to keep staring at her, tell him to get rid of his 1970s shirts.

The phone was ringing as she opened the door to the cottage. 'Hi, Tess.' Her heart leapt. Her favourite sounds: the sea retreating over a pebbled shore, a distant church clock striking the hour, and Fergus's voice. She felt a rush of immense tenderness for him. There was no doubt about it, this was love, she couldn't wait to be on that plane down to London next Friday evening. Up into the sky and the start of the journey south to London, 400 miles away, down the coast to Dundee and the bridges over the Tay, and then a veering westwards and inland, down over the sprawling green hills and ridges of the Lake District, through the fug of Manchester and Birmingham to London - toy town of redbrick houses and patchwork gardens, and cars whizzing along like trains on a model railway. And Fergus at the barrier with the collar of his jacket turned up, watching her as she got nearer and nearer to him. They would spend two whole nights and days together.

But he had exciting news for her. He'd been asked to go on a tour of Eastern Europe and Russia as part of a string quartet. The cellist who would normally have gone had broken his finger. They'd be away for nearly six months!

'I can't believe my luck. We'll be starting out in Prague and a few other places in Czechoslovakia or whatever it's called now, and then we go to Bratislava and then Hungary and lots of places with unpronounceable names. And we'll be playing quite a lot of Bartok - I don't know how I'm going to cope with that. But it's exciting, isn't it?'

'Yes, it's wonderful,' she said, feeling like someone who'd returned home to find their house burned down.

'What about me?' was what she was screaming to herself. 'When am I going to see you?' Trotsky had joined her at the phone, purring noisily and brushing up against her cheek. She pushed him away.

'I'm sorry I don't know if it's going to be possible to meet up before I go. We're frantically busy rehearsing. We're leaving next week and we still haven't got our visas fixed up - luckily I got my passport renewed last year, thanks to you. I don't know if it would be worth you coming down this Saturday … But maybe you could come out Christmas time - to St Petersburg, or Bucharest or wherever it is we'll be? But I'll phone you again. And I'll phone you when I'm there whenever I can.'

'That will be nice.' She'd never known anyone so

incompetent with a phone as Fergus.

If it was love she felt for Fergus she ought to be glad for him. **Love** - *that disposition or state of feeling with regard to a person which manifests itself in solicitude for the welfare of the object* He'd been out of work for ages, busking outside Chancery Lane tube station in his old Oxfam jacket, men in grey suits throwing him coins as they hurried past. And he wasn't having any success with the film music he was writing either. This was a great opportunity for him. If she loved him she ought to be glad.

But she just felt anger that he could go off like that. He hadn't even sounded all that concerned that he wouldn't be seeing her for six months. He'd tried to put regret into his voice but what had come across was mainly excitement and happiness. What sort of passionate relationship was this? No, it wasn't love she felt for him. He didn't deserve love. What she was beginning to feel was more akin to hate. The story was turning into something nasty. *Woman stabs lover for desertion.*

She went out into the garden and started tearing at the long grass around the water butt. That was the end of that story. That was the end of Fergus and whatever there had been between them. Fergus was just a source of pain interspersed with brief - too brief - spells of pleasure. What she needed was love, a love she could depend on.

The grass was becoming smeared with her blood. She stared at the bright beads oozing from her finger. 'You should have worn gardening gloves,' she could hear her ex-husband Bob saying. She caught hold of another tuft of grass and yanked it out.

Chapter 4

She woke up feeling calmer. It was mean and unreasonable of her to be so angry with Fergus. This was probably the end of the road for them but she could at least go down to London on Saturday after all, just for a final goodbye and to wish him well.

'Goodbye,' she would say and give him a long hug and a last wave and then he would be out of her life. She wouldn't tell him this at the time but she would write it in a letter. 'Dear Fergus, it is clear that we do not mean enough to each other to keep this relationship going ....'.

Driving in to work, she tried to focus her mind on what she would do with Dominique whom she was seeing at nine. Not that it needed much planning. Dominique was a top executive, a whizz kid, a product of the Ecole Polytechnique, the highest educational institute in France. If you got in there you were made for life, all the top jobs were destined to be yours.

She was working through a book with him called *Making Your Mark at Meetings: what to say and how to say it.* It was all about how to agree, disagree, make suggestions, offer compromises in English. How to say things like 'I agree with a lot of what you have to say but I can't help feeling you mightn't be altogether right when you suggest ..... '.

'I just say 'Rubbish' one Frenchman had told her once. He had no time for what he thought of as typical British hypocrisy. He hated his boss's indirect way of criticising him - 'I thought your report was quite good but maybe you could have...'. Why couldn't he just say 'Your work is shit'?

On the phone to Fergus yesterday evening could she possibly have come out with something like 'I am very happy for you but do you not think that ...?' 'Perhaps I could make a suggestion ....'.

'It's all the same useful to study these expressions,' she'd tried to convince the Frenchman. It was to learn how to talk in meetings that he'd been sent to her by his boss. 'Then you'll know that *talking at cross purposes* has nothing to do with being cross, and saying *he backed them up* is different from *he got their backs up.*'

Did she make her point? Maybe, but he still never came back.

No problem with Dominique on that score. He was bent on being a match for any of the British as regards his language. His ambition was 'not to be taken for a forEIGner.' 'A what?' she'd asked. Today they were due to practise the language used for expressing degrees of importance. *It is essential/vital/desirable/preferable that you be there* etc.

'It is essential/vital/desirable/preferable that I see you, Fergus, before you go away,' she found herself saying as she got closer to Aberdeen. And then suddenly she was angry for being so obsessed.

'It is completely unnecessary/not at all desirable that I see you before you go away,' she began to shout as she came to a stop at the lights. The man in the car next to hers looked across. It wasn't often men spared her a glance these days. Maybe she should behave in this manner more often, become mad as a bicycle, become known as crazy Tess. She gave him a little wave as the lights turned to green and she drove away.

A lorry had broken down at the roundabout before the Institute and she was ten minutes late as she rushed up the stairs to her room. Dominique was never late, he arrived always on the dot of nine.

> *Name: Dominique Truffaut*
> *Age: well-preserved early 40's, helped by curl on forehead*
> *Position: something very important*
> *Clothes: Armani suits, silly ties*
> *+++: curl on forehead, possibly coloured glasses*
> *---: self-seeking, self-centred, self-important*
> *Lesson Plan: helping him to make a fool of himself at meetings*

He was, as she predicted, there waiting for her, impeccably

dressed as usual in what was probably an Armani suit in a light grey. Light blue shirt and a dark blue tie with a motif of white swans across it. The previous week it had been rows of little golfers all swinging their clubs at the same angle. She was glad he'd chosen his swan tie this morning.

He began by asking her about something that was preoccupying him - a stylistic question. He really had a very sweet boyish face all the same and today there was a tendril of hair on his forehead (was this deliberate?) and glasses with deep turquoise frames.

'Because in France we have a rule - never use the same word twice. We must find synonyms. But here they are saying *at the end of the day* all the time.'

He was just back from a meeting in Cambridge. He'd been very impressed by their wide vocabulary there. And also by their pronunciation - you could hear the ends of their words

'So we know if it is one problem or two problem'

'Problemsss, Dominique. Two problemsss.'

He looked surprised. Was that not what he had said? He continued.

'And they had a very educated vocabulary. For example one of the lecturers had used the word *wade*. 'What is *wade*?' I asked the Texan sitting next to me. He didn't know half the words they were using either. He explained me *wade* meant *walk*. Was *wade* a formal word for *walk*?'

'The lecturer probably said 'when we've waded through all this stuff' or something like that. Not formal at all, in fact very informal and just a bit more picturesque than 'when we've got through all this stuff.' The thing about English is you mix the formal and the informal. This is what is known as introducing a light touch. The French think: 'This is a formal lecture so I must use formal language.' It's like the French way of dressing - unadventurous. Even when you break the rules you all break them in the same way. For example, somebody told me there is a fashion in France at the moment for turning up to big weddings in casual clothes. But you will all wear the same sort of casual clothes - designer jeans carefully pressed and immaculate designer t shirts on top, that sort of thing.'

She hadn't realised she was in such a bad mood this morning. It was Fergus's fault. Maybe she could practise her Irish accent, to take her mind off things. Dominique was stirring in his seat, opening his mouth to reply but she cut in before he could begin.

'We'd betterr getH down to *Making Yourr Marrk AtH Meetings: whatH to say and how to say itH,'* she said. 'We gotH as farr as page 72, oi tink.'

"Yes, I hope we could finish the book before I leave,' he said.

He was leaving? This meant that he'd cancel out the new arrival. The numbers would remain at six.

'Oi'll be sorry to lose you,' she said, meaning it.

He was going back to France to work - just outside Paris.

'Near Chateau Fort,' he said, looking at her and pausing.

Chateau Fort? Oh yes, she'd told him once about how she used to drive out there for lunch. No more, but he'd remembered. Did they speculate about her among themselves? She sometimes encouraged this, dropping little hints here and there, about her life in France in the years just after she'd stopped being a student. Maybe to them she was someone quite different from the person she felt herself to be, someone they had invented.

Though the reality had been romantic enough, even at the time. Chateau Fort and a little restaurant crowded and noisy with French people having lunch in their hour - or two - off from work. Marc and herself would arrive late after the drive out from Paris at the end of her morning's teaching. They always chose to sit outside on the terrace. A woman with a kindly face and a flowery pinafore wrapped round her stocky figure, the same woman always, would limp towards them. (Was she lame? arthritic? They never did find out, indeed weren't particularly curious, absorbed as they were in each other. She was just 'the woman with the limp'). She would recite the menu.

'Eh bien, nous avons des escalopes avec purée de

pommes de terre, poulet roti, truites aux amandes ...'. And always the same question put as she looked at them with what seemed to them to be extreme tenderness.

'Vous voulez les légumes avec?' Do you want the vegetables served at the same time?

No need to give these students these details, let them invent their own. What passions had she lived through? What passion was still being reined in behind that ladylike exterior - long smooth grey skirt, black jumper? This morning she had selected to wear her wine coloured hat to give herself an air. She'd got out of her car with it pulled down over one eye, imagining herself looking like Vali in *The Third Man*. Maggie, arriving at the same time, had started to say something and then stopped. Tess had pressed her to continue, had had to drag it out of her.

'Well, you look a teeny weeny bit like Miss Marple,' Maggie finally admitted. 'I think it's just that she's the only other person I've seen wearing a hat like that,' she added quickly, seeing the expression on Tess's face.

'Yes, well, let's try to do as much as possible of the book today,' she said briskly, reverting to her normal accent. *'It's essential/vital/desirable/preferable that you be here.* It sure is.

'Now think of something else that is essential.'

It is essential that I be nice to this man, she said to herself as she waited for him to come up with a sentence. It is essential that I find somebody with whom I can have a loving, lustful, stable, reliable relationship.

'It is essential that we find oil,' he said at last.

'It is indeed,' she agreed. What would she do for a job if all the oil companies left Aberdeen?

'So, I'll see you next Tuesday,' she said ten minutes later as they got to the end of the section and he started gathering up his papers. Oh no, he couldn't manage Tuesday. He suggested the Thursday instead, at the same time, nine o'clock.

'Is that a suitable time for you?' he asked her.

'Yes, that's convenient,' she replied. All times were

convenient, practically.

What was the difference between *convenient* and *suitable*? Was *suitable* wrong? Should he have said *convenient*?

'No, both are equally good,' she told him, which was probably not the case but it was near enough to the truth. She closed the door behind him. She would phone Fergus straight away and tell him she was coming down this weekend. Why should she torment herself like this? Even if he was busy rehearsing during the day they could still have the nights together. Before they said goodbye for ever.

She picked up the phone and dialled his number. It rang and rang. Ten o'clock on a Tuesday morning. What could he be doing out on a Tuesday morning? But of course this Tuesday was different, he was busy, preoccupied, buoyant, rushing round fixing up his visas. What would be the point of her being there at the weekend, struggling to look cheerful? She put the phone down and picked up the Personal Details form destined for the new student and started to fill it in.

Name: Thierry Fouchard
Age: indeterminate (attractive, older man)
Nationality: French with a Spanish or maybe Polish mother
Occupation: geophysicist
Marital Status: free as air, still looking for true love/lust
Hobbies/Interests: capacity for falling in love/lust totally and unconditionally with Tess McGuire
Level of English: poor, in need of intensive tuition

Chapter 5

A knock on the door. 'Come in,' she called and there he was. Tall, lean, a bright smile on an intelligent face, lively brown eyes and his clothes a long way away from the Armani suit. Not only was he in a pullover but she noticed immediately a little hole on the left hand side. He shook her hand vigorously

'Thierry Fouchard. Good Morning. I hope you will help me do progresses in English. Only one thing, I do not want to lose my French accent.'

There is little fear of that, Tess thought to herself. She had rarely heard such a robust one. Her low spirits were lifting already. How long had he been in Aberdeen, was this his first time in Scotland? And was he married, was his wife here, and children? She was used to firing off questions. Annie had interrupted her once when they were talking to people on a train. 'Mum!' she had protested. But here it was part of her job to ask questions.

'I have no wife. I am a widower.' He had the word ready like his money for the bus. He was obviously used to answering this question.

'Oh, I'm sorry,' she said politely. But this was maybe better than someone who had never loved at all. Of course it was sad but, at the same time, it was undeniably attractive to imagine him as a solitary male with no one to mend the little hole in his pullover.

'And I have a son who has nineteen years and a daughter who has sixteen year.' He was used to giving that information too. 'They are in France with their aunt.'

In Paris? Let it be Paris. No, not in Paris, in Versailles. Oh well, Versailles, it could have been worse, it could have been one of those towns in the north of France, like Mauberge or Sotteville. Did she know Versailles? She'd been on a very disagreeable visit to Versailles once with Bob, and Annie aged six - queuing for the lavatory, queuing to get a drink with the temperature at 80 degrees, queuing to get in to the palace. And then standing in a great crowd of Italians, Americans, Spaniards, Japanese, listening to a French guide intoning. They'd all returned home with nits.

'Yes, the gardens were wonderful,' she said.

'Ah, le parc de Versailles. But it is not so beautiful than your parks here.' It was not often she heard such praise on the lips of a Frenchman. She gave him a warm smile. He has nice hands, she thought, very nice hands. But then so has Fergus. Fergus's hands on the wheel of the car as they drove towards a night together.

'It's true, public gardens in Britain are much more informal than in France,' she said. Was he interested in visiting gardens? There were lots of beautiful gardens attached to big houses here in the North East of Scotland but soon they'd all be closed for the winter. But there were the parks. She hesitated. Should she offer to show him round Seaton Park - Aberdeen's wildest park - one weekend? Next weekend, for example? They would walk along the path beside the bank of the River Don that ran through the park, looking up at the tall beech trees, if they were lucky catching sight of a heron.

No, she should take a hold of herself. An invitation at this point - she'd only known him ten minutes - would smack of desperation. Instead, would he like a cup of coffee? Together they made their way to the coffee room. Pete was there, gulping down a large glass of water.

'This is Pete, he's teaching ten Japanese businessmen this week,' said Tess, proud of Pete. Thierry looked round. The Japanese tended to be small, but not that small, where were they?

'I've sent them away,' said Pete. 'I've told them to go out and walk around the town for half an hour and then come back and talk about what happened to them.'

'And that is what you call teaching?' asked Thierry.

That sounded like a boring way of looking at it. She hoped he wasn't going to turn out to be what her mother-in-law used to call 'stuffy'.

'All the same, we'd better get back or he'll be saying the same about me,' thought Tess. 'Is this what you call teaching, standing around in the coffee room making conversation?'

26

'We'd better get back. I want to give you a test, to see what your level of English is,' said Tess, avoiding looking at Pete. Pete didn't approve of tests.

They walked side by side back down the corridor to her room, Tess enjoying the way her step matched his. She took a copy of the test out of the filing cabinet and handed it to him. He shook his head. He hadn't expected this. She suddenly had an image of Annie aged nine, recalcitrant in front of her homework, succeeded by an image of a woman in high boots with bouncy blond hair and a short red leather skirt brandishing a whip.

She explained what he had to do. The first part was a listening activity. You had to decide which sentences on the test paper matched the sentences read out on a tape. *Would you say that a man who was interested in girls/gulls was a bird-watcher? It's my birthday/bathday today* and such like. One hundred items.

'Underline the word you think you hear,' said Tess. The tape took about ten minutes. How old was he? Late 50s? About the same age as herself. She'd forgotten to give him the Personal Details form to fill in. The one she'd filled in herself was protruding from underneath her desk diary. Was he really free as air, looking for true love/lust?

'And now a grammar test,' she said as the tape came to the end of the hundredth item - *The play's about three wishes/witches.*

The grammar test consisted in choosing between three possibilities, only one of which was correct. For example *I have not seen them a) for a long time b) since a long time c) since long.* Some of the students got 90% on this test. But no one had been known to get 100%. You had to be a native speaker for that. They all made mistakes with things like *I think it's hardly worth it, a) don't I? b) is it? c) isn't it?*

She marked the listening test while his shoulders were hunched over the grammar. Wavy grey hair curling up at the ends, quite thin on top. He looked up suddenly and their eyes met and her heart inside her jumper gave a lurch. She looked down at the listening test and began to count up the number he'd got wrong. Thirty five, including *gulls/girls* and *birthday/bathday*. About average. That should mean that she would be sure of regular attendance, though it didn't always follow. Often it was the worst who never found time to come. His score on the grammar test looked as if it would be even lower. She watched him as he struggled with the complexities of choosing between *I enjoy to do/doing/do English.*

He finished at last.

'I am a very, very stupid,' he said as he handed over the test. He watched her marking it, exclaiming over every cross.

'What does the cross mean? It mean I am good?'

'No, bad. A cross in English means you've got it wrong.' In French a cross against what a student had done just meant that the teacher had seen it.

'Oh. I am how you say - dreadful? I am a dreadful pupil.'

He had indeed got nearly half of them wrong.

'Good,' she thought. 'We'll do a review of the English tense system, beginning with the present,' she announced.

The present had suddenly begun to have a buzz about it. She might even start in a while to be glad that Fergus was going to be away for six months. Or for ever - would she care if she never saw him again? When would Thierry be free for his first lesson? Tomorrow? No, not tomorrow, but the next day, Thursday. Would Thursday be all right? Yes, Thursday would be fine.

'But just one thing. I am getting up very early in the morning.' He wanted to start at eight a.m. That way he could be at work for just after nine. She saw the rationale of this from his point of view. And for this man she was beginning to feel that she wouldn't mind jumping out of bed at seven (or jumping into bed either?) She saw herself driving in to the Institute, the darkness lifting from the fields, and the cattle just becoming visible through the early morning mist, to find him there waiting for her.

'Yes, eight o'clock will be okay,' she said.

.

Chapter 6

She made her way to the coffee room. Pete was still by the window, looking out at the sea gulls on the roof opposite.

'Pete, would you like to come to lunch with me and Kirsty on Saturday?' She thought he was going to fling his arms around her, but then he remembered. This coming Saturday he was going down to St. Andrews to see his daughter who'd just started at university there.

'She hasn't settled down at all. She's really miserable. The place is full of Ra, Ra people from England. I'd warned her it would be like that.'

Maggie arrived and started reassuring Pete that it was early days and she'd make friends and get herself a boyfriend and everything would be all right. Tess made her way back down the corridor to get her coat. Would she try Fergus again? No.

As she left the Institute later Quentin was standing by his car. Quentin did a bit of Spanish teaching at the Institute but he was also its owner, though he left all the administration to Stephen. His mother had been a clairvoyant who late in life had remarried some rich financier. And then they'd both died in an air crash over Cyprus and Quentin had inherited everything.

He was trying to rub off the mess some careless seagull had made on the bonnet of his car. The best thing one popular travel writer found to say about Aberdeen was that there were seagulls in the streets. But then he didn't own a car in the city.

'It's incredibly corrosive this stuff.'

Tess knew, but her car was so old it hardly mattered.

'I'm on my way to Emilio's, I just stopped by to drop in some books. Do you fancy coming along?'

Why not? She didn't really need to get back to Kineldie that early. She got into Quentin's car.

The Tapas bar was surprisingly crowded for a Tuesday, mostly students. Emilio was doing well. He'd only started doing tapas about a month ago. In the evenings they had paella on the menu and things with squid, and upstairs there was salsa dancing, run by somebody else. Lunchtime was self-service. Tess helped herself to some Spanish omelette, and would she have a glass of wine? Why not? It wasn't every day she had lunch at Emilio's. They squeezed into a table next to the kitchen.

'We're trying to buy the upstairs room and turn it into more restaurant,' said Quentin.

Tess liked the *we*. This was Quentin's restaurant. It was exclusively Quentin's money that had gone into it. Emilio had nothing. He'd come to Aberdeen from Valencia as a waiter in the French restaurant.

'Emilio certainly knows how to make churros.'

Quentin dunked a third one into a large cup of foaming chocolate. An odd thing to be eating for lunch but it was really his breakfast, he explained. Emilio didn't get back from the restaurant till after midnight and then they ate and went to bed about three and up about eleven.

'Hi Tess. Everything okay? Is good?' Emilio's face emerged from behind the kitchen door, dark, smiling.

'Is very good,' said Tess, putting another forkful of the omelette into her mouth and taking a gulp of wine.

'Stephen wants me to run this intensive course next week, starting at *nine* every day - can you imagine? I've told him to find someone else,' said Quentin. Quentin, as owner of the Language Institute, could afford to say No to Stephen.

'He's putting on weight,' thought Tess as he started into his fourth churro.

'I wish *I* had an intensive course coming up,' she said.

A shout from across the room.

'Quentin! I'd been going to come to see you.' A plump young woman with dark brown hair framing her face in art nouveau curves.

'This is Janet. Janet, this is Tess.' Janet beamed briefly at Tess. Lots of white teeth.

'Quentin, any chance of a few hours teaching foreigners English while I'm looking for a proper job? I know this Frenchman who says he comes to the Institute every week to learn English. He says he has one-to-one lessons. I did a bit of that sort of thing when I was in Italy and I wouldn't mind doing it again. I need the money.'

'You'd have to ask Stephen. He's in charge.'

Not a proper job. She's talking about the job I've been doing all my working life, thought Tess.

'Or Tess would have an idea. She teaches English as a Foreign Language.'

'Oh do you? Oh, you're probably Laurent's teacher.' Janet turned to give Tess her full attention. And what had Laurent actually said to her? 'There's this old woman - I'm sure you could do it better ….. '.

'I don't think there's any chance,' said Tess, a trifle on the brisk side, pouring herself a glass of water and wishing now she hadn't had the wine. One glass was always too much and not enough. 'There are three of us there already teaching EFL and there isn't really enough work for us as it is. What are your qualifications?' Hah.

'Well …. '

'Tess, I'd better be going,' said Quentin.

'Me too,' Tess said, finishing off her water.

'Anyway, you could always call in at the Institute and give Stephen your name,' said Quentin as they said goodbye to Janet. Mr Nice Guy.

They stood outside in Golden Square - Aberdeen's only square, practically. Pity about all the cars crammed into it around the marble statue of the fifth and last Duke of Gordon (1770-1836), looking very noble staring into the distance.

'Would you like a lift, Tess? I'm going back to the Institute.'

'No, I think I'd like to walk,' said Tess.

The Institute was only quarter of an hour away, along the stretch of Union St. where Annie aged eight had done cartwheels one evening, and into Market Street, down past the harbour and the boat for Orkney and Shetland and the Russian boat in from Marmansk, and the fish market.

Union Street, inspired by Edinburgh's Princes Street, built to celebrate the union of the two crowns of Scotland and

England in 1800. Two straight miles of grey granite. The day had changed. The sun had come out, giving a sparkle to the stone. It was the sort of day when it was almost possible to believe in the description of Aberdeen as *the silver city by the golden sands*. Almost but Tess found the uniform greyness, even on the brightest of days, depressing..

The *golden sands* were real enough though. That was an idea. She'd pick up her car and go for a walk along by the beach before going back to Kineldie. A walk from the River Dee to the River Don, at the place where each of them came out into the sea. Four miles there and back of brisk walking. It wasn't yet two. She'd still be out of Aberdeen well before four, missing the commuter traffic.

At the intersection with Market Street people were waiting patiently for the green man. All except for two very drunken men, fresh from the fishing trawlers via The Sea Inn, who were staggering diagonally across the wide expanse of road, swaying between the cars and buses, waving imperiously at them to stop. In Aberdeen at intersections both sets of lights changed to red, allowing pedestrians to cross the road diagonally. But you had to be quick. Old age pensioners, someone had once observed, had just about time to get to the middle of the intersection before the traffic started up again. Tess crossed smartly, not wishing to be taken for anybody remotely resembling a pensioner.

She parked her car opposite the Beach Ballroom and started to walk northwards along the promenade. A supply boat was out there, motionless on the water, waiting for the call to load up with pipes for an oil rig. An east wind was turning the foam on the waves into powder. She hadn't thought about Fergus for at least an hour. She took a deep breath, filled her lungs with the sea air, fastened up her jacket and set out..

Chapter 7

Name: Denis Marcandier
Age: 43
Nationality: untidy French
Occupation: employed by Termoil to find oil
Clothes: baggy
Level of English: mistakes spilling out of his mouth like
smarties out of a tube
Remedy: no idea

'Good morning!' Dodgy Denis was standing there, large and untidy in baggy cotton trousers, rolled up sleeves, a Fair Isle slip over, and a smile on his face which said *Now aren't I a good boy and aren't you're pleased to see me.*

She had met Denis at the entrance to the Belmont cinema last week. All the French in Aberdeen were there because it was a French film that was on. Catching sight of her familiar face he had momentarily taken her for another Frenchwoman and had kissed her on both cheeks. His son of sixteen had followed suite and then his wife. Six kisses in all. The next day he'd telephoned her to apologise.

'I am confused,' he'd said. He meant *embarrassed* but he had indeed also been confused. The experience had not been unpleasant, she'd thought.

'No need to apologise at all,' she told him, but she'd seized the opportunity to remind him about his English lesson.

'I'll see you on Monday,' she'd said in a tone aimed at precluding any excuses for why yet again he wouldn't be able to manage an English lesson that week. She hadn't seen him for four weeks – which is why she called him Dodgy. Could the Aberdeen Language Institute go on getting money out of Denis's oil company for such sparse attendance? She couldn't afford to lose him. Anyway here he was and was she glad to see him!

Well no, she wasn't, not at that precise moment. She'd just started applying a discreet amount of blusher to her cheeks, intended to give a healthy look to her face. She'd slept badly. Fergus had phoned the previous evening just as he was on the point of leaving for this house in the country they'd been lent for rehearsals'

'So there's no point in my coming down,' she'd said, trying not to sound plaintive.

'Well, no,' he'd said – hesitantly. Regretfully?

'What we should do ...' Denis began as she ran her fingers lightly over her cheeks and sat down to face him.

Surely it was for her to be saying that, not him - though in fact she had no idea what she was going to be doing with him. Had he sized her up, noticed how she never did seem to know what she was about? Had he decided to take over?

'Okay, Denis, what do you think we should do?' she interrupted with just a hint of condescension, of amused tolerance in her voice. What he suggested was that he should talk and whenever he made a mistake she should correct him and give him exercises to do at home so he didn't make the same mistakes again. Little by little his English would move towards perfection.

'Mmm,' she said. It sounded like a reasonable idea but it wouldn't work. The language was too chaotic. But no, that was being unfair to the language. The language wasn't chaotic, it was complex. But was it not her job as the teacher to explain and to clarify and simplify the complexity, instead of creating more muddle?

But Denis himself didn't help, Denis was a stirrer up of muddle. Throw him one ball and you found he was juggling with five, or give him a nice simple fact as you'd give a child a nice simple toy and in moments he'd taken it to pieces and was there with six ill-fitting bits trying to put them together again. For example, you said 'Aberdeen has a population of well over two hundred thousand people' and he would say 'Why you cannot tell *persons* instead of *people*?' or 'Why you cannot tell *two hundred thousands of people*?'

'Well, let's begin by looking back at what we were doing in the last lesson,' she said. She had no recollection of what they had been doing in the last lesson, it was so long ago.

Denis opened up his green folder. On the top was an exercise full of crossings out, an exercise on what she called *Tricky Verbs,* verbs like *steal* and *rob, let* and *leave, rise* and *raise, say* and *tell. Fill in the blanks in the following sentences choosing an appropriate verb* was what she'd told him to do. *Let the book on the desk. Say me what you want. Who has robbed me my pen? I have been stolen,* he'd written.

'No, Denis, you have not been stolen,' she'd said.

'I cannot tell *I have not been stolen*? What is this other word meaning the same *...bunged ...buggered...*? I cannot tell *I have been buggered* ?'

'You mean *burgled*' She had written the word up on the board. 'It is important to pronounce it properly.'

He'd had nought out of ten for the exercise. No wonder he hadn't come back for so long. What had possessed her to give him such a complicated exercise?

'Okay. Let's focus on *say* and *tell* today.'

Denis was always saying things like "Did I say you what he told?" instead of "Did I tell you what he said?" She went over again the difference between the two. A bit like reciting the rosary when she was a child, she'd explained the difference so often over the years. What sort of state were her cheeks in? She could go and see Hilary and check them on the way.

'And now, Denis, I'm going to leave you for a moment and while I'm away I want you to do this exercise. Another blank filling exercise! Fill in the gaps with either *say* or *tell*.'

She left him with his very handsome bald pate bent to the task and made her way quickly up to the next floor to the toilets. Hilary was there, standing in front of the mirror examining a lurid black eye. She looked sheepishly across at Tess.

'I banged into the front door coming in Saturday evening. We'd been on the town. I'd had rather a lot to drink.'

More like it her husband, Cecil, had had too much and he'd got into a rage and lashed out at her. This had happened before. Why she didn't leave him Tess could never work out. She'd known Hilary for longer than almost anybody. They'd worked in Paris together in the same place. And Cecil, who was a writer and had to be protected, had always been there. An image Tess often had was of frail little Hilary carrying this huge palouka of a man, Cecil, on her back, staggering under the weight but never letting go of him.

Cecil had been writing a novel at the time about his childhood in China. Had he ever finished it? Had he ever finished anything, except for the odd article about life in Paris for an English paper? And Hilary had been writing a thesis about Shelley. She hadn't ever finished that either. Did either of them care? Their main commitment was to a way of life - to what nowadays would be called an Alternative Life Style, but which Hilary and Cecil still called bohemian.

'If I keep my hair down over it, you don't notice it so much, do you?' she asked Tess. Hilary had lovely long curly auburn hair that had hardly faded with time and she usually wore it tied back. But this morning she had it coming round her face. She looked like an elderly Ophelia about to go on stage for the mad scene.

'What about a pair of dark glasses? I have some in the car. Then you can put your hair back and you'll look fine.'

Had she time to go out to the car? Denis had surely finished the exercise by now. She had a recurring dream in which she was in the middle of teaching a class of students when she ran out of chalk. 'Back in a minute,' she'd tell the class but once out of the room she'd decide there was just time to nip down the road to do a bit of shopping. And then she'd meet a friend and they'd go and have a cup of coffee together and suddenly hours later she'd remember the waiting class.

'I'll just finish with Denis and then I'll be back. I'll bring them to your room and we can have a natter.' She badly needed the comfort of Hilary's wrapt attention.

Denis had obviously finished the exercise some time ago. He was examining the map of Europe she had pinned up on the wall. She looked at what he'd written.

I used to stand at the door and **say** *to my daughter when she was playing in the street with her friends "Your dinner's* *ready." But then she **told** me to call it "tea" not "dinner". So then I stood at the door and **said** "Your tea's ready." But then her friends **said** "Tea? Haven't you had your tea yet? It's half past six." So then my daughter **told** me just to stand at the door and **say** nothing. "Just stand there," she **told** me "and I'll see you and come in straight away."*

He'd got it all right.

'Well done, Denis,' she said.

'You see, I said you the best is to choose one mistake I am doing.'

'You're right,' she said as she ushered him to the door.

She rushed out to her car to get the sunglasses for Hilary. Stephen was just emerging from his aquamarine Mercedes - a nice time to be arriving, eleven o'clock.

Hilary's room was two doors down from Tess's - Tess at the top of the stairs, then Pete, then Hilary; the three EFL teachers all in a row. She was sitting by the open window almost hidden by the cloud of smoke emanating from her Gaulloise. Ever since her Paris days and no matter how hard up she was, Hilary always smoked Gaulloises.

'You'd better be careful. I can smell it in the corridor and Stephen's on the way.'

Hilary shivered, hunched up her thin shoulders.

'Anyway, here are the glasses,' said Tess. She had a sudden idea. 'Hilary, are you free at the weekend? Let's go and have a curry somewhere and afterwards we could go clubbing or something.' The idea of herself and Hilary clubbing was ridiculous but ridiculous was what Tess felt like being. What need had she of Fergus?

'Clubbing?' said Hilary. 'What's that?'

Chapter 8

Tess returned to her room. She'd been going to talk to Hilary about Fergus. Hilary was the only person she could talk to freely, though often she wondered if she should be talking - Hilary maybe took too much pleasure from hearing about 'bohemian' tales. Her eyes had gleamed when Tess first told her about Fergus, the clandestine lover.

Had Tess felt guilty about Fergus in those early days? She hadn't. The elation she'd felt at her first meeting with him outside the Music Hall when she'd tripped up over his cello had lasted.

'Is there a place you can go for a drink round here?' he'd asked her. They'd ended up in the Café Rouge round the corner. He lived in North London, in a flat just off the Seven Sisters Rd, he told her.

'That's the end of the Number 73 bus route, isn't it? It passes King's Cross where I catch the train for Aberdeen.'

'Well next time,' he'd said with a quick smile, 'why don't you stay on the bus and come and see me?' And she had. After years of being the dutiful wife and mother she was embarking on an adventure.

But Hilary had been supportive, too, when two years ago Bob had announced to her out of the blue that he'd fallen in love with someone else. Her feelings for Fergus had vanished then like swallows at the end of the summer at the threat of losing Bob. He'd turned into somebody essential to her survival and she'd fought to keep him. But to no avail - he'd gone off with this other woman. (Liz, the other woman was called, but Tess could never bring herself to say the name.). Tess had returned from work one day to find the cupboards bare of his clothes, the shelves clear of his books, the racks empty of his CDs and his toothbrush gone from the bathroom.

All of them at the Institute had helped her through that terrible time. 'You'll be able to eat rice pudding in bed in the morning with lots of cherry jam on top,' Kirsty had tried to joke with her. 'And toast in the middle of the night' (Maggie). 'And have Bob Marley playing at full strength'

(Pete). 'And come to Valencia with me and Emilio' (Quentin). But it was Hilary who had continued to say how Fergus was much better for her than Bob. Bob was conventional and boring and carried a personal organizer and was only interested in his research into bats.

'And his research into that woman,' Tess had thought to herself.

And then like swallows in the spring her feelings for Fergus had returned. Now she was free to spend long weekends with him - every weekend with him - down in London or up in Kineldie. He'd spent the whole of June with her there - his first time in the cottage now it was transformed into a completely Bob free place. She'd turned what had been their bedroom into a study, moved into Annie's room, bought a new double bed and painted the walls poppy red. It was Fergus who had chosen the poppy red.

But was Hilary right? Was Fergus really better for her than Bob? The pain as well as the excitement of living apart, of never being sure. And now this departure without a bye-your-leave.

She looked out of the window. The horizon was a band of turquoise blue, the sea a deep blue grey. Only a few wisps of clouds brushing the sky. It would be a nice drive over to the university in Old Aberdeen for the first class of the year with the new intake of foreign students. Not much time now to prepare what she was going to do with them but the first class was always easy.

She needed to work out how she was going to fill the three hours a week for ten weeks right up to Christmas, though. She needed to make a plan. But she already had a plan. In fact she had a whole ten week course she'd made up four years ago. She got the file out. First week: *Listing* using words like *firstly, secondly, lastly, last but not least, moreover, furthermore.* Second week: *Classification* with *These can be divided, classified, arranged into several, various, broad groups, categories, classes, types.* And so on to Week 10: *Punctuation (including further uses of the comma and the colon).*

Yes, but she'd been going to do things differently this year, adopt a more creative approach, inspired by Pete, have brainstorming sessions, word games, get them writing poetry. Or at least incorporate some of the stuff from a newly published book on writing that she'd lashed out on - £15 plus p.and p. She took this out now and flicked through the pages - *themes, expansions of themes, misleading parallelism ..... .* No, she'd stick to her own course for today.

Anyway it would be nice to be in Old Aberdeen where the streets were cobbled and the granite was pink and the crown tower of the 16th century chapel patterned the sky and the students never got any older.

Maybe Hilary was going over there today, in which case they could have lunch together. Hilary spent a lot of her time browsing among the books in the university library. She went along the corridor to the door of the classroom where she was teaching.

'The subjunctive in English occurs in a number of set phrases .... ' Tess heard her announcing. Pete had got nowhere in converting Hilary to his style of teaching. She'd be on about the subjunctive for at least another half hour. Franck went hurrying past with a 'Gutbye.' Stephen emerged from his office, shrugging his way into his Burberry raincoat. She went back into her room and, waited till the coast was clear.

She took the long way round by the sea, still undecided about how she was going to handle this group of students who'd come from the four corners of the earth here to Aberdeen to study Marine Biology, Animal Nutrition, Forestry, Medical Physics ..... . How was she going to teach writing to this hotchpotch of foreign postgraduate students - one from Ethiopia according to the list, two Mexicans, an Iraqui, a Thai, an Indonesian, a Chinese-speaking Malaysian, a Sudanese, a Greek and a Japanese? Would they really want to know about further uses of the comma and the colon in English?

'I want you to write an account for me of what brought you to Aberdeen,' she told them as she stood in front of them.

'What brought you to Aberdeen?'

'An aeroplane,' called out the young Mexican man. The young Mexican woman sitting next to him burst into a great laugh at this and gave him a push on his shoulder which nearly knocked him off his chair. The young woman from Thailand looked alarmed, turned nervously towards Tess and gave her a big smile which Tess interpreted as: *Do not be insulted by the behaviour of these students who seem so disrespectful of your age and your status as our teacher. They know no better. You must make allowances for their ignorance.*

'In other words I want you to write me an account of why you're here and what you are going to study,' Tess went on, ignoring the disturbance that Xavier's remark had created.

The first hour and a half had been a getting-to-know-them session. The Sudanese, Mousa, had lost his umbrella that morning and was in great distress about this. The loss of the umbrella was no doubt the last straw. He'd arrived in Aberdeen a few weeks before with his wife and child but she had immediately decided she could not survive the winter in Scotland and had flown back to Sudan with their little boy the previous weekend. The two Mexicans, Concepta and Xavier, were actually married to each other, they told the class. They'd got married just before leaving Mexico. Concepta waved her left hand with the ring upon it around for the class to admire. The beautiful Ethiopian girl next to them, Sheba, was here to study Animal Nutrition. Tess had been obliged to tell her not to sharpen her pencils onto the floor and from then on she'd adopted a sulky look which Tess was unable to banish. The Japanese man next to her, Mr Sakura, seemed to have only a minimal understanding of the spoken language. After asking him repeatedly in an increasingly slower and clearer voice 'Where are you living?' his eyes had suddenly lit up and he'd opened his mouth and enunciated an energetic 'Yes'. He was here to study Forestry

'Horses? You have come to Aberdeen to study horses?' asked the Iraqui, Hunein, who looked at first sight like Sadam Hussein but who had a nice smile and seemingly a sense of humour.

'No, Forestry,' Tess replied for him. 'Mr Sakura is studying Forestry.'

It was true that it had sounded more like 'horses'. The Thai woman, who was studying Marine Biology, had arrived with an apology for the absence of the Chinese Malaysian gentleman, Chai. With a bright smile she'd told Tess that he'd been rushed to hospital with something wrong 'with his berry.'

'His belly' corrected Tess. 'Well, actually, no, his stomach.'

'Perhaps the nicest of them all is Joseph from Indonesia,' Tess thought as she sat looking at them bent over their writing. He'd left a wife and six children behind in order to come to Scotland to study marine biology.

'There are good times in life and there are bad times,' he'd said as they looked out at the rain that had begun to fall heavily.

'You're right there,' thought Tess. But for her maybe these were not bad times, maybe she was at the start of good times, the beginning of a completely new and utterly loving and lustful relationship. How lucky that Thierry had walked into her life at this particular moment. All the time she'd been working at the Institute this was the first time there had been what could be called an 'eligible male.' At least she hoped that's what he was. The hole in the pullover surely suggested there was no tender and devoted woman in the background.

But maybe he had left some glamorous career woman back in Paris.

'Aberdeen? Where is that? Mon Dieu, mon pauvre Thierry, my poor dear. But you will fly home to me every weekend, no? We will spend *white nights* together to make up for all the nights we will be apart.'

As they wrote Tess was relieved to see that Mr Sakura's command of the written language seemed to be better than his spoken. His head bent, he was filling the page with apparent effortlessness. Sheba, on the other hand, with her row of nicely sharpened pencils in front of her, seemed hardly to have started. Her page was blank apart from one sentence. It was still that way when they handed in their pages at the end of the class. Along with his inky scrawl Hunnein produced from his brief case a present for Tess - a wooden box with neat rows of dates inside.

'See you next week,' said Tess as she left them, wondering how many of them would have fallen by the wayside between now and then.

Chapter 9

Kirsty was beside her in the car. Kirsty wasn't pleased. To begin with she didn't appreciate having to get up an hour earlier so that Tess could be in for eight o'clock to suit the convenience of this Frenchman. Try anything on, they would. She should have said 'No, can't do. You'll have to organise yourself better, can't have other people disrupting their lives just for you.'

The other thing was, Stephen's wife had come back earlier than expected. Horror yesterday evening. Just as she and Stephen were sitting down to eat the vegetable curry they'd made together the phone rang. Cynthia phoning from the train - had left the conference early, train arriving in ten minutes, could he be there to meet it? Of course he could. Yes, darling, of course. Really despicable, the tone he'd adopted. Yes, darling, anything you say, darling, of course I'll be there, lovely to have you back, I've missed you terribly. He hadn't actually said he'd missed her but Kirsty could well imagine him saying it as he snuggled up to her in bed later that evening. And he was probably already thinking how he'd say that he'd cooked the curry specially for her return. Would he remove the candlesticks from the table? Anyway she'd had to rush around collecting all her things and checking the pillows for blonde hairs and remembering to grab her green silk dressing gown from where she'd hung it on top of Cynthia's yellow chenille one on the back of the bedroom door.

'And he couldn't get me out of the house quick enough. He was going to let me go without even a kiss but I gave him a big one on the cheek and I could just see him thinking - now I'll have to check I don't have lipstick plastered all over me.'

On her drive back to Kineldie Kirsty had remembered her earrings - still on the shelf in the kitchen where she'd taken them off half way through their meal on Monday. They were getting in the way of Stephen's tongue rooting around in her ear like a hungry kitten. She'd got Tess to phone to speak to him on some pretext.

'Stephen, when is it you want my report on Teaching Termoil? Oh, it's not till the week after next. Thank Goodness for that. I'd had a sudden dreadful thought that it might be this week. There's something on the shelf next to the cooker that needs removing. Okay, well, see you tomorrow.'

Stephen as the person who ran the Institute knew about everything going on. At least he liked to feel he did. He liked to feel he controlled everything. Only he can't have felt that much in control yesterday evening, Tess imagined, standing there saying 'Yes, dear, okay dear.'

'You don't need to drive so fast, Tess. What's he like anyway, this new man?'

'He's all right,' said Tess. She didn't want to embark on what she thought about Thierry with Kirsty. She hadn't even felt like confiding in her about Fergus. What did she know about Thierry anyway? In today's lesson she would do her best to find out a little bit about him. They'd do a review of the English tense system starting with the Present - before moving on to the Future.

'In French, Thierry, you only have one form to express the present time, don't you?' she began. He'd been waiting at the door when she arrived and the smile he had given her had made her feel like embracing him. 'French only has *je parle* whereas English has *I speak* and *I am speaking*. So if you want to say *I speak French* then you say *je parle français*. If you want to say what language you are speaking at the moment you use the same words *je parle anglais en çe moment*. But in English you say *I speak French but I am speaking English at the moment.*'

Though anyone overhearing Thierry when he spoke English would almost certainly have thought that what he was speaking was French not English. He was still in his green pullover and the little hole was still there. Quite a boring garment, a V neck pullover in a dull shade of green - maybe he wasn't too interested in clothes. Had he noticed what she was wearing today? She thought she looked quite stylish in what she called her Russian army outfit - a long green serge dress with epaulettes. It emphasised her height, and made her look willowy, she hoped.

'We use what we call the simple present tense to make general statements. The form is easy. It's just the verb itself - *I play the piano, I work at home, I eat a lot of bananas, I drive a Porsch* and so on. What we call the continuous present tense is used to talk about things happening at the moment. *At the moment I am not playing the piano, I am not working at home, I am not eating a banana, I am not driving my Porsch.'* He knew all this of course, he'd done it at school. He was looking bored.

'Ah, yes, driving.'

Driving in from work he'd been listening to *sooth of the day* on his car radio. Sooth of the day? Was this some programme coming from London?

'South,' she corrected.

'No, no, *sooth.* It was a man telling us to sink about all the people who are dying in Africa. It is stupid. What can we do about it? It is stupid to say us this.'

'Ah, *thought. Thought for the Day.'* *Pronunciation practice next time,* she scribbled down in her diary. Was he right? He worked for a multinational oil company. Was it true he could do nothing? You could give them some of your fat salary, for starters, she thought.

'So we use the simple present to talk about statements of fact. For example we say *The sun rises in the west and sets in the east.'*

'The sun is rising in the west here in Scotland? That does not surprise me.'

He was meant to correct her, using the simple present tense. 'The sun doesn't rise in the west. It rises in the east.' Realistic use of language, Pete would have been pleased with her.

'*The sun rises*, not *The sun is rising*. It is a statement of fact.' 'We only use *the sun is rising* if it is actually rising at the moment. Is the sun rising?'

They looked out of the window. Day had already broken and the sky was streaked with pinks and golds.

'Look at that sky. Isn't it fantastic?' she said 'You could even say it was stupendous.'

'Ah, *stupendous*. I will write that down.' He got a sheet of paper out of his battered briefcase. 'And are there other words I could use? There is a word they are using in the office- *gorgus* ... .'

'Ah, *gorgeous*. Yes, you could say that. What did she know about this man? She could hear them talking about some young woman colleague. 'She's gorgeous, isn't she?' 'Yes, gorgeous.' 'Gorgeous legs.' 'Yes, gorgeous'. She wrote the word up on the board. Was Thierry watching *her*, thinking she was *gorgeous*?`

'You could also say that the sky is *staggeringly* or even *breathtakingly beautiful* this morning.' Had anyone ever thought, or at least said, that *she* was staggeringly or breathtakingly beautiful? She wrote the words up on the board under *gorgeous*. Even to write them up and say them out loud was pleasing.

'Say *the sky looks stupendous this morning. The sky looks gorgeous this morning.....*'

She sat back in her chair, listening to him going carefully through the sentences in his crushed blackberries and cream voice. And now say it all again, changing *The sky* to *You. You look stupendous this morning - gorgeous.*

'To get back to the Present Tense - as opposed to the present,' she added with emphasis, 'we also use the simple present tense to express a habit. For example *I get up at seven every morning. I go the hairdresser's once a month.* The mistake French people make is to use the Present Continuous. That's because in your first English lesson the teacher teaches you this tense and you go on using it all the time, because you think it is typically English.'

'Ah, typically English. Typically British, you mean!' Since coming to Scotland he'd obviously been told to avoid applying the words *England* and *English* to the whole island.

'Let's practise the Simple Present to express a habit.' A chance now to find out more about him. Where would she start? *How often do you go to the cinema? How often do you eat oysters?* How often do you make love?

'I never go to the cinema and I am hardly, no I hardly never eat oysters.'

(And you hardly never are making love?)

'And you?' he asked. 'You are going to the cinema?' He seemed eager for a reply, eager to know something about her.

'Yes, I am going – I go to the cinema a lot. I like the cinema.'

Standing outside a cinema in the Latin Quarter trying to decide which film to go to, not sure she wanted to see any film. It was nearly a year after Marc's death. 'Vous etes dans le cirage,' the mother of one of her pupils had said to her that morning. She'd looked the phrase up in the dictionary when she got home and found that it meant that she was *lost, completely at sea.*

'I think you'd like this film better,' a voice behind her, talking to her in English.

She turned round to see a thin young man with fair hair pointing to *Kind Heart and Coronets.* How did he know she was English? Was it that obvious? Afterwards he'd told her it was because there was a copy of Evelyn Waugh's *A Handful of Dust* sticking out of her raincoat pocket. They'd gone in to it together. It was his third time seeing it, he told her. He also told her he was called Bob and he came from Scotland. Scotland, after years of living in France, began to seem like a strange place of great appeal.

And so it was, when she arrived there a year later as Mrs Brodie. The enjoyment of being treated politely in shops and of sitting in a café with a scone and a cup of tea listening to people talking about the weather. And then Bob - never exciting but loveable, good company - and dependable, until that Saturday morning just as she was putting her coat on to go out to do the supermarket.

'Tess,' he'd said 'I've fallen in love.' That was not something that she and he had ever done. Theirs had been a gentle beginning, heralding a gentle union.

'For next time, to practise the simple present tense, why don't you write an account of what you usually do at the week-end?' said Tess. 'I want to know all about what you do,' she said as she accompanied him to the door. Did that sound coquettish? Not businesslike enough? Too businesslike? *Thierry, the widower, The widower, Thierry. Le veuve Fouchard.* Which sounded best? They all had a pleasant ring to them.

Chapter 10

Seagulls making a clatter outside. What were seagulls doing so far inland? Then she remembered. Of course she wasn't in Kineldie, she was in Hilary's flat in the centre of Aberdeen. What time was it? She'd been without a watch for a week now and Hilary didn't have anything so down-to-earth as a clock that worked. It must be getting on for eight, a cold grey light was coming in through the window. That must be what woke her up. When they got in last night she'd gone to draw the curtains and then remembered that Hilary didn't have anything so bourgeois as curtains on the windows either.

Likewise comfortable chairs. Hilary called this room the sitting room but there was very little in the way of anything you could conceivably sit on, except for the sofa she was now stretched out on. Certainly nothing so unbohemian as a three piece suite, that's for sure. Only mountains of books and piles of newspapers going back several years, probably with mice nesting among them. She'd heard little scuffling noises in the night.

She closed her eyes. Did she have a headache? How much had she drunk of the *voros bor* - the Hungarian for red wine, she'd learnt yesterday evening? They'd eaten in Aberdeen's Hungarian restaurant. She felt slightly queasy. Better not to think about anything to do with food or drink for the moment, except that a cup of tea would be nice.

'I bet Hilary is out of milk and I bet she forgot to buy any bread. Why didn't I think of that yesterday? Where is there going to be a shop open this early on a Sunday morning?'

Tess buried her face in her pillow and tried to get back to sleep. What was that table doing in front of the door? Oh, yes, it came back to her now, she'd dragged it there on Hilary's advice when they'd come back from the restaurant yesterday evening. Otherwise Cecil would be barging in, 'pissed out of his tiny mind' as Hilary put it, at three in the morning, forgetting that Tess was there, staying the night. Or maybe not forgetting, thought Tess. There was that time in Paris. But that was many years ago now, Cecil a lot thinner, gaunt even, and very soulful in his advances.

'Tess, you are so beautiful, so clever, so sensitive, so human. I can't get you out of my mind. I want you, I need you. Tess, please, please be my muse, please come to bed with me.'

Tess, who was usually very susceptible to flattery, on this occasion had no problem about refusing him. In fact she'd done the worst thing possible, she'd laughed in his face and he'd been very hurt. He was probably still hurt after all these years. No, he would never come on purpose into the room where she was sleeping.

No good, she wasn't going to be able to get back to sleep and the need for a cup of tea and a bit of breakfast was growing. Maybe they could all invite themselves round to Pete's for breakfast. She could phone Kirsty who was spending the night at her mum's and she could join them and Pete would be pleased. And then Kirsty and herself could drive back to Kineldie together.

Would Pete be up? What time did Pete get up? He'd started on a fitness regime, he'd told her, which involved an early morning run along the beach. He wanted to get rid of his flabby belly in order to make himself more attractive to Kirsty. Kirsty doesn't seem to mind Stephen's flabby belly, Tess had thought when he told her this. Should she try phoning him? Surely it must be getting on for nine o'clock now. She'd at last located the phone - on top of a pile of books, the receiver off the hook, the cord dangling. She rolled off the sofa and crawled towards it.

'We could walk around North Square and then back around South Square and by that time he should be back,' said Hilary, shivering in her long coat.

'I'll put the bag beside the door,' said Tess. They'd found a corner shop open and bought milk and half a dozen Aberdeen butteries, (or Aberdeen greasies as Hilary called them). Pete, when she phoned, had said he was off for a quick run but should be back by ten. It was now ten past. Nobody else was up in the old fishing village of Footdee. The austere little chapel in the middle of South Square was firmly closed. Half a century ago Tess imagined all the fishermen and their families emerging from their houses to attend the morning service. Now most of the houses were lived in by people like Pete.

As they turned into North Square they noticed a figure ahead of them, huddled into a thick jacket, his head bowed against the wind. Was that Thierry? No, it couldn't be. The previous evening in the restaurant and later in the pub she'd constantly been scanning faces, staring at the backs of heads, wondering if she would see him. And here she was, at it again. But no, this time it *was* him. Should they try to catch up? But he'd stopped in front of the old fountain.

'Thierry! Hello!'

'Ah!' A smile. Of delight? He held out his hand. She hadn't touched his hand since their first meeting. She introduced Hilary. What were they doing here, did they live here?

'No, but a friend does - Pete. You've met him in the coffee room. We're going to have breakfast with him. Why don't you join us?'

The plastic bag was gone from Pete's door. He had returned. The smell of freshly made coffee and of butteries heating up in the oven was coming from the kitchen. And then Kirsty arrived and the smell of freshly shampooed hair.

'Let me see your new computer, Pete,' she said, refusing a buttery, making Tess, about to reach for a second one, feel gross.

'She must be in a good mood this morning,' thought Tess 'if she's actually offering to help Pete with his computer.'

Hilary had installed herself in the window seat with a new anthology of modern poetry. Pete had put on a Miles Davis disc and Tess was sitting by the little coal fire hoping Thierry would join her.

'Have a buttery.' She held out the plate to him. 'They're Aberdeen's version of the croissant.' He took one and she decided she'd have a second one after all to keep him company.

So did Tess live nearby? This must be the nicest place to live in Aberdeen, in one of these old houses built round a square no bigger than a large courtyard.

'I used to live in the house opposite,' she said. 'When I was married,' she added. Maybe he was going to think she was widowed like himself.

'I'm divorced,' she said. 'I've been on my own for the last three years.'

'And you like being with yourself?' What could she say?

'Well, I'm not really by myself,' she said. Wasn't she? Did Kirsty count? Or Fergus? 'I share a house out the country with Kirsty and then I have a lot of friends. We meet up a lot, like now.' She gestured to Kirsty and Pete bent over the computer and to Hilary in the window seat.

'Ah yes, but ... ' He gave a Gallic shrug. He'd taken his jacket off. Underneath a black shirt, black cords, a leather belt. He looked lean, nice

'How about you?' she said. How long had he been a widower? Did she want to know? Did she want to find herself sitting by the fire listening to Thierry talking about his dead wife and how much he missed her?

'Listen to that,' he said without answering. Miles Davis's trumpet was soaring.

'You like jazz?' he asked her. Tess wasn't sure that she did. Louis Armstrong maybe and this CD yes.

'I like this,' she said and they sat in silence listening to the last notes.

Kirsty came over to join them, leaving Pete staring at the computer screen. Did she need to sit so close to Thierry?

'*Tirez sur le pianiste* is on at the Belmont at 2 o'clock,' said Tess. 'Do you feel like seeing it with us, Thierry?' She and Kirsty had talked about going.

It wasn't his sort of film, he said, and in any case he'd been invited to lunch by some French colleagues. Not that he liked these Sunday lunches that went on for hours. It was nice of them to invite him but it was *borring, borring,* sitting there listening to French people grumbling about Aberdeen and eating and drinking too much. He'd prefer going for a walk in the country. So, a pity about *Tirez sur le pianiste* but very good that he preferred a walk in the country to Sunday lunch.

'He's nice, isn't he?' said Kirsty as they drove home after the film.

'You mean Aznavour? Yes, he looks so sad playing that piano.'

'No, I mean Thierry. I like the way he moves. I can just see him on the dance floor.'

The dance floor? Tess had never mastered the art of dancing. She saw herself sitting there watching while Thierry twisted and turned in Kirsty's arms.

'How are things with Stephen?' she asked.

Chapter 11

Dominique phoned. He was very sorry but he would not be able to come today. No explanation of why he was cancelling. Was this a cultural difference? Did the French think explanations unnecessary? Did this sort of behaviour in the political world lead eventually to warfare? Anyway, it meant she had the rest of the day free and it was only nine o'clock. She gazed out at the sea and the sky. The view today was far from being stupendous - a grey mist had descended, obscuring everything.

She looked at the map of France on the wall and wondered which part of France Thierry came from. Had he always lived in Versailles? The map was an old one with hardly any autoroutes marked on it. She ought to replace it along with the one of Scotland, which still showed the old county boundaries. Apart from a Jack Yeats poster, all streaks and smudges of colour, entitled *There is No Night*, a picture of a man sprawled on a bog and a white horse beside him (had he been thrown from it or was it a vision, of death maybe?) her walls had nothing on them but maps. No photos anywhere either. The others had posters on their walls and photos on their desks. Maggie, who taught Italian, had posters of the Coliseum and St. Mark's Square and a photo of her husband and three teenage children. Quentin had a poster of a village in Spain cut out of the rock, and one of a Greek statue of a fine-looking young man. Kirsty had a photo of her brother Angus, in his survival suit, about to get into the helicopter to go off-shore. A fat lot of use survival suits had been that night he along with so many others had died in the Piper Alpha explosion. Stephen had an enormous photo of Cynthia and one of him with their two children when they were young, an arm around each of them. Tess liked keeping her room impersonal, not even a photo of Annie.

She noticed a hole in her black tights near the ankle and reached for a black biro to colour in the pink flesh. Thierry would have a job doing the same for his green pullover with the hole, unless he had a matching green shirt underneath.

Easier get a bit of thread to it, or buy a new jersey altogether and use that one for gardening. What sort of garden did he have here? The French didn't usually bother about doing anything in their gardens until they got communications round from the oil company - *It has been brought to our notice that you are failing to maintain your garden to an acceptable standard. We would like to remind you that the grass should be cut regularly and the hedges trimmed and all borders kept tidy.* Aberdonians in the areas where the French had their houses were scrupulous in the upkeep of their gardens - a neat border with tulips in the spring, a careful nine inches apart, and a few carefully placed rose bushes. Front gardens that looked like floral pinnies.

What was Thierry going to be doing next weekend? Maybe she could suggest a walk to save him from one of those Sunday lunches. Fergus had phoned Sunday evening to say he was off the following Wednesday.

'I'm sorry we haven't had a chance to see each other before I go. Do you think you will manage to come out to wherever we are over Christmas?'

'I could come down for the day on Tuesday, just before you leave' she just managed to stop herself from saying.

'I don't know,' she said, 'I'll have to see.'

There was a knock on the door. She quickly laid the pen on the desk, rearranged her skirt and called 'Come in.' Dodgy Denis. Surely he wasn't meant to be here today.

'I have a good new,' he announced as he sat down opposite her. His wife had just had a baby, a girl. They already had a boy of three. Was that not all the more reason for him not to be here? But maybe he was feeling neglected, maybe he'd come to her for comfort.

'That's marvellous,' she said. Even more marvellous as far as Tess was concerned was that the problem of what to do with him for the hour was solved. She allowed a brief pause before launching in, happy at this unexpected opportunity to leave Fergus behind.

'But you cannot say *a new. New* is not the singular of *news. News* is already a singular noun. *No news **is** good* *news*, not *No news **are** good news*. The *s* is not a plural *s*. So you should say *news*.'

'So, I have a newsssss.'

'No, *News* is what we call an uncountable noun. In French you can say *one news* (*une nouvelle*) or *two news* (*deux nouvelles*) but in English you can't. You have to say *some news* or *a piece of news* or *two pieces of news*. Like *advice* and *information* and *luggage* and *furniture* and *equipment*.' She reeled off the words. She even had a filling-in-the-blanks exercise on the subject which she now gave him to do.

Information and *advice* had reminded her of the visit from the slater, a young fellow. *Nail sick* he'd said her roof was and it would cost five thousand pounds to have it repaired. How was she to know whether the nails holding the slates were sick or not?

'What does that mean?' she'd asked, sounding like she was talking to one of her students. Five thousand pounds was what that meant, but he'd come back an hour later.

'The roof is probably all right for another ten years or so.' (By which time you'll probably be thinking of sheltered housing, was that what he was meaning?) 'I could just do a few patching up jobs on it for you.'

So he gave her another ten years, did he? She'd straightened up at this, tried to put a bright look on her face to banish any suggestion of haggardness. She'd made herself a cup of coffee after he'd gone, thought maybe she'd contact another slater. Ten years. But people lived into their eighties these days. She'd turn into a chirpy old woman hobbling around in her garden and catching up on all the reading she hadn't done. Which books would you choose to read if you knew you only had a limited amount of time? Would it be a re-read of *The Brothers Karamatsov*? A bit heavy in more than one sense for a frail eighty year old. Maybe Proust, the first book of *A la Recherche du Temps Perdu*.

She looked across at Denis. He'd obviously finished the exercise minutes ago. She asked him to read out what he'd written. Very good. Now they'd practise using the words in real situations.

'So did your wife get much advice from the hospital? Did she get much information from them?'

'Yes, she got much advice and much information,' he replied. That didn't sound right but it was approaching the hour.

'So what sort of advice did she get?' He didn't know. He'd only said that in order to practise using *much*. In fact they hadn't been at all impressed by the maternity services compared with France. He was all set to launch into criticism of the National Health Service. A few years ago she would have argued with him but as the service had deteriorated she'd become less inclined to argue. Now she preferred to avoid arguing altogether.

'So what are you going to call the baby?'

'Celeste.'

'Ah, that's nice.' The name conjured up angels playing celestial music. Better than listening to complaints about the National Health Service.

Chapter 12

She glanced down at her foot on the accelerator, same tights, same hole. Or maybe she had two pairs with a hole near the ankle? Maybe Thierry had two pullovers with a hole on the left hand side. Would she have time to fill it in? She waited for a straight bit of road and then began rooting in the bag beside her for a black biro. A pity Kirsty wasn't there. Kirsty had the morning off and she'd left her still in bed. Stephen might call, she'd said. Promised nothing but if he could manage it on his way in to the Institute. His way in? Only ten miles out of his way.

That meeting with Thierry on Sunday had been such a piece of luck, to have been in Footdee just at the precise moment he was walking through. Or maybe it had been fate. When she saw him tomorrow morning could she suggest a drink after work one evening, with Hilary? She could explain to him how Hilary was deeply homesick for Paris and cafe life and sitting there sipping Pernod and talking about Sartre and Camus and existentialism and smoking Gaulloises. How nice it would be if he would join them one evening for aperitifs.

But where in Aberdeen would they find a place where they'd be able to recreate the atmosphere of Les Deux Magots on the Boulevard St Germain or the Dome at Montparnasse? There was a café down near the beach where there were tables and chairs outside but you'd be mad to sit on them in the slitting wind. Plenty of café bars but all throbbing with young people and loud music. The place she usually went to with Hilary had definitely nothing in common with a Paris café. Maybe with Thierry there it would be different.

She was seeing Laurent at nine. One thing for sure, she'd better be more disciplined with him than last time, all that clunking and whimpering and leaping, demonstrating words for sounds and movements. She imagined him recounting it to Janet and the two of them laughing. Today she would start *Making Your Mark At Meetings* with him and they would practise bringing people into a discussion

You are in a better position than me, Ms Bright, to answer this question.

'What does *Ms* mean?' Laurent asked, half an hour later..

She explained. Why should women have to declare their marital status by choosing between Mrs and Miss, some women had asked back in the seventies.

'Yes', he said 'but I think it is ridiculous nowadays that you have to be so careful what you say. You cannot even tell a woman she is attractive, if she is.'

'But I think the problem is there is too much focus on women as sexual objects,' she said.

'And what is wrong with that? In France women do not 'ave a problem with that.'

She began to feel like she was standing on a sand bank with the tide coming in fast.

'Well, the problem is' she said boldly, 'that women are fussed over and spoilt by men until they reach the age of forty or fifty so they think they don't need to do anything except just be there looking attractive. And then after fifty - more or less - they don't exist any more.'

This is getting tedious, thought Tess. She'd had the argument too often and maybe it was out of date anyway. Women these days did do things, they had careers.

'Notice the use of *should* in sentences like the following,' she said, returning to the book.

Yes, I think that it is very important that we should think carefully before acting.

Here she was on firmer ground and the sun was streaming into the room. She had a friend who had written a thesis on *should*. She had read numerous detective stories, noting down every sentence with a *should* in it and then she had analysed them. She had found five different uses.

'There are five different uses of *should* in English,' she said. If he passed that information on to Janet she would be impressed. 'But that will have to wait until next week.'

'Hilary, when we go to The Blue Fortune on Friday I could invite Thierry along as well. You remember, you met him last

Sunday.' Tess, rehearsing what she might say to Hilary, began to have doubts. What would they talk about, anyway, she, Hilary and Thierry? He probably wasn't the slightest bit interested in Sartre and he wasn't at all bohemian. He'd start on about how this socialist and that, if they were allowed to pursue their policies, would be the ruin of France. And Hilary would get more and more pissed on rum and black. And then Cecil would come staggering in because Hilary would surely have told him where they were and Cecil was not a one to pass by the chance of a free drink, or two, or three. So she hadn't suggested a drink to Thierry as she'd said goodbye to him at the end of his lesson.

'So I am seeing you on Monday,' he'd said a little too briskly for Tess's liking. He'd seemed busy, pre-occupied.

But then, she began to wonder if maybe she'd got it wrong, he'd been not busy and pre-occupied but sad and lonely, waiting for her to suggest a meeting. So she phoned him up with the invitation and he accepted.

There was a definite scowl hovering on Hilary's face. Thierry was talking about how his oil company had just discovered a new oilfield.

'This is where most of our existing fields are,' he said, moving his own glass to the edge of the table. 'And this is where the new field is.' He took hold of Hilary's glass and placed it in the middle of the table. Hilary immediately leaned forward, grabbed it back.

'It is not a very big field,' he continued, ignoring Hilary 'but the technology has improved so much….'

'How's Fergus?' Hilary interrupted, turning to Tess.

'Fergus is okay.'

Who'd like another drink?'

'Not for me,' said Thierry, who'd barely touched his glass of white wine.

'I'll get you another one, Tess,' said Hilary fishing a tired leather purse out of her shoulder bag. She set out across the crowded room like a frail craft braving the ocean.

'Thierry!' Two young women in leather jackets and short

skirts, one tall, one short, holding pints of lager.

'Elaine! Tess, this is Elaine and this is Elaine. No, I am pronouncing it wrong.'

'I'm Helen. She's Elaine,' said the tall one. 'Do you mind if we join you?' They dragged chairs across and threw themselves down into them, stretching out their shapely legs.

'So where's the blonde bombshell? What have you done with her?' Helen asked Thierry who laughed and turned to Tess.

'Elaine and Elaine are working in the same office than me.' Tess could see Hilary making her way back unsteadily with two glasses of red wine.

'This reminds me of what Sartre was saying about free will in *The Roads to Freedom*,' said Hilary as she sat down.

'Oh, Sartre! We could discuss him for hours,' said Thierry in the tone of voice of someone who had no desire or intention of discussing him at all.

Elaine and Helen were off to the Lemon Tree to hear some jazz band.

'Do any of you want to come along?' Helen asked, looking at Thierry

'No, I have to go in a moment,' he said with a slight shrug of his shoulders. The blonde bombshell awaiting him?

'I am sorry I cannot stay longer,' he said, turning to Tess.

There's always tomorrow… a voice behind her had burst into song … *and what can I do? Your kisses all tell me that you've been untrue.*

Helen and Elaine started to laugh. Thierry got up and began dancing his way to the door. Tess turned round and there was Cecil swaying on his feet, beer dripping from his moustache.

'Tess, my darling …'. He was holding his arms out. Thierry was disappearing out the door with a wave of the hand.

'Oh Cecil,' said Hilary 'for goodness sake sit down.'

Chapter 13

The phone rang. It was Vincent, who she was due to see at eleven. Please don't tell me you can't make it, Vincent. *Termoil* wouldn't go on paying indefinitely for non-existent students.

'I have not written in my agenda ...'

'Your diary,' she corrected. Why did she have to jump in there to correct him? Professional deformation, they called it. 'I have drowning,' she imagined someone some day calling, and her reply from the bank 'Not *have* drowning. *Am* drowning.'

'I have not written in my agenda,' he continued, (okay, she didn't need to worry about having undermined his confidence) 'when is my next lesson.'

'It's at eleven today so I'll see you then.'

Long pause and then hesitantly 'Why not?' He couldn't see any possible reason for not attending. 'But I did not read the article you gave me.' Was this the beginning of an excuse not to come?

'That's okay, Vincent. Just bring it along and we can read it together.'

Name: Vincent Béart
Age: 33
Nationality: nice French
Occupation: drilling kilometres into the earth's crust in search of hypothetical oil wells.
Clothes: neat red check shirt, neat matching tie
+++: thinks I'm nice
---: mad about golf
Level of English: not bad except for pronunciation of 'th' and 's'
Lesson Plan: keep him attending

Vincent was soon going to be going to Angola to work. The country was poverty-stricken and it was going to be dangerous for him there - he could get blown up. The problem was the land mine.

'Just one land mine? It is important to pronounce the *s* of the plural,' she said. 'In French you don't pronounce it but you know whether it's singular or plural because you say *la* or *une mine* if there's just one and *les* or *des mines* if there's more than one.'

He was sitting there preoccupied by the danger of being blown up by a land mine and here she was fussing about the pronunciation of the letter *s*. At the outbreak of the Iraq-Iran war long ago she'd been teaching an Iranian doctor. One day he came to tell her he'd been recalled to serve in the army and that this was his last lesson. She'd planned to teach him the most complicated of the English tenses - the Present Perfect - so, in spite of his news, she'd embarked on a careful explanation of this.

'Are you following me?' she'd asked him

'No,' he said. 'I am sitting here thinking the next week maybe I am dead' And maybe he was. She never heard from him again. Of course this Frenchman was in a different position, he didn't need to be working for an oil company.

'It's important because in a meeting you might say 'I'd like to discuss the problem' when what you mean is the problems. You could mislead people.'

'The people are poor,' he continued, 'but if the profit were distributed among the people instead of to go to buy armament, there is enough money to give each person one dollar a day - which is enough to leave.'

'To leave the country?'

'No, no, to leave.'

'Ah, to live, to live on. Really? That's shocking. But does the oil company not bear some responsibility for this?' He raised his shoulders and his hands in a *don't expect me to state an opinion about that* gesture.

'It's *profits* and *armaments*, not *profit* and *armament*. You said 'profit and armament'.' She wrote up the words on the board: *land mines, profits, armaments* and added some more: *oil companies, dollars, problems*.

He read out each word, hissing like a snake as he came to

66

the final *s*.

He apologised again for not having read the article she'd given him - an article about a planned *Festival of the Midge* in the West of Scotland - a typical example of British humour, he'd thought.

'But you have festivals in France.'

'Yes, but they are to celebrate nice things like flowers and wine. Only the British would have the idea of having a festival for something as unpleasant as the Scottish midge.

'But I have brought a report I want that you check,' he said now. He was a drilling engineer and had to write regular reports on the progress of the well they were currently drilling.

The eighteen and five-eighths drilling phase was completed at 658 metres ...

He didn't need any correction. His written English was always faultless. She must stir herself and teach him something.

'Read it out,' she told him. He stumbled, as she knew he would, over *eighths*.

'You can always say *t* instead of *th*,' she said. 'That will make it easier. And nobody will notice. Some Irish accents don't have a *th*.'

Which reminded her, she was supposed to be practising her Irish accent. *Dat's one ting more to tink about.* And something to take her mind off the blonde bombshell.

'You could say *the eighteen and five eights drilling phase*. It wouldn't be as bad as saying *eighthththththuuz*.'

'Really?' he said. She felt like God.

'Yes, no problem, no one will notice. It's like *clothes* and *months*. You can leave out the *th* and say "close" and "mons". No one will notice.'

'Really?' he said again.

When was he leaving for Angola? Not till the end of November? So he'd be able to have lessons for the next few weeks? Well, he had a lot to do, finishing off work.

'Let's make an appointment anyway,' she suggested.

She watched him as he walked smartly down the stairs in

his dark coat. The French really were very neat.

Though not Denis. Nor Thierry - it wasn't like a Frenchman to turn up to work with a hole in his pullover. Except that he was a widower, of course. Could she see herself mending that hole and ironing his shirts? No, she couldn't, but then a blonde bombshell didn't sound as if she'd be too nifty with the needle either.

'Oi'm haappy, Oi'm very haappy and why wouldn't Oi be?' she asked herself as she looked out of the window at the grey mist coming down. 'Happier than if I were living in Angola anyway.' Surely Angola was where that friend of Marc's came from. She'd only met him that once.

'Let's go and see Marc,' she'd said to Jennifer at the end of a sunny Thursday morning as they'd emerged from their first lecture on *French Culture and Civilisation*.

'Who's Marc?' They'd only been in Paris a few weeks and knew hardly anyone.

'He's the man who was sitting next to the one you were talking to in the university restaurant the other day?'

They'd learnt that if you paid £10 you could register as a student and get a student card, which meant you could avail yourself of the subsidised meals. So Tess and Jennifer had got themselves cards. As they'd sat, on that first visit to a university restaurant, trying to imagine what bit of the pig was involved in the production of the slices of cold sausage that were on their plates, they'd begun to wonder if it had been worth the trouble gathering together all the necessary papers to prove that they were bona fide students.

'What's this?' Jennifer had asked the bearded student sitting opposite her.

'It is made of the pig's lip, no, not lip .....'

'Cheek?' Jennifer had suggested, patting her own in a very charming way. The bearded student's gaze had softened as he watched her.

'No, no ... How you call ...?' and his hand had descended dangerously close to the region of his testicles. Surely not.

'You mean Bertrand? I'm seeing him this evening.'

'Well, his friend's called Marc and he said if ever we

were walking along the quais we should look out for a barge called the Atalante. He lives on it.'

He and a lean and handsome black man were busy working on the deck with hammers and chisels as Tess and Jennifer strolled past.

'Jump on and we can have something to eat,' said Marc. Only no, they'd nothing on board either to eat or drink, he suddenly remembered, and it was after one o'clock and the food shops would almost certainly all be closed.

'We could always try,' said Tess. She was starving. 'We might find one open.'

The four of them had set out down a deserted street, the clatter and smells of people preparing their *repas de midi* coming from open apartment windows high above their heads. To their joy at the end of the street they'd found a little grocer's still open. They'd together managed to collect enough money for two baguettes, a head of lettuce and a litre of vin ordinaire.

To this day if Tess had been asked to say what was the best meal she'd ever had in her life she'd have said that it was fresh French bread with salad smothered in garlicy vinaigrette and a large glass of rough red wine, sitting in the sunshine on a Paris quai separated from the man she was about to fall in love with by a decorous two feet of murky Seine water. Jennifer had been too nervous to make the leap onto the boat so Marc had passed across two camping stools for them to perch on.

'Have some more wine,' Marc had cried, picking up the bottle with the same theatrical gesture he'd made eighteen months later in the Boulevard St Michel. *My taileur eez reesh* …

She started to wipe the board clean of *land mines, profits, armaments, oil companies, dollars, problems.* What had become of the man from Angola? She couldn't even remember his name. Hilary was passing outside.

'I've something to tell you,' she said, her face lighting up as she saw Tess. She came into the room and closed the door behind her.

'I saw Thierry yesterday evening. I'm sure it was him. He was leaving that Indian restaurant in Summer Street with a blonde woman. I slowed down so he wouldn't see me and Cecil. They turned into the car park and she had her arm through his. I thought you said he was a widower.'

'Yes, he is, but he's allowed a girl friend, isn't he?' said Tess as she finished wiping the board. 'What did she look like?'

'I couldn't really see her. I only saw the back of her. Elegant, I suppose, in a conventional way - hair done up in a chignon, long black coat, and those shoes with gold bits on the heels. Oh, and she walked in a funny way.'

'Oh, really?' Thank you so much for telling me all this, Hilary.'

Chapter 14

Laurent had asked all the women he worked with whether they used *Ms* and most of them had said they didn't like it because it gave the impression they were feminists. Same old story. In her opinion the mistake had been to choose a completely new term. What was wrong with *Mrs* to refer to all women, not just the married ones, like *Mr* was used for all men? But of course *Mrs* had an older woman ring to it. You imagined a stalwart of the Women's Institute. *Madame* sounded more glamorous.

'But women still like to be called *Mademoiselle*. It makes them feel they are still young,' he said.

I rest my case, she thought. The subject depressed her. She turned to her copy of *Managing Meetings*.

'You said you'd explain *should*,' said Laurent. So she had. He was looking particularly stunning today in a blue tweed jacket. No tie, just an ivory cotton twill shirt buttoned up to the neck. Was he buttoned up? She didn't think so. That humorous smile. Maybe he'd be more fun than Thierry with his bombshell in tow if there weren't any Janet around.

'Well, there are five different uses of *should*,' she began. 'First of all there's the *should* which is used to say what is desirable or to give advice - *You should try harder.'*

'And *should* is stronger than *must*, no?'

No, in theory *must* was stronger. *You must try harder* was stronger than *You should try harder. Must* and *have to* were for giving orders. *Should* was for giving advice. *We must meet some time for a cup of coffee.* (Was that an order?). *We should have lunch together one day* (Was that the expression of something desirable?) Only joking. He really was much too young. She would just feel depressed, in constant fear of being taken for his mother.

'Only you have to be careful. Some people when they say *should* really mean *must* but they don't like to sound as if they're giving orders. It's to do with the freedom of the individual. *It's up to you, you have the choice.* But this is misleading because often you don't have a choice. So *You should finish it by Friday* could mean *It would be better if you did but it doesn't really matter.* But it could also mean *If you don't finish it by Friday you're sacked.*

'So beware *should* on the lips of an Englishman!' she cried. What was it about this man that tempted her into behaving like an actress in a B movie?

'The second use of *should* is to express a prediction.' She got to her feet, drew in her stomach and began to write on the board but he was looking at her now as if he wanted to say something.

'You are not free to come to dinner this evening, are you? I invited these people when Janet was still living with me but we have split up and now there is only me to receive them. I am going to cook them monk fish.'

'Oh, I love monk fish.' Was she going to follow this with 'but …'? She shouldn't really be jumping at an invitation delivered at such short notice.

'That will be lovely,' she said. He wrote out his address for her.

After he'd gone she looked down at her feet, at her boots with traces of mud on them from her walk that morning up to the top of the hill. She could slip into town and buy those black shoes with the stiletto heels she'd noticed the other day reduced to a ridiculous price in the sale in John Lewis's. And, while she was there, squirt herself with some of the perfume from the cosmetics department - maybe *Mitsouko*, specially created for the Ballets Russes in 1910, she'd told the salesgirl last week, who'd simply said 'Oh well.' No, something more modern for black stilettos. She undid the button on her skirt. That was another thing she'd need to buy if she was to survive the evening - a large safety pin.

The shoes just about fitted. Her hand hovered over the perfume bottles. Should it be the *Mitsouko* or should she choose *elle* – the new fragrance from Yves St Laurent. Or something more seductive like *Insolence*? She'd no idea how the evening was going to go, but his flat was just round the corner from where Hilary and Cecil lived so that meant she had three options. Option 1: don't drink and drive back to Kineldie. Option 2: drink and fall into Laurent's arms. Option 3: drink and then totter round to Hilary's. As she dithered before the waiting salesgirl she caught sight of her face in the mirror on the counter. She chose *elle*.

His flat was in a very modern building. Any furnished accommodation Tess had ever inhabited had been full of ill-assorted furniture - tables, chairs, settees picked up cheap in the local junk shops. Here, everything was brand new and co-ordinated - two cream leather sofas, a beige fitted carpet, halogen lamps on golden stands, smart coffee tables, white blinds, music Tess didn't recognise coming out of what looked like a miniature television screen.

'This is Neil and this is Sandra,' said Laurent and disappeared into the kitchen with the bottle of wine she'd brought. They looked about thirty, the same age as Laurent. Neil was very tall and going bald. He was in smart blue trousers and a bright check shirt. Sandra had on black trousers, a black lacy top with shiny bits in it and very high heeled boots. A pale face, brown eyes scrutinising Tess, lots of dark eye shadow, cyclamen pink lipstick and red highlights in her long black hair.

Neil was admiring the miniature television screen that the music was coming out of.

'That's an iPod dock and in front of it's the iPod,' Neil explained to Tess who'd just bought herself the cheapest MP3 player she could find but hadn't yet got round to recording anything on it. Kirsty was supposed to be helping her.

'Oh, that's near where I live.' She'd suddenly noticed a photo of the Aberdeenshire countryside on the wall above, with Bennachie in the background.

'We all work for *Termoil*,' said Laurent, coming back in with a large glass of red wine for Tess. That meant Neil and Sandra would know Thierry.

'It looks as if Option 1 is about to be crossed off the list,' thought Tess as she took the glass from him. With her other hand she checked that her sweater was still hiding the large safety pin with the pink end to it that was keeping her skirt together. Option 2 isn't very likely either, she was thinking. What was she doing here with these people not much older than Annie?

'And what do you do, Tess?' She was a teacher of English as a Foreign Language who specialised in pillow talk. She bought shoes with killer heels and then set out to seduce her students, one by one, a sort of female Bluebeard. This evening it was Laurent's turn.'

'I work at the Aberdeen Language Institute.'

'Ah, so you're Laurent's English teacher. You must know Stephen, Stephen Grant.' Stephen and Kirsty in the bath with froth up to their chins, sipping pink champagne.

'Not very well,' she said.

I will show you my magnificent apartment before we eat,' said Laurent. 'First the bathroom.'

All chrome, and tiles with boats on them. An array of bottles on the shelf over the washbasin - *Impulse... Poison ...* Janet had left her trail. And a large bottle of Armani's *Acqua di Gio*. That's what that faint smell was that always accompanied Laurent. She wondered if they could smell the *elle* she'd squirted on her wrists and behind her ears. She'd been about to spray some down her jumper when she saw the assistant approaching her. 'I'll just live with this for a little while' she'd said, moving away.

'And this is my bedroom.' Laurent threw open the door next to the bathroom onto more cream and white and beige and a golden laminate floor.

The Ile de France, a little auberge, the door slowly being pushed open by a heavy wooden tray loaded with croissants and café au lait, carried by the woman who'd served them dinner the previous evening. The sun shining on the faded flowery wallpaper and Marc beside her in the bed, still fast asleep.

'Marc, wake up.'

'This room must be east facing - which means you get the sun coming in in the morning, no?' Tomorrow morning, sunrise about six - if there was a sun - lying there beneath the heavy white counterpane. No, out of the question.

74

'This is really fine,' said Sandra as they started to eat nearly an hour later.

Laurent explained how he'd poached the monkfish gently in cream and white wine. It was now sitting on their plates, enveloped in a tarragon flavoured sauce. They talked about how in Scotland people on the whole tended not to eat fish, except for fish and chips when it was enveloped in batter. That was the only way you'd get Neil to eat fish, Sandra started to say and then stopped and Neil said that if she could cook fish like Laurent did he'd eat it every day.

'How about you, Tess?' Neil asked her. He had a nice way of looking at you that made you feel you were worth something.

'My ex-husband ...' There, she'd answered the question they must all have been asking themselves 'hated fish so we never ate it. But since we split up a few years ago ..... I go to a little shop in Torry ...just off Victoria Rd .... '

It was a long time since she'd been in the company of strangers. She felt on the edge of losing herself, of inventing a completely different personality that would fit in with how they must be seeing her now, a woman in her late fifties with a lived-in face.

'We'll have to go, Neil,' said Sandra. They'd finished their chocolate eclairs from Marks and Spencers and were drinking coffee made from Laurent's newly bought espresso machine.

'I promised the babysitter we'd be back not long after ten,' she said to Tess as they got into their leather jackets. Tess wondered if she should ask them about their children, but Option 2 was hovering in the doorway.

'I must be going too,' said Tess after they'd gone.

'You *must* or you *should*?' Laurent was smiling at her. She looked across at his collection of DVDs.

'I notice you have *Jules et Jim*,' she said.

'Yes, I brought it back from France. Would you like to watch it with me? It is only ten o'clock.'

'I saw it in Paris years ago.' Before the film they'd had a drink in a smart bar called the *Pam Pam* across the road from the cinema in the Champs Elysées.

'I like your coat,' Marc had said. She'd been thinking of throwing it away - a camel coloured coat her mother had bought her when she was 18. She'd gone on wearing it after that but months later he admitted that he hadn't liked it at all, he'd only said that because he'd wanted to say something nice to her.

'But I'd love to see it again,' she said. She slipped off the stilettos and curled up in a corner of the cream leather sofa. Laurent settled down at the opposite end but then he jumped up again. Would she like another glass of wine? When he came back with it he sat down beside her, their shoulders almost touching.

The film began - Jeanne Moreau in baggy trousers and a peaked cap racing these two men - one fair-haired, the other dark - across a bridge. Which of the two was she going to end up with? Tess stared at the screen, realising that her foot was only inches away from Laurent's knee and that if she wanted to move it, and it was already beginning to feel uncomfortable, she wouldn't be able to avoid touching him. She stirred.

'Are you okay? Would you like a cushion?' What did that mean? *Maybe someone of your age needs some support?*

'No, no, I'm fine,' she said, at the same time taking the opportunity to withdraw her foot and uncurl herself. She was now sitting primly with her feet side by side on the floor, the way she'd been taught to sit by the nuns, waiting, wondering 'if he was going to make a pass at her' as they used to say.

And then it occurred to her that maybe Laurent was waiting for her to make the first move. All her talk about feminism and women being independent, taking responsibility for what they did. Yet here she was, waiting to be seduced, overpowered, the decision taken out of her hands. Even at her age.

Maybe all it required was a little movement on her part. Laurent's arm was now extended along the back of the sofa. If she lent back - as if by accident - her head would find itself resting on it. How lovely that would be, to feel the pressure of his arm, and then his fingers playing with her hair, caressing her cheek. They'd go on watching the film in silence but then, with the closing credits, they'd move towards the bedroom, and the bed with the heavy white counterpane. All she had to do was to lean her head back just a little.

Jeanne Moreau had now abandoned the dark-haired man in favour of the fair- haired one. She'd also abandoned the boyish peaked cap and was wearing a wide band in her long hair.

'She's wonderful, isn't she?' Laurent murmured and Tess remembered how Marc also had fallen in love with Jeanne Moreau that evening and she'd started wearing a wide band in her hair too and Marc had said she looked like she was sixteen.

'Oh, I've been there! I've seen that!' Laurent had removed his arm from the back of the sofa and was leaning forward in great excitement, his elbows on his knees. 'I've seen that statue!'

The two men had gone to Greece together in search of perfect beauty and harmony and they'd found it in this statue.

Tess looked at her watch.

'Laurent, I think I'd better go. I've seen the film already and I think I'd better get to Hilary's before they go to bed.' She managed to get her feet back into the stilettos. Laurent was already standing holding out her coat for her. Should she give him a light kiss? She held out her hand.

'That was a lovely evening.'

Chapter 15

'He's got a meeting down in London the week-end after next. Cynthia cannot decide if she wants to go with him or not. If she doesn't ...'

'When will he know?' This sort of situation had arisen before. Cynthia tended to leave off making decisions till the last moment, as if she knew what was going on.

'Well, he said she would have to make up her mind in the next day or two, if she wanted to get a cheap fare. But she is earning so much money I don't suppose that bothers her.' Cynthia was a financial advisor.

'I think I'll tell him I'm finishing with him if we can't have this weekend together.' Kirsty was always talking about finishing with Stephen.

'How's Jacques?' Jacques was someone who'd worked for a time as a waiter in the French restaurant in Aberdeen. Kirsty had got quite friendly with him.

'You could always buy your ticket to London and then if Cynthia decides to go with Stephen you can continue on your way to Paris and spend the week-end with Jacques.'

Silence. This sounded a much better proposition to Tess, but unfortunately Jacques didn't have Stephen's appeal for Kirsty. Better still, Kirsty could stay behind in Aberdeen and Tess would suggest to Pete to invite them for a meal and then Tess could develop a migraine at the last minute? Tess glanced at her. She was definitely looking as if she could have done with an hour more sleep. She wasn't even wearing lipstick this morning. For some reason this made Tess feel better about herself.

'No, I don't think Jacques will want to see me. He's got this new friend, Sylvie. I think maybe they're becoming an item.'

She still hadn't decided what to do with Thierry, who would be waiting in her room when she arrived, installed at the table, a fresh page in his exercise book open in front of him. Should she go on with the present or start on the past? Or the future? What future was there with Thierry? Was there still the possibility of a future? She didn't need to give in to this blonde bombshell without a fight. Who was she, anyway?

He was actually standing at the entrance to the Institute when they arrived. He was looking at the window boxes that Maggie and herself had put there in the Spring to brighten up the grey granite, though Stephen had thought it a waste of money.

'What is the name of these flowers?' he began. Kirsty disappeared into the entrance hall with a little wave, Thierry following her with his eyes. What's he looking at? thought Tess. The answer was obvious - Kirsty's short skirt, Kirsty's beautifully shaped legs inside skin-coloured tights, Kirsty's bouncing fair hair, Kirsty's elegant bag slung over a slender shoulder, Kirsty's youth.

'They're marigolds,' said Tess, wishing she'd taken the trouble to put on some blusher that morning. In French, he told her, they were called *oeillets d'Inde* - Indian carnations. She'd thought the word for marigold in French was *souci*. Ah yes, but that was for your ordinary marigold - *soucis des jardins*. Did he know what forget-me-nots were? And poppies? And wall flowers? And columbines and nasturtiums? She wrote the words up on the board.

'And *lilas*. That is *lily*, no?'

'No, *lilas* is *lilac* in English.' Jennifer had sent flowers to Marc's funeral. She'd wanted to send lilies - white lilies - but she'd made the same mistake and ordered *lilas* over the phone. She was very embarrassed but Tess had preferred the lilac.

'Look at that stupendous sky. Isn't it gorgeous?' said Thierry, going to the window. Day had just broken over the North Sea. He seemed to be on very familiar terms with this word *gorgeous*. 'But here it is too cold. Me, I am from 'ere.'

He turned to the map on the wall beside him and with his finger jabbed at a place somewhere south east of Paris. Ah, she was right. He was not a native of Versailles. His family was from near Dijon, from Burgundy.

'I have a big big house here and a lot of land. I am - what

you call it - a farmer? No, not a farmer. I grow ... .'

'Carrots? Tomatoes? You are a market gardener?' She'd spent a summer once picking and grading tomatoes in the south of England.

'No, no. I am growing wine.'

'Ah, wine! No, you don't grow wine. Though you can say you're a *wine-grower*.' That doesn't make sense, she thought as she wrote it up.

But her mind was beginning to be elsewhere. How nice it would be to live in a big, big house in Burgundy - a chateau, or maybe a manoir, a manoir sounded even better, more manageable, more homely, more like a large rambling house - in yellow stone that turned a warm orange in the setting sun, and surrounded by vineyards and orchards. She could see herself sipping sundowners on the terrace, or, in the morning sunlight, in a floating negligee, drinking café au lait out of an enormous blue bowl. He was a widower. Why not? The blonde bombshell, who was surely much younger than her, would go better with Laurent. Thierry and herself had age on their side.

'Today we will do the future,' she said. 'We will talk about the difference between *will* and *shall*. In fact it makes very little difference which you say. You can say either *I shall go* or *I will go*. Most people say *I'll* in any case. But if you're getting married you say *I will*,' she added a propos of nothing and everything. She wasn't sure about that, she realised, as she said it. Nowadays she rather thought people said *I do*.

'Why don't we get married?' Marc had taken her by surprise as they made their way southwards to the Côte D'Azur. He'd come in for a bit of money that he wanted to blow on a week in the sun in November in a posh hotel and he'd asked her to go with him. She was surviving on fromage blanc and baguettes in her attic room and the cheapest cheese you could buy - a nasty rubbery thing called *Bonbel*. Neither of them had ever stayed in a posh hotel before. She'd never even been south of Paris but she hesitated all the same. She'd only known him a few months. Would she be turning herself into an adventuress like Becky Sharpe? (She was reading *Vanity Fair* at the time.) She wasn't sure she wanted to be an adventuress. But she'd agreed to go all the same. And agreed to marry him.

'Why not?' she'd replied looking roguish in the manner of Becky Sharp, feeling a little drunk and very reckless, after lunch in Beaune in a Michelin three star restaurant that specialised in cuisine bourgoise. She would live the rest of her life in the heart of the country in France. (Marc came from a little village in the east of France and was going to take over his father's farm). What would she do there? She hardly posed herself the question. Had she read Madame Bovary yet? Certainly children were not on her agenda. That came much later, married to Bob, the desire not to miss out on the experience of being a mother.

'But returning to *will* and *shall*...'

'Ah yes,' he interrupted. 'How you pronounce *I will not?* I cannot hear a difference between *I weun't* and *I weunt*.'

'Between *I won't* and *I want?* That is serious. That could lead to misunderstandings.' What sort of misunderstandings? *I want to see you/I won't see you. I want to be with you/I won't be with you. I want/I won't ....*

'Listen: *I want to go/I won't go; I want to go/I won't go.* She recited the two sentences. 'Your lips are much more rounded for *won't*,' she said. 'Watch me.'

What was she thinking of, inviting him to stare at her puckered lipstickless mouth? Better get him to concentrate on listening for the difference.

'The vowel in *want* is short. It's the same sound as you have in *hot*. The vowel in *won't* is long. If I speak with a Scottish accent I pronounce it as a pure vowel as in *beau*.'

'Bo?'

How was it they never understood when she introduced a French word? What is this strange word *bo*? Ah *BEAU!* Yes, that's what I said, no?

'I'm using a French word - *beau*' She tried to pronounce it more carefully this time. 'The French for *beautiful* - or *handsome* if you're describing a man.'

Nobody could call him handsome. His face looked like the sort of face you'd produce during your first steps in pottery. But there was an aliveness about it, yes.

'If you speak with an English accent you pronounce it as two vowels which run into each other, that's to say, as a diphthong.'

She wrote the word up on the board. Only how did you spell it? Should there be an *h* after the *p*?

'You begin with a little hesitating sound like *euh* and then you turn it into a *oo* like in book - euhoo. But if you want to sound like the queen you start with an *e* like in *get*. "Eoo neoo I deoon't think seoo." '

She was rather pleased with her imitation of the queen. He laughed.

'What are you doing next weekend?' she asked suddenly with a surge of confidence in her powers of seduction. 'Would you like to come out to my house in the country for lunch on Saturday? I could show you my garden - my fuchsias, my lobelias and ... and ... '. She tried to think of the names of the flowers they'd started out with - marigolds, columbines, lilies.

'You want to come? You won't come?' she asked playfully, tantalisingly, seductively.

He seemed very pleased at the invitation. He was - how you say? – 'tres touché'. And he would bring a bottle of wine - of very good wine. Burgundy.

'The village is here,' she said, pointing to a spot on the map on the wall beside her, 'and the house is up this track.'

He came round to her side of the desk to have a better look and she got up to make room for him. There was hardly an inch between them.

'I hope the weather will be good,' she said, trying to push her chair against the window to allow herself to stand upright. He's going to be in my lap in a minute, she thought. Slight smell of sandalwood mingling with gaulloise.

'I have a plan in my car, I will find the house,' he said, going briskly back to his seat, leaving a strangely empty space where he had been.

'What's *nasturtiums* in French?' she asked, trying to fill it. Ah yes, *capucines*, like the Capuchine monks. And it also means a lady's hood, no? Thierry in a cowl pursuing her down the garden path, and she, dressed in a cloak with a hood like that woman in the Scottish Widows advertisement, playing hide and seek with him.

'Well, I'll see you on Saturday.'

After he'd gone she began to wonder how people from Mayo would pronounce the *o* in *No*. Of course there was no word for *no* - or *yes* - in Irish, which was why when Irish people spoke English they tended not to use the words. *Do you like me, Tess? I do. Would you like to have dinner with me? I would. You won't be offended if I put my arms round you? I won't.*

Chapter 16

Jean Louis Truffaut
Age: 30 going on 60
Job: accountant
+++: can't think of anything
---: everything
Clothes: blue-striped shirt, white collar, orange tie with
diagonal green stripes
Level of English: tedious
Lesson Plan: take him down a peg or two

He turned up in a tight blue-striped shirt with white collar and cuffs, orange tie with diagonal green stripes. How did he expect her to sit there for the next hour and look at that? She looked out of the window. A grey brooding sea, untidy patches of light in the sky, swollen clouds.

'What does *to put up with* mean?' For once he was asking her a question.

'It means *to tolerate*. It's a phrasal verb'

He had never heard of phrasal verbs. Were they like irregular verbs? Irregular verbs struck terror in the hearts of people learning English as a foreign language. Regular verbs were easy, you just added *-ed* to the stem of the verb and you got the past - *I played* - and the past participle as in *I have played*. But with verbs like *cut* and *break* and *drink* you'd no way of guessing what transformation they mightn't undergo once you were foolish enough to embark on talking about yesterday.

In the old days learning English was largely a question of being able to rattle off the principle parts of irregular verbs. "What's your name?" Blank look. "Where do you live?" Even blanker look. But "What's the past of the verb *to cut*?" and *cut, cut, cut* came at you like a machine gun. And *smite*? And *cleave*? More machine gun fire.

'No, *to put up with* is an irregular verb ...'

'*Put, put, put*' he puffed. He's a young boy again, his first year at the big school. 'but it is also a phrasal verbs' she continued, 'because it is made up of three bits - *put* + *up* + *with*. English has got thousands of verbs like that.' She smiled proudly. 'There are maybe a hundred irregular verbs but more than three thousand phrasal verbs. And it's often impossible to guess what they mean unless you know already.'

And there he was thinking she had nothing more to teach him.

'For example ... ' She wrote up on the board:
They fell out over a trifle and never made it up.

'Do you know what that means?' she asked, leaning back in her chair and looking at her watch. What would she give Thierry for lunch on Sunday? She could make a fish pie today and then freeze it. Fish pie. She was pretty sure that was a dish that would be new to him.

'Well *trifle* is a sort of desert,' he began.

'Dessert' she corrected.

'No, I do not understand. They fell when they were making a trifle. It is not making sense. Ask to all the other student and nobody will know the meaning of that.'

'I'll leave it up for the rest of the week,' she said. 'It will be interesting to see if anyone can guess what it means.' A fish pie would be good. She wasn't going to risk any imitation French dishes. Go to the trouble of putting together a Salade Niçoise - celery, peppers, tuna fish, a few potatoes and damn I've forgotten the anchovies and blast Kirsty's eaten all the olives and rushing in to the supermarket to get them and then... 'We have something in France which is a little bit like this. It is called *Salade Niçoise*.' Oh really?!

'But to get back to *to put up with*, the reason English has such a big vocabulary is that it has the old Anglo-Saxon way of saying things like *to put up with* and it has words from Latin and French like *to tolerate,* which mean more or less the same thing.

He didn't see the point in having several ways of saying the same thing.

It was true that if you turned up in any other country in the world you'd expect to be served a typical national or

86

regional dish. It was only here that people felt obliged to give you Coq au Vin or Thai Chicken or Mexican Tacos instead of Scotch Broth or Lancashire Hot Pot or Roast Beef and Yorkshire Pud.

'Well, there was this American in this country railway station,' she began. Jean Louis looked at his watch. 'He noticed that there were two clocks on the platform and they each told a different time. He drew the stationmaster's attention to this but *he* said that if they both told the same time there wouldn't be any point in having two of them. It's the same with language. If two words meant exactly the same thing there ...'

'What is the difference between a stationmaster and a guard?' he interrupted and when she didn't reply 'I think English clothes suit me'.

He'd bought a tartan tie - a Stewart tartan - and he was intending buying a pair of trousers to match.

'Soon people will be taking you for a Scot, your English is so very good.' She smiled. 'And you are right. I'm sure none of your compatriots are going to understand *They fell out over a trifle and never made it up.*' She showed him to the door. 'We'll go on with phrasal verbs next week,' she said. Yes, fish pie and maybe Kirsty could do a pudding.

She had the afternoon off. Pete had asked her if she wanted to go to the matinée at the Belmont but Tess resisted the temptation. She'd go home and do a bit of gardening. Tidy the place up in preparation for Thierry's visit on Saturday.

Drops of rain began to appear on the windscreen as she came to what had been John Wood's cottage and Finochty House half a mile on. She glanced down the drive and caught a glimpse of Colonel Forbes getting out of his Range Rover. She stuck her tongue out at him as she passed. Fat lot of good that would do. She should have spoken up at the time but what good would that have done either?

'We don't think you should put John Wood out of that cottage after he's lived there for the past thirty years looking after your cows.' Organised a petition then? Yes, they could have done that, instead of just sighing and shaking their heads in the village post office. John Wood had had to go and live with his sister and her husband in Aberdeen in a top floor tenement flat looking out onto more tenement flats after a lifetime of looking out on fields and trees.

As she drove up the long avenue of beech trees that ended in her pink granite cottage the drizzle had definitely turned into rain. Hurrah, she thought, that meant she wouldn't be able to do any gardening. She got out of her Russian officer's dress, put on an old sweater and skirt and woolly socks and installed herself with a cup of coffee and the newspaper in the summerhouse she'd had built on to the side of the cottage.

Summerhouse? Why not a sun porch? In fact it had been the joiner who had called it a summerhouse and she had taken over the name. But *summerhouse* did have a ring of Enid Blyton and middle class children to it. The headline in the paper she now unfolded read *Class distinctions a thing of the past.*

When she'd mentioned her summerhouse the other day to Laurent he had understood that she had a holiday home, a house she went to in the summer.

'No, the stress is on *summer*, not on *house*. It's really just one word. It's what we call a compound noun.' She was anxious to get back onto a teacher-student relationship with Laurent after the other evening.

'With the main stress on *summer* and less stress on *house* you have one word - a compound noun - a *summerhouse*. But if you put the same amount of stress on each word you have two separate words. You have *a summer house*, which is a house you go to in the summer. It's like *blackbird* and *black bird*. A *blackbird* is a sort of bird and a *black bird* is any bird that's black. Another example is *walking stick*. With the main stress on *walking* it means a stick you carry when you're walking. But a *walking stick* with the same amount of stress on both words means a stick that is walking. Which doesn't make much sense, unless, of course, you're talking about someone very thin.'

'SUMMERhouse - Summer house   BLACKbird - Black bird   WALKing stick - Walking stick.' She'd read out the words slowly, exaggerating the stress patterns, enjoying the feeling that this was all there was between them, these contrasting rhythms and the memory of a pleasant evening spent together. Would it be the same with Thierry after Saturday?

Anyway here she was now in the summerhouse with Trotsky noisily crunching a Daddy longlegs. She'd forgotten to stop off at the village shop to buy cat food. Would a diet of Daddy longlegs suffice?

It had been a poor year for sweet peas. She'd planted them up against the window of the summerhouse in the hope that she'd be able to look out on a profusion of pink and red and purple and lilac flowers and drink in their honeyed scent as she passed. But all she'd got was a scrabble of leaves and suckers and a few white petals on the end of long stems. Beyond them, though, a single coral-coloured rose, And then the michaelmas daisies, purple and puce, fully recovered from the deer trampling they'd got the other week.

She wondered what Thierry would think of her garden. Pity about the rain, all the same, it really did need tidying up a bit. She hoped it wouldn't be raining on Saturday and that the coral rose would still have all its petals.

A skein of geese passed overhead. She opened the door of the summerhouse to hear their - what was the sound? - honk? caw? She remembered the first skein of geese she'd seen that winter, the evening she was waiting for Fergus to phone, the day before she learnt that he was going away.

She'd had two postcards from him since then from towns in Hungary with unpronounceable names. He seemed very far away and not just physically and this suddenly made her feel immensely sad. The only other time there had ever been any distance between them had been briefly one weekend they were spending together - Bob was away at a conference on The Anatomy of Bats. Fergus had a concert in Inverness so they'd chosen to stay in this pretty little town in the Moray Firth. Some quarrel had developed between them as they walked down the main street.

'I'm going back on the early train,' he'd shouted and set off in the direction of the hotel to collect his bag.

'Good riddance,' she'd shouted after him. She'd stayed on the old stone bridge, looking down at the river, with wild daffodils growing up its banks. Then she'd looked up and seen him coming back, walking towards her in the absurd hat he'd bought in Oxfam just a few hours earlier.

She heard the phone ringing in the house. She'd forgotten to bring out the cordless. By the time she reached the hall where the phone was hanging it had rung off. She dialled 1471 and recognised Stephen's number. She hesitated. Should she press 3 to ring back? Kirsty had said that she and Stephen were escaping out this afternoon to this house in the country owned by a friend who was away. She stood there holding the phone. Maybe there had been some muddle and Stephen had missed Kirsty and was phoning to see if she had come home. She pressed 3 and got Cynthia's voice on the other end.

'You rang,' said Tess, trying to sound relaxed.

'No, you rang me. This is the Wilkinson phone,' said Cynthia. 'I dialled 1471 when I got in just now and yours was the last number that had dialled us. Are you ....?'

'Oh, yes, of course.' Curse the 1471 exposure device.

'I'm Tess McGuire. I work at the Institute. I think we met once. I was ringing Stephen to know about a student who'll be arriving next week.'

'Did you not try him at work or on his mobile? He's never here in the day time.'

Any moment now, if they're not there already, the seeds of suspicion are going to be sown, thought Tess. Kirsty is a fool. Surely she had understood the dangers of 1471, surely she should know to dial whatever it was you dialled first to make it impossible to trace the call. Or just dial him on his mobile always.

'Yes, I got him at work eventually,' she said. She was about to add 'He's always so busy. He's quite difficult to get hold of,' when she heard the front door open. She turned round and there was Kirsty, with Stephen just behind her, the lovers in from the rain.

'Hi Tess!' Stephen boomed out.

'Goodbye, sorry to have bothered you,' she said hurriedly down the phone and hung up.

'That was Cynthia. I wonder if she heard your voice, Stephen.'

Part of Tess wanted to laugh but Stephen was obviously not amused.

'I'd better be going,' he said immediately to Kirsty.

'Have a drink first,' said Kirsty. 'I mean a cup of coffee.'

'No, I'd better be getting back. I'll just use your bathroom first, if I may.'

He made off down the corridor. Kirsty stood there looking as if she was going to cry. After Stephen had gone she burst out

'I see him just one afternoon in the week - not even that, it is three weeks since we had an afternoon together - and even this is spoiled by him having to rush away.

But you'll be spending a whole week end in London with him soon, won't you?'

'Yes, but did you see how scared he looked when you told him Cynthia was on the phone? If she heard him she'll certainly want to go down to London with him herself.''

'Do you think he'll ever leave her?' Tess asked her later as they were on their third glass of wine. And what would Kirsty's reaction be if he even began to contemplate it? Kirsty up to now seemed to specialise in impossible love/lust situations.

'I don't think he'd have the courage.'

Was it really courage - or ruthlessness - that he lacked, or was it that Kirsty for him was just an occasional life-enhancer, like Fergus used to be for her? Was Stephen passionate enough about Kirsty to leave Cynthia for her?

'But they have nothing in common any more. They lead completely separate lives. The children are grown up, there's no need for them to stay with each other. Only she's Catholic you know so she believes in what God has joined together you mustn't tear asunder sort of thing. But they don't need each other any more. There is no reason for them to stay together.'

Not so, Tess was thinking. There had been plenty of reasons for her and Bob to stay together even though they led such different lives.

'You want that chair in the garden painted green, no?' asked Kirsty, jumping up.

'But you can't paint it now in the dark. Besides it's wet, it's been raining all afternoon.' Maybe she and Stephen had hardly noticed. 'And also I'm beginning to think it looks quite nice white under the laurel tree. You could paint this window sill instead if you like.' She was suddenly seeing the room through Thierry's eyes.

Chapter 17

Eight o'clock, Monday morning. Thierry turned up purring

'Thank you for the lovely lunch on Saturday and what a charming person your friend Kirsty is.'

She should have known better than to have included Kirsty in the invitation. He'd turned up very late - 'You said me turn right in the village' - and it had rained steadily all the time he was there so they hadn't gone into the garden at all. Worse, she had miscalculated the amount of time it took for a fish pie to defrost.

'Help yourself,' she'd said, presenting him with the dish and she'd watched as the serving spoon encountered a block of ice.

'No, no, round the edges it will be good,' he'd said gallantly.

They'd finished by spooning helpings onto their plates and putting each plate in the microwave in turn.

'We could have another sherry while we're waiting,' Kirsty had suggested.

'And some more of your delicious cheese straws.'

Kirsty had made cheese straws from a recipe her grandmother had taught her. She'd made them the evening before to cheer herself up. She hadn't seen Stephen all week after their afternoon in the rain, except briefly at the Institute. What Tess had actually asked her to do was the pudding. She wasn't going to spend the time scurrying around in the kitchen while Kirsty flirted with Thierry at the table.

'Do a Pavlova or something,' she'd told her, imagining her wrestling with a Pavlova while Tess finished off the wine with Thierry. But Kirsty'd made little raspberry and blackberry tartlets the evening before also so all she'd had to do was disappear into the kitchen for a few seconds and emerge with this stunning display of tartlets arranged on a white napkin covering a rush tray made by some friend of hers that made baskets.

'How wonderful, how delightful, how charming,' Thierry had cried.

He'd liked her cottage, though - the stone fireplace and the old heavy wooden table and chairs - furniture from an old farm - and the kilims on the walls that she'd brought back from her wanderings round Turkey with Bob. And he'd asked Tess if she'd like to go with him to his furniture man the following Sunday.

'He is making up this old mill and selling furnitures,' he'd explained to Kirsty as they sat drinking coffee after lunch. 'Every Sunday I am going there and discussing with him but I am buying too much furnitures. I have to stop."

For a moment Tess thought he was going to include Kirsty in the invitation but he didn't. He wanted her by herself.

'*Doing up*,' she corrected. 'He's doing up an old mill. Yes, that would be nice.'

'And why not *making up*? I never know when it is *do* and when it is *make*. I am always doing mistakes.'

'I'll explain on Monday.' She'd managed to make this sound conspiratorial.

Anyway now it was Monday morning and the view of the sea was completely blotted out. Nothing but a grey mist. She didn't feel up to launching into the difference between *do* and *make* and besides, they should really revise the future. *What do you do, what are you doing, what are you going to do, what will you do,* and then the Future Continuous: *what will you be doing this evening, tomorrow, next year and for the rest of your life?* Above all, *what will we be doing together next Sunday?*

'You said you will explain me *do* and *make*,' he said.

Okay. She actually had an exercise on it. And it would be easier than getting lost again in the future.

She opened the drawer of the filing cabinet marked *Vocabulary*. I must get round to organising all this, she thought, and typing out fresh labels. She'd thought this for several years now, every time she opened the drawer. Bob, soon after they'd got married, making a joke of her untidiness, had typed out labels for her for her newly acquired filing cabinet: *maps and old envelopes; bits of string; letters from*

Aunt Susie; old Christmas cards and shopping lists ....

She'd crossed these out in some irritation at the time and scribbled beside them things like *Idioms; Newspaper headlines; Discourse markers; Taboo Words used in the oil industry.* She now took out *Do and Make,* run to earth in the file entitled *Suggestopaedia* and gave him a copy of the exercise.

'The problem for French people,' she began 'is that in French there is only the one verb *faire* which means both *do* and *make.*'

The exercise began with a general explanation. She decided to read it out to him. ***Do** is less specific than **make**. With **make** there is the idea of constructing something. You **do** a job, you **do** the cooking but you **make** a bookcase or you **make** a cake.* And you *make* love - how constructive was that? Or was it one of the exceptions. She ran her eye down the long list of exceptions she'd added - *make an effort, a fuss, a noise, a mistake ... .* M*ake love* wasn't there.

'This list of exceptions is not complete,' she said. Could he think of other expressions with *make*?

'*Compliment?*' he suggested. 'You *do* or you *make* a compliment in English?' Was he about to say something or was he thinking still of Kirsty and her cheese straws?

'Neither,' she said. 'You *pay* people compliments.' How Breeteesh.

'I will pay you a compliment,' she said, taking the initiative. 'Your English is improving.'

'I am doing progresses?' he asked, looking pleased.

'No, look at the list. You are *making* progress.'

What sort of progress was she making with him? What about the blonde bombshell? Are you doing progresses with the blonde bombshell?

'I forgot to put *to make love,*' she said. 'You *make* love in English, you do not *do* love.' Are you making love with the blonde bombshell? 'And if I might *make* a suggestion, or a proposal, or a proposition ... you could now *do* this exercise and try to avoid *making mistakes.*'

He stared down at the list of sentences that occupied the

rest of the page. Would he remember about his invitation to the antique man?

'Oh, by the way,' she interrupted when he came to this last sentence, 'are we going to see your man by the river next Sunday? Did we make a plan?'

Yes, of course, that was *wondairfool*, he hadn't forgotten, he would phone her on Friday to do a rendez-vous. And they would book a table for lunch? Would she like that? After he'd gone she put her feet up and unfolded her newspaper. The day had changed. The sun was streaming in and the sea was bright blue.

Pete was in the car park surrounded by his six Japanese businessmen. Smiles and low bows which Tess returned, not sure what Japanese etiquette would have to say about an older woman bowing to younger men. They were on their way into town to buy strong walking shoes and waterproofs for their expedition up to the top of Bennachie on Sunday.

'On Sunday I'm going to take you to the top of Benachie - Aberdeenshire's best loved landmark,' Pete had told his Japanese. 'Bennachie is a rocky 500m high mountain with a Iron Age fort at the top.'

'OOOh! Aaaahh' they'd exclaimed.

Tess had completely forgotten that, on the spur of the moment, on Wednesday at the university she'd asked her foreign students if they'd like to come along as well. Of course it's optional, she'd told them but they were all coming. Maybe they hadn't understood the word *optional*. But what about her visit with Thierry to the antique man? She'd have to phone him to put him off - or invite him to come with them.

'We must meet to talk about the arrangements, Tess. I've managed to organise two minibuses. Oh, and did you mention it to Kirsty?'

Cynthia had finally decided not to accompany Stephen on his trip to London so Kirsty was going instead.

'No, Kirsty will be away.' Just as well. Pete could easily fall off the top of the mountain gazing at her. 'I've told the students to be in the university car park for ten,' she said.

She should have checked if her students possessed the right clothes and foot gear. They certainly wouldn't be able to afford to buy anything specially, not Hunein anyway, or Mousa or Joseph. Maybe she could persuade Hilary to turn up at the car park to take the unsuitably dressed and/or the reluctant off to the Art Gallery instead.

Sunday turned out to be a lovely day. It wasn't far to the top, even the slowest walkers weren't going to take more than two hours, the path was nicely graded, and there were blackberries and blaeberries to be picked along the way. At one moment Sheba fell over backwards in a panic, having been attacked by what turned out to be a nettle. And Mousa, at a section where the path petered out, sank ankle deep into the bog and almost had to leave one of his polished shoes behind as Pete grabbed hold of his leg to pull him out. But there was a lot of laughter as they sat all together, huddled in the shelter of some rocks just down from the top, sharing out sandwiches and thermos flasks of soup.

'You can just see my house down there.' Tess pointed.

'Oh, it is very big!'

'No, not that.' That was a large grey granite house, built in the Scottish Baronial Style, now a hotel, with a walled garden and a lake. 'The little house to the left of it, just the other side of the road.'

At the top, Pete's Japanese businessmen stood on the rocky summit in their quilted anoraks, exclaiming at the view below them of large fields of golden corn, and Pete pointed out to them the remains of the Iron Age fort, still visible in places. Two thousand years old? "Oooohh Aaaahh". A few yards away from them a couple were looking at the fort, puzzled. They didn't remember seeing it last time they were at the top. Maybe it was the Scouts built it.

But then Tess became aware of Mousa and Sheba standing beside Pete's Japanese in their thin clothes, shivering in the icy wind. Hilary hadn't been at all attracted by the idea of turning up at the university at ten on a Sunday morning to take the doubtful ones to the Art Gallery instead. Tess interrupted Pete's explanation of iron age forts to tell him they were starting down.

It wasn't until they were back in the minibus that they noticed that Concepta and Xavier were missing. Had they turned right instead of left just down from the summit? If so they would have ten miles of wilderness in front of them, always supposing they walked in a straight line, before they reached a road and it was already getting dark. Pete's Japanese had their own transport so they went off while Pete and Hunein went back up the mountain and Tess stayed in the minibus with Joseph, Mousa, Mr Sakura and Sheba. Nobody was talking much.

'They're cold, they're hungry, and Concepta and Xavier are going to perish on the mountain and I am responsible,' Tess was thinking.

'Let's each of us sing a song in our own language,' suggested Joseph.

He started out with an Indonesian love song, tears in his eyes. Sheba came next, warbling in Amharic. 'Maybe I should take a turn and teach them Cockles and Mussles,' thought Tess - though that was a pretty sad song too. But to her surprise Mr Sakura got in before her, volunteering a song in Japanese about cherry blossom. The word for cherry blossom in Japanese was the same word as his name, *sakura*, he explained. Only it was pronounced with a different tone, which gave a different meaning to the word.

'My name means *warehouse*. I am Mr Warehouse in English,' he told them. They were all managing to laugh at this when the car park was lit up by the headlights of a car arriving - with Concepta and Xavier inside. At the top they'd taken the path which had gone straight on and which had led down through trees to a different car park and a little house with an obliging man inside who, when they managed to explain themselves to him, drove them round to the waiting minibus.

'Are you running an Outdoor Enterprise Course?' he asked Tess. Was he being sarcastic?

Chapter 18

It was 8.10 by the time she got to work and Thierry would be waiting at the door. Kirsty's fault again, she'd got back from her weekend with Stephen late the evening before. To her surprise he wasn't there. It was well after eight o'clock and day had broken over the North Sea. Had he forgotten? Why was she foolishly imagining that his English lesson with her was the highlight of his week? The phone rang.

'I am very very sorry. I 'ad forgot. I am just arriving in my office when I remembered me.' Profuse apologies which she struggled to receive gracefully.

'How's your ankle?' she asked him. She'd invited him to come with them yesterday but he'd hurt his ankle, he'd told her. Was it dancing with the gorgeous bombshell that had caused the injury?

'It's a pity you weren't able to come yesterday, it was ... ' She searched for an adjective.

'But the antique man ...' he interrupted. 'You are coming with me next Sunday?' Yes.

She put down the phone and sat, like Aramis in *The Three Musketeers,* with her elbows on the table and her hands in the air, watching as the blood drained out of them making the skin lily white, ready to face the day. For no reason at all the memory of Professor Kupka, who'd taught her linguistics, came into her mind. 'Professor Kupka with his Central European charm' one of the (male) students had once said. What had he meant by that - gentleness, courtesy, gallantry, a custom of kissing a lady's hand on meeting? Not that Professor Kupka had ever kissed her hand. Though he'd kissed her on the cheek at the end of the year as they said goodbye and she'd instantly fallen in love with him, interpreting that parting kiss as a declaration of concealed and contained passion. She'd day dreamed about him for years after that.

But it was not just his Central European charm. It was also the fact that in one magical hour he'd transformed grammar from nightmare to - it was not too strong a word -

pleasure. One hand resting casually in the pocket of his suede jacket he'd with the other written up sentence frames on the board:

A .... came into the ....

This .... deserves some ....

A noun was no longer the name of a person, place or thing but any word that could fill the slots. Any word that filled the slot after *a* and *the* and *this* and *some* became a noun - words classified on the basis of what words could go in front of them and after them and not on the basis of vague notions.

So excited had she been by this discovery that she'd immediately wanted to pass it on to the day release class of junior shop assistants that she taught on a Monday morning to pay for the linguistics course.

'Give me a sentence beginning with *A*,' she'd asked a little pale-faced lad - Fred? Len? - sitting in the front in a navy blue suit that was too big for him. This was in the days when work of any sort except manual labour required a suit. Silence. A word which comes after *A,* she'd prompted. More silence, and then: 'A was mucking about with mi friend yesterday.'

She'd tried again, this time addressing the whole class and using a different approach: 'Give me words to fill the blank in this sentence:

I saw a .... at the week-end

This time the words had come hurtling through the air. Most of them she had pretended not to hear. She'd been unable to arouse in the class of shop assistants any interest whatsoever in *parts of speech.* (She had been unwise enough to use the term). It was like trying to persuade them of the seductiveness of slugs, she was a total failure as a teacher.

But maybe not, who could tell? Maybe out there

somewhere there was a now ageing manager of a department store who'd got where he'd got because of his ability to recognise a noun. Stan was the name of the little lad with the pale face, not Fred or Len.

Jean Louis sat before a blank table looking organised, neat and tidy, waiting.

'What have you planned for me today?' he asked.

He'd written on the questionnaire she'd given him at his first lesson that he wanted 'to have a corect riting' so a few weeks ago she'd asked him to bring along some of the writing he had to do in his job. Had he brought any along? Ah yes, he had a report to show her. She looked out at the sea as he rummaged in his brief case. The horizon today was like a dark blue line drawn by a ruler.

He couldn't find it, yet he was sure he had put it in his case before leaving. He didn't even have pen or paper with him. They would do something else, but what? She remembered then: Phrasal Verbs. But surely he could have remembered too. *Put off, put up with, put on, put forward.* She would test him on these. He couldn't remember any of them. It was as if he was hearing them for the first time.

'I am very contrarié. How you say that in English? Annoyed? Upset? *Annoyed* and *upset* mean the same thing, no?'

'Not really.'

'Yes, they do.'

'No, they don't.' Who was teaching who here?

'There are other ways of saying *annoyed*,' she said, 'but *upset* is not one of them. You could say *hacked off* or *incensed* or *outraged*.' She wrote up the words. Inside herself, thinking of Sunday and the visit to the antique man, she was singing the words *happy, delighted, over the moon*.

'Okay. To get back to phrasal verbs ....' Would he please learn the ones with *put* for next week? And along with them today they would do phrasal verbs with *make*. She wrote *make* in the centre of the board.

'How many lines could you draw radiating from *make*

with *up* at the end of each of them?' she asked him. By the end of twenty minutes they had six: *to make up a face, a story, one's mind, a quarrel, a dough, an amount of money.*

He had been familiar with only one of them - *to make up one's face.*

'The ladies are always making up the faces.'

Not this lady, she thought, though this morning she'd had time to get her lipstick out at the traffic lights and draw a line lightly across each cheek. Had she rubbed the lines in at the next set of lights? She couldn't remember. Had she been sitting there all morning looking like a clown? Just as well Thierry hadn't turned up. But the mention of ladies and make-up had started him off on another tack.

'The wives are not happy here,' he was saying. 'They have to find things to do and people to meet to feel their time. Their situation is not normal. They have to manufacture interests - following flower-arranging courses, becoming friendly with people they do not normally have anything in common with just because they are here because of their husbands.

He's quite right, Tess was thinking. Maybe Jean Louis was not so bad after all. Dominique, on the other hand, had told her his wife was perfectly happy here and was very sorry that they were leaving since she had such a nice life with hill walking, upholstery classes, English lessons … What sort of life would Tess have if she married Thierry and he was posted to Jakarta or Venezuela?

The phone rang. It was Thierry. He was very sorry but he had completely forgot.

'This weekend there is a geologic field trip so I will not be there on Sunday for the antique man.'

'Never mind. It doesn't matter. Maybe the following Sunday?'

'Yes, I 'ope so. I am very sorry.'

'He might have suggested a drink after work this evening instead,' she was thinking. Then she would have had the pleasure of saying she was otherwise engaged. It was true, she was going to the cinema with Pete.

'And as for home-making,' Jean Louis continued relentlessly, 'if you care about your home it is frustrating because we are forced to live in furnished houses with other people's taste. All of us are grumbling. None of us is happy with the standard of interior decorating here in Scotland. It is comfortable but ugly. How you say? Cosy!'

Yes, cosy. A word she hated, signalling a judgement based on material rather than aesthetic grounds. 'Please don't tell me you think this room looks cosy,' she'd mutter to herself whenever she brought anyone out to Kineldie. After all her trouble making the place look colourful, imaginative, unusual, creative, to have it described as if it were a pair of carpet slippers. Thierry had not called her cottage cosy. He'd appreciated the tweed curtains with the colours of the countryside woven into them, the water-colours of seascapes discovered in junk shops, the chairs with carved backs, the kelims.

'Even the bachelors are noticing,' he was continuing. His own bathroom for example - the bath was orange and the tiles were green like the colour of frogs. It made him unhappy to go in there every morning. What would he make of Fergus's bathroom down in London with half the tiles fallen off because of the damp? Fergus - she suddenly had a picture of him on a stage somewhere in Eastern Europe playing to an audience of enraptured young woman.

'Yes, well .... ,' said Tess, allowing a silence which could have been interpreted as sympathetic. Why hadn't he phoned? Surely there were public phones in places like Budapest. Or he could borrow someone's mobile, couldn't he?

A really funny French film about a man who worked for a company producing condoms. He was being threatened with the sack so his neighbour suggested he should pretend he was homosexual and then the company wouldn't be able to sack him without being accused of prejudice. The ruse worked - he didn't get the sack.

'Twenty years ago I lost my job because I was gay,' his neighbour told him. Today you've kept yours for the opposite reason.'

'Let's go for a drink in *The Wild Boar*,' said Pete. It was a few yards down from the cinema.

They'd just got inside the door when, in spite of the gloom, Tess noticed, a few tables away, Thierry. Sitting opposite him a woman, a blonde woman, looking up at him, laughing, her pale hand with its long pink nails caressing her soft pale cheek. Tess turned to get back out into the street, pulling Pete with her.

'Why do men always go for young blondes?' she asked him as they sat in *Qui*'s. She imagined the pale hand by now stretching across the table to catch hold of his brown one and him whispering 'Let's go, chérie.' She looked past Pete out into the street to see if she would catch sight of them passing.

'You mean me and Kirsty?' Kirsty was also a young blonde - well, youngish. Younger probably than the woman she'd seen with Thierry.

'But mature redheads have their charm too.' Pete grinned across at her. *Mature?* She wasn't sure how she felt about that word. Certainly the blonde couldn't have been described as mature, the coy way she'd been looking at Thierry in the café.

She sensed Pete wanted to talk about Kirsty but all Tess could think of regarding Kirsty was her account of her weekend in London with Stephen. It had been wonderful only they'd had a narrow escape. Just as they were disappearing into their hotel room on the Friday who had they caught sight of down the corridor but Maggie and her husband? Kirsty had known they were going to be in London the same weekend, but in the same hotel?

As a result Kirsty and Stephen had had to spend the weekend carefully avoiding arriving or leaving together, preparing themselves separately for an encounter with Maggie in the lift. How extraordinary, you too! The whole of the Language Institute seems to be here this week-end. Have you seen Stephen/Kirsty? He/she is here too!! We bumped into each other at the reception desk. Actually I'm down visiting a friend/attending the conference. Not that they'd done much coming and going anyway, Kirsty had added with a little smile.

'I had an argument with Stephen this morning,' said Pete. Tess took her eyes off the street outside. Did the mention of Kirsty bring Stephen to Pete's mind also?

'I was saying how I objected to the way they always talk about us as *customers* on the trains now instead of *passengers* but Stephen couldn't see what was wrong with customers.'

'He probably thinks of the students as customers too, everything reduced to buying and selling and making money.

'What's wrong with that?' he'd say.

They became absorbed in defaming Stephen and it was some time before Tess thought to look out at the passers by again.

'They'll have gone by now,' she thought as they emerged from the café, but no, there they were in front of them, a man and a woman walking slowly along in the moonlight engrossed in conversation, he waving his arms and she nodding her head slowly. Yes, she did have a funny walk, in fact it was a definite limp.

'I keep asking Kirsty out for a meal but she's always busy,' said Pete. Was he too noticing the loving couple in front of them?

Chapter 19

So had Thierry had a good field trip? Her weekend had been sabotaged by Kirsty being there the whole time, very twitchy, hanging round the phone. 'Anyone phone?' she'd say if she went out for five minutes.

'Are you going to be free Monday afternoon?' Kirsty had asked Stephen as she left the Language Institute on Friday.

'I don't know,' he'd said. 'I'll phone you over the weekend if I get a chance.'

'Get a chance?' Meaning 'if Cynthia goes out.' His phone call didn't need to be dependent on Cynthia being out. Or he could have gone down the garden and phoned her on his mobile, no?

Should she ring him? Could Tess ring him? Not again she couldn't. They'd be starting to think she was in the early stages of senility. 'Sorry to bother you Stephen but I can't remember if I have a student on Monday.'

'He's probably quite attached to Cynthia, you know,' Tess had said. Like she'd been attached to Bob - faithful Bob. Fergus had been like Marc back from the dead, all colours and patterns like a Persian carpet, while Bob was all black and white. But she'd never contemplated leaving Bob and Fergus seemed happy with things the way they were.

Thierry had picked up mushrooms on his way home from the west, along with a group of French who knew themselves in mushrooms.

'*Pick*, not *pick up*. You pick up something you've dropped but you pick flowers and mushrooms.'

He was opening his briefcase. He handed her a paper bag with yellow chanterelles spilling out of it. Every year the French were picking up kilos and kilos of mushrooms, yet they had never thought to bring her even one or two to have with her pork chop.

'It's a very good year for chanterelles,' they'd say and she'd coo 'Oh, I love chanterelles' but they never took the hint.

'Today I want to do the future with you,' she said,

cheered by the gift. She moved towards the board. She'd dressed extra carefully today, she'd be a match for any bombshell. She was almost certainly a very dull and conventional woman - Hilary had discerned this. Tess had hennaed her hair yesterday and this morning she'd put on the wine-coloured camisole knickers she'd bought in a sale two years before and never worn up to now. She didn't expect to reveal them in the course of the day but they said that wearing sexy underwear made you feel, and so look, good. Who'd said that? Mrs Thatcher of all people, if she remembered rightly. A programme on television long ago about the clothes she wore and her underwear. Had she actually said *underwear*? Or had she said *lingerie*? No, probably a circumlocution: 'I do believe that what one wears underneath one's clothes is very very important,' in the same tone of voice she might have used to say 'I do believe that it is very very important that people should not be allowed to become dependent on the state.'

Well, the wine-coloured polyester camisole wasn't making her feel good at all - it felt scratchy and uncomfortable - but the purple dress she'd selected to wear on top was fine, plus the purple suede shoes. A bit over the top for a Monday morning maybe but what the hell.

On the board she wrote up five different ways of expressing the future - *I go, I'm going, I'm going to go, I will go* and *I will be going*. What was the difference between them? Had he any idea what the difference was between these sentences? No, the English was too complicate for him. This was a terrible way to teach *Ways of Expressing the Future in English*. Was she indulging in a sadistic activity? Outside the sky was a rosy dawn pink and the sea a milky blue.

'Well,' she launched into her well-worn explanation 'you'd be more likely to use *I go* if you're talking about a string of planned activities. For example, *I go to London this evening and then I take the Eurostar to Paris tomorrow and on Wednesday I fly to Athens.*' How thrilling.

'If you're just going as far as London then you'd probably

108

say *I'm going to London this evening.* But Fergus won't be there. He was looking down at the sheet of paper on which he'd dutifully written the five forms. Should she move towards the board showing off her purple outfit instead of sitting there sedately? Maybe if she introduced a suggestive note into her voice.

'*I'm going to go to London* has a more determined ring about it, it's your intention whether other people like it or not. So you might say *I'm going to give up smoking in the New Year.*' No, no, that sounded too moralistic, too censorious, too interfering.

'You want that I give up to smoke?' he asked. A rush of tenderness towards him. She smiled an answer. Yes, I do want that you give up to smoke, I don't really fancy kissing someone who smells of Gaulloises.

'*I will go* can mean that you are less certain about going. You might add *hopefully.* Or *insha' Alla* if you're Muslim or *Please God* if you're a devout Catholic.' Was he a devout Catholic? He might well be. But she could go along with that. She'd been a Catholic once herself, and it wasn't as if there would ever be children that she'd have to promise to bring up in the faith.

'You also use it to make promises as I said last time. *I will love you till I die* and things like that,' she said rather boldly. Or until she dies, his wife, or rather *until she died.* That was an ill-chosen example. Was she imagining it or had a shadow come over his face?

'You use it usually about the weather,' she hurried on. 'At the weekend hopefully it will be fine.'

'And *I will be going to London this evening* is the tense known as the future continuous. It is less definite, less positive than *I am going* because you use *will.* You could say *Are you going to France at Christmas?* Or you could say *Will you be going to France at Christmas?* The second is less direct, you often use it to ask a question politely.'

She opened her mouth to ask 'So, will you be going to France at Christmas?' Christmas was quite a long way off but it would be nice to know. She certainly wasn't going to try to meet up with Fergus wherever he was. But he had a question.

'What means *to pop*? ' At work everyone was always popping out and up and down and round and in. She explained the meaning of *pop*.

'So on Sunday I am popping *out* or *up* or *down* or *round* or *in* to see the antique man? And you are coming with me? That is a planned future activity, no?'

'That will be lovely,' she said. She had done right to put on the purple dress.

Today she would do something about Denis's intonation, his habit of saying *Yes* in such a way as to express irritation, impatience, even annoyance. *What a stupid question to have asked me* sort of thing. Fergus had said something similar of her once, about her message on her answer machine. Breathy, hurried, sounding as if she was saying 'I've much more important things to be doing than talking to you on the phone.' She'd spent some time trying to change the message after that to sound friendly and encouraging and had ended up somewhere between the efficient company director away at an important meeting and the sultry call girl busy with another client but 'do call back soon.'

She was sitting with a mug of coffee in her favourite place in the house, in the sitting room at the small table that looked out onto the garden and the view of the other side of the valley. Fields with motionless sheep in them, giving way to gorse bushes and heather and pine trees and at the very top of the hill rough grass and rocks.

She had the house to herself and didn't need to be in Aberdeen until eleven. Kirsty was at Stephen's - Cynthia was at a conference in Birmingham.

She made herself another mug of coffee and gathered around her all the books she had on intonation. *The Intonation of Colloquial English; Speak Clearly! Sound Right! English Pronunciation; Better English Pronunciation; Better English Pronunciation Still.* Some of the books dated back to her days in Paris. Her heart sank as she flicked through them trying to make sense of them.

Intonation consists of the continuous changing of the pitch of a speaker's voice to express meanings. This continuous changing had been analysed into numerous tunes. Basically the voice either went down at the end of what was called a *sense group* or it went up. Though it could also have it both ways, first rising and then falling in a Rise-Fall tune, or falling and then rising in a Fall-Rise tune. All this falling and rising took place on the most important word in the sense group. One of the books had represented these tunes with blobs and tadpoles to accompany sentences such as

Oh, do you, indeed! But you can't do that. That's a very smart suit you're wearing. It was an unusually clear night. You brute!

As for meanings these ranged from grumpy to ponderous to airy to indignant, surprised, tentative, assertive. *'Do you love me?' she asked ponderously, grumpily, indignantly, reluctantly.* How was she going to get through this thicket created by scholars?

She looked out at her own thicket of hawthorn and escallonia and beyond to the trees. They had lost enough of their leaves for the tower of the church to be just visible. It wasn't a church any longer. It had been converted into a house and sold for a great sum of money to an American family, people to do with the oil industry, Pam in the post office had told her. What must it be like to live in a church? A Church of Scotland church would at least not be reeking of incense, though incense had quite an exotic smell if you didn't associate it with Benediction at the end of a tedious Sunday afternoon and altar boys gathered round the priest and the priest striding forth to swing whatever you called that clanking thing on the long chain, up and down the aisle. Why no altar girls, she used to stand there thinking. The priest was a man, the Pope was a man, the apostles were all men, Christ was a man, God was a man. The only important woman in the story was Mary and she was only important because she was the mother of God and the handmaid of the Lord. Not much of a role model. Even at aged ten she'd rebelled at the idea of being any man's handmaid. She'd two brothers and had no evidence whatsoever that they were in any way superior to her except when it came to wrestling.

She hunted among the pages of the books for an explanation that would be relevant to Denis. Ah yes, that was it. He was using a Rise-Fall intonation instead of just a Fall. He started his *Yes* with his voice going up before it started coming down. This could signal enthusiasm, she read, but in certain contexts it could imply impatience. What he needed was to use a simple High Fall. She started practising different ways of saying *Yes*, starting high (enthusiastic), starting midway (normal) and ending low (mechanical, dispassionate). A female pheasant, a gentle speckled brown, was walking across the grass. Any or all of her students would be reaching for their guns.

'Pheasant? Oh yes, very good at this time of year. Later, after the winter, they are thin and do not taste so nice because they have been eating rubbish. But in the autumn their flesh has the taste of corn and berries. It is very good.'

She hunted for a suitable exercise she could give Denis to practise a falling tone. *Repeat each of the following sentences three times*:

*She is making a red **dress**. It'll soon be **spring**. Help your**self**. The birds are singing in the **trees**. It would be better to phone for the **doc**tor. Let's go for a little **walk** ......*

Could she decently spend the hour with Denis reading out each of the sentences three times? Maybe she should just stop asking him questions, or tell him to smile to soften the effect of the impatient *Yes*. He had a very nice smile, something about the eyes that seemed to caress you as he spoke - lucky Celeste, lucky whatever his wife was called.

All the same she had to fill the hour with something. And learning how to say *Yes* in a foreign language in such a way as to avoid the risk of being hit over the head seemed to her to be a lesson worth learning. She put all the books back on the shelves and decided she'd make up her own exercises on her way in to the Institute.

Instead as she hovered behind first a tractor and then a

bus she found herself spending the time trying to see the landscape through Thierry's eyes - the curves of the hills, the granite cottages just like her own with the dormer windows, and the washing blowing around madly in the wind, the rowan trees still with their berries on. What was rowan in French? Then the names of the places, some of them very bizarre, like Ythensie. The other Saturday he'd arrived asking her to explain a whole string of place names: 'How you pronounce …?'

In the distance she could see geese circling round the lake where she'd gone with Fergus one winter evening. Could she take Thierry there? Would he understand the joke she'd made waiting with Fergus for the geese to arrive to spend the night on the water. As they waited for the air to be filled with the sound of wings she'd whispered

'I hope I haven't brought you on a wild goose chase.'

The memory usually brought a smile to her lips but now she tried to crush it like an empty packet. Fergus was in the past, that story had come to an end.

She arrived at the Language Institute without having given a thought to Denis and intonation. Fortunately he was late.

'How is Celeste? Is she a good baby?' she asked him

'Yes,' he replied in his what-a-silly-question tone

She leapt to her feet and drew a long downward curve on the board.

'Now say *Yes* as I trace my finger along the curve and down. Begin high and slowly, slowly bring your voice down with my finger. Ye-e-e-s Ye-e-e-s Ye-e-e-s.

She said the word along with him. It began to sound like the most beautiful word in the English Language.

'Would you like to come and live with me in my manoir, Tess?'

'Ye-e-e-s!'

Chapter 20

The antique man was standing outside the old mill talking to Thierry when Tess arrived. The Dee was silvery and calm under a grey sky.

'This is my English teacher I am telling you about,' said Thierry, touching Tess lightly on the shoulder as he introduced her.

'Hello,' she smiled.

The furniture was kept in the mill itself. Apart from two or three chests of drawers the walls were lined with nothing but grandfather clocks. Thierry was in love with grandfather clocks, he told her. He showed her the one he was thinking of buying for his flat in Versailles, much simpler than the others, in a dark oak case with no ornamentation.

'Listen to its lime, Tess,' said Thierry. She liked the way he pronounced her name. The clock had a very musical chime but someone had said once that the chime of a grandfather clock could drive you mad if you were lying awake listening to it in the small hours. Tess liked one in mahogany better, with a tag *1785* on it. She wasn't sure if that was its price or the year in which it was made.

'Both,' said the antique dealer, who was called Jim. Was he wondering what her relationship was with Thierry? Thierry seemed very matey with him. They were talking non stop as they stood there - about the shooting of pheasants and rabbits, about politics (Thierry kept saying 'Oh, the enveerronmentaleests' as if it was a rude word), about food, and about mending clocks. Jim had all those clocks because he was clever at mending them, it was his hobby.

It was cold standing there. He gets more English practice here on a Sunday morning than with me during the week, Tess thought. She looked on as he wrote out a cheque. There were no mirrors for sale and even if there had been they would have been more than she could afford.

'Jim has a house in the Dordogne,' Thierry said to Tess.

'How nice,' she said. Along with hundreds of other British - *Dordogneshire* she'd heard it called. Sour grapes.

'I 'ave told Jim that when he will be in France in the summer he must make a detour and come and visit me in Burgundy.' So Thierry was naturally friendly, his friendliness towards her didn't mean very much. She was his teacher, it was normal that he should be courteous towards her, and that he should invite her to lunch. What sort of story was this?

'Where shall we go for lunch?' he asked as they got into his car.

'To Raemoir,' she said. 'It's a nineteenth century country house hotel with stags' antlers in the hall and a library with oak panelled walls and a large open fireplace with real logs burning. Very Scottish, and it's just a few miles away. I'll introduce you to a typical British Sunday lunch.'

Large plates of roast beef and Yorkshire pudding, roast potatoes, gravy, sprouts and carrots, served by a homely looking waitress in black with a grey bun.

'Have you seen *The Thirty Nine Steps*?' she asked Thierry. 'The waitress reminds me of a woman in that.' He'd never heard of the film.

'It's an early Hitchcock,' she said. But he'd seen *Psycho* and *The Birds* and they talked about these as they ate. The cold air had given them an appetite and the food was good - the best of Scottish cooking - and they had a bottle of Burgundy chosen by Thierry to go with it. He was very impressed by the wine list, some of the bottles costing over £100. He chose one for £18.50. That was okay. She'd been a bit worried he might choose the house wine. The dining room was full of families - parents, grandparents, children.

'This is making me thinking of Sundays in France,' said Thierry. And of his own family? One question from her and maybe he would start talking - about his childhood, his wife, his children.

'Yes, and then the parents will make the children go for a walk,' she said. 'I remember when I was a child I always had to go for a walk on a Sunday.' Ask me about my childhood. 'There's a good walk you can do from here up through the forest and onto the Hill of Fayre. Have you time this afternoon?'

116

He had to get back. He'd been invited to a little party - a baby that is born a few weeks ago.

'Oh, a christening,' said Tess.

'Yes,' said Thierry. 'If you like you can come along with me. It is Denis's baby, I think you know.'

That was very nice of him but a christening was not quite her 'cup of tea'. He laughed. He was amused by the expression - 'not someone's cup of tea.'

'But the meal isn't over. You've got to have the apple pie and custard.'

'Ah, les desserts chauds. Hot puddings. Your rosbif was excellent but apple pie - we have it every day in the restaurant at work. I will have a little sheese. Oh and, by the way, I am having a little lunch party next Friday in the restaurant, it is my bayerrtday. I invite you.'

'Thank you very much. That *is* my cup of tea,' she said. They both laughed.

They had a little cheese to finish the wine and coffee by the fire in the library and then Thierry drove her back to the old mill and her car. As they stood saying goodbye he suddenly put his arms around her and kissed her on the cheek and then before she had time to respond he'd bent down and opened her car door for her. She had drunk only two glasses of wine, surely she was safe to drive home.

She went carefully nevertheless. Had the day been a success? Did she feel she knew him better? Did she feel closer to him? They'd avoided talking about anything personal but they'd been very relaxed together and then there'd been that goodbye. But how abnormal was that? The French were always kissing each other, it maybe didn't mean very much, no more than his invitation to Jim had meant to him. It was maybe up to her to make the next move. At the lunch party next week? She imagined holding his gaze across the table.

Kirsty had spent the weekend obsessed by Stephen again. How much did he care about her? Why hadn't he phoned her? He had been away at a conference in London all week. She'd expected him to phone her mid week - *missing you, please please come down at the week-end* - but no phone calls, no text messages.

Tess had made a list of dos and don'ts for her on Friday evening. What to do and what not to do when you're suffering the pangs of ill-requited, not to say non-requited-at-all, love. Surprising how easy it was to give advice when you weren't in that state yourself.

1. Stay as far away from a phone as possible. Like a watched pot never boils a watched phone never rings.

2. Leave your mobile at home if you go out. Tess had gone to the supermarket with Kirsty on Saturday. Every ring at the cash desk had had Kirsty diving for her phone in her handbag.

3. Think of all the things you don't like about him. Tess could think of plenty of things she didn't like about Stephen - his egocentricity for starters - but Kirsty couldn't think of anything. His qualities rose in her mind like milk on the stove whenever she thought of him. All she could think of was how clever, witty, entertaining, kind, sensitive he was and how good he was in bed. Was he that marvellous? Come on now, Kirsty. You remember telling me how he was beginning to bore you, how the novelty was wearing off? No, no, I was totally wrong, not boring at all.

4. Think of how much more attractive and desirable you'd be if you stopped whimpering beside the phone. Go out and do things. What is it they say? *Follow and they flee. Flee and they follow.* But there was nothing Kirsty wanted to do except follow.

5. Associate yourself with all those others who have been unlucky in love, who have had tragic lives. Listen to Chopin or Schubert. Or put on Marlene Dietrich singing *Falling in Love Again* or some Billie Holiday. Or we could watch the video of *Anna Karanina* or *Wuthering Heights*. Oh no, they would only depress her, after all Heathcliff had loved Cathie passionately - *I cannot live without my love, I cannot live without my life.* So think of *Gone with the Wind*. At the end what was important to Scarlett was Tara, the house, the land,

118

not any man.

When Tess got back on Sunday they put on a compilation of songs from the sixties. They turned the volume up and started to dance and got so carried away they didn't hear the phone when it rang at about six o'clock. Call minder rang them back later in the evening. It had been Stephen phoning from Heathrow before catching his plane for Aberdeen. He hadn't phoned because he'd been down with flu all week, had missed her, would see her Monday at the Institute. Joy on Kirsty's face. Meanwhile Tess felt like an orange with the juice squeezed out of it.

'*Oat*' Lauren settled himself opposite her.

'You mean *ought*?' she said.

'Yes, *oat*.' She'd told him that whether he said *You should do it* or *You ought to do it* was the same thing, they meant the same. But somebody in his department had told him that *oat* was old-fashioned.

Who was this person, who, just because she - or was it a he? - was a native speaker of English, thought (s)he could pontificate on the language? She struggled to adopt a reasonable tone of voice.

'Pick up any newspaper or watch the news on television or tune in to any radio programme and you will see and hear *ought* being used all the time,' she said. 'Of course it's more difficult for French people to pronounce, which is why it's better if you say *should*. Anyway, let's go on with *should*. A third use of should is after words like *recommend* or *suggest* or phrases like *It's important/necessary/essential* ... She was about to make for the board to write these up when she remembered that she'd undone the button on her skirt as she'd sat there with her feet up and the zip had worked its way down. She remained seated.

'Give me a sentence beginning *It's important that* ...

'It's important that men and women who are living together should discuss about the homework.'

'Should discuss the housework. Yes. Good. And what would you suggest? What would you recommend?'

'I suggest that they should share it.' Very good.

'My girl friend and I we are sharing but I am a good cooker so I am making the cooking.' Had Janet returned or was this a new girlfriend?

'*Cook*, not *cooker*. A cooker is a thing. A cook cooks on a cooker. And a cook *does* the cooking.' Outside a mist had descended, the sea was now completely obscured again. Should she go on with the other two uses of *should*? What were they anyway? She was sure there were five. There was a handout entitled *Should* in the filing cabinet. It would be better if she gave him that, if she could only get her skirt sorted out.

'Write me out a recipe for your favourite dish using lots of *shoulds*,' she told him.

He bent his head to the task. She started to fiddle with the skirt button, trying to bring it across with one hand to fit into the hole which was at least an inch away. How had she allowed herself to get so fat? Impossible to do with one hand. She brought her right arm across her body. He looked up and she gave him a smile.

'Have you finished already?' Surely not.

'No,' he said, 'I am thinking.' She brought her arm back to her side, took up her pen and made as if to write something down in her diary.

Ah, inspiration! He bent his head over his sheet of paper again. Quickly she brought her arm back and, using both hands, managed to put the button through the hole. Then she took up her pen again, at the same time pulling gently with her left hand, wriggling slightly in her seat. The zip was up.

Laurent laid down his pen and handed her the sheet of paper.

'I'll take this home with me and make the dish myself, following your recipe exactly,' she said. She noticed it was the recipe for the Monk Fish dish he'd cooked for them that evening. She got to her feet - she could hardly breathe - opened the drawer of the filing cabinet marked *maps and old envelopes* and finally located the handout on *should*.

'You could read through this at home,' she said -

examples taken from Jill's thesis of all five uses of *should*. She'd better do the same herself.

After he'd gone it came to her that what the know-all in his office had been talking about wasn't *ought* but *aught* as in *For aught I know* ... Probably she'd assumed that Tess was quite capable of teaching them English that was completely out-of-date. 'Wouldn't put it past that schoolmarm to be teaching *aught.*'

School marm. Huh. She undid the button on her skirt again, collected up all the bits of paper scattered around her desk, arranged them in a neat pile and got into her coat.

Thierry had left a luncheon voucher for her at reception and told her to make her way to the restaurant. She hadn't seen him since Sunday, he'd had no lesson that week, as he'd had to go over to Paris for meetings. It was not her first time in the building. She'd visited several times to talk to the bosses of her students about their language needs and *learning curves* and *aims and objectives* and she'd often been invited to stay for lunch.

Aberdeen Language Institute had peeling paint and worn carpets and windows that needed jobs doing on them and, despite Stephen's efforts to impose order, rooms with books scattered around and untidy people of all ages and sizes, and a caretaker who was a refugee from Hungary in the fifties whose English had remained picturesque. Here everything looked newly furbished in state-of-the-art office interior decoration with, in the entrance lobby, a magnificent specially commissioned stained glass wall hanging of an off-shore oil rig set in the midst of bottom-of-the-sea vegetation. Also everybody at Termoil was young and well-dressed with a smile on their faces. She was glad she hadn't made it to the hairdresser's and that she'd decided to wear her oldest shoes.

The restaurant was at the end of a long straight beige carpeted corridor with stunning pictures of North Sea oil platforms on the walls. She'd many times tried to make out a case for visiting a platform - 'in order to research language needs' but this had only ever produced a mirthful response.

'Language needs? I tell you even *my* ears curl up when I hear the sort of language they use on the rig,' one driller had told her.

As she queued up at the self service lunch bar she caught sight of Thierry already installed at a table in the far corner of the restaurant. Opposite him the blonde woman she'd seen him with in the *Wild Boar*. 'Breathe slowly and deeply.'- the only thing she could remember from her few yoga sessions. She made her way across to them with a tray of leaks in vinaigrette, roast lamb, cheese and biscuits. There was just one place left at the table - next to Thierry. He had been saving it for her. She flashed him a smile.

'This is a stupendous occasion, I think,' she started to say. She had decided that a light-hearted, bantering tone would be appropriate. She'd wondered about buying him a present, or at least a card, decided that a warm kiss on the cheek would be enough. But in the circumstances even this seemed inappropriate. Thierry, greeted her with a big smile and helped her with her tray and then briefly introduced her to the blonde. 'This is Barbara, she's from Poland'. A round plump face, lively dark eyes.

.Denis, who was sitting directly opposite Tess and next to Barbara, gave her a bright smile and offered her some wine from a bottle which had Médoc written across it.

'Where is the Médoc region? I can never remember,' she raised her voice slightly to ask Thierry, feigning ignorance. She even caught herself about to flutter her eyelashes. He picked up the salt cellar.

'This is Bordeaux and here is le Médoc.' With his hands he described the tongue of land north of Bordeaux. 'The wine from 'ere is very good but the best wine in the world is from Burgundy,' he proclaimed.

'Come now, Thierry.' A voice with all the assurance of a public school accent came from the other end of the table. 'How about that bottle of South African wine we were drinking the other evening?' Thierry lifted his shoulders.

'Well, this wine is certainly...' Tess began, but Barbara from the other side was claiming his attention.

'How long have you been a teacher at the Aberdeen Language Institute, Tess?' a young woman with short spiky hair across the table from her leaned forward to ask..

'Oh, a long time,' said Tess.

Of course it was just possible he was overcome with embarrassment and emotion at having her sitting so close. She cast a glance sideways. No, she had to admit that what she saw was not the behaviour of a shy man. He was leaning towards Barbara, gesticulating, laughing, totally absorbed in charming her.

She took a large drink of the wine. The young woman with the spiky hair had started talking to Denis so Tess turned to the man on her left. He was something in Safety. And Tess taught English as a Foreign Language? His wife had done a bit of that when they lived in Saudi Arabia, had given conversation lessons. Oh yes, the sort of thing anyone could do just as long as they were native speakers of English. No need for a training, no need to know anything about the language other than being able to speak it, just sit there and chat, no knowledge and skills involved. Tess plunged her fork into a roast potato.

'I've been doing some research into the language used over the Public Address System on the platform,' she began. That would put her at least three cuts above his wife teaching conversation in Saudi Arabia. For example, she explained, men were ordered to *cease* doing whatever they were doing and *don* life jackets - words they'd never use in ordinary conversation.

'I see,' said the man in Safety politely and turned to his neighbour on his right.

'But your English is much better than mine,' Thierry was saying to Barbara. Tess glanced across and caught the Polish woman's eye.

'I was wondering if you gave private lessons,' she said, leaning forward to talk to Tess. 'I feel my presentation skills could be improved.'

'Oh really?' Your presentation skills seem to be more than adequate, Tess was thinking.

'I'm sorry. I don't give private lesson.' She'd had enough of private lessons in France, sitting there always wondering if you were giving them their money's worth. And then the cancellations. 'Sorry I cannot come today. I am fatigué,' and bang would go the money for your week-end meals. The French were always fatigué. Tess had thought the word just meant 'tired' but it seemed to be much more serious than that.

'But I could maybe find somebody else who does,' said Tess. She was thinking of Battleship Norma newly back from the Middle East with her sleek Egyptian oil engineer boyfriend.

'I have told her you are the best teacher I never have.' said Thierry. Not much of an advertisement.

'You have time for coffee?' Thierry asked her at the end of the meal. Barbara too had time for coffee.

'You are not joining us, Denis' Barbara said to Denis as they got up from the table.

'I have too many works to do,' said Denis.

She's watching him moving away like he's the last bus, Tess thought. Maybe bombshell Barbara fancies Denis as well as Thierry. Together the three of them made their way across to the coffee area. Thierry told her that the grandfather clock was now standing in the hallway of his house in Aberdeen and one day she must come and see it.

As they sat down Barbara turned to her and asked her if she could recommend a good hairdresser in Aberdeen. Tess was surprised, surely her hair didn't look like an advertisement for any hairdresser. She felt flattered in spite of herself. Maybe Barbara was quite a nice person after all. Should she in return admire her rather flashy necklace?

'I love your necklace,' she said and then told them about the hairdresser she did actually go to occasionally.

'She's very interesting. She's doing a degree in sociology. Only last time I saw her I was feeling quite tired and she was standing with the scissors explaining some obscure bit of research to me and I was there wishing she'd ask me if I was doing anything nice with the rest of the day.'

Thierry laughed but Barbara shook her head and thought

she'd rather have a hairdresser that concentrated on the job of cutting her hair.

She parted company with the two of them at the end of the long beige corridor and drove back to Kineldie, thinking. Thierry's behaviour was certainly not that of an aspiring lover. How could she have been so foolish as to imagine that there was anything between them? She might well be his favourite teacher but his interest in her seemed to end there.

When she saw him on Monday she would keep her distance. She would greet him pleasantly enough and suggest a cup of coffee as usual but then, with an irony that would almost certainly be lost on him, she would say:

'We began by studying the present tense. We then went on to talk about the future. Today we are going to concentrate on the past.'

'What is the difference,' she'd ask him, 'between ...' and she would write this up on the board in green ink:

She was happy for a month

She has been happy for a month?

And there would be no smile on her face as she turned to face him.

Chapter 21

Monday morning. It was barely light as she set out at half past seven - shadowy seagulls coming in to land on the newly ploughed fields. Why was she getting up in the dark just to suit Thierry? That lunch last Friday. Stupid ever to have imagined he might fancy her. Her hands on the steering wheel - beginning to look as gnarled as the roots of the beech trees along by the roadside. Fergus had always liked her hands.

Fergus. Maybe she would try to see him at Christmas after all. She'd had another postcard from him this morning saying he was going to be in St. Petersburg then. She'd phone a Travel Agency to see if she could get on one of the cheap flights. Maybe it was not all over between them.

She'd left Kirsty behind, still in bed. A large piece of paper on the floor outside her bedroom: *3 a.m. Still awake. Don't bother waking me IF I manage to get to sleep. Tell Stephen I've swallowed a bottle of sleeping tablets.*

She met Stephen as she went up the stairs, looking bright and business-like in a brown (was brown the *in* colour this season?) suit. *He's* not losing any sleep over *her*.

'Oh, Kirsty's not very well this morning. She asked me to tell you to let her class know.' Bastard.

A Sophie Hannah poem ran through her head as she walked down the corridor to her room - *'...he treats houses like hotels/and she, hotels like houses.'*

But was this true? She wondered again about Kirsty. If Stephen did start talking about leaving Cynthia Kirsty would probably be off. She wouldn't want any metamorphosis of Stephen into humdrum husband.

Thierry was late. When he eventually turned up at a quarter past eight he looked much more like her idea of Monday morning.

'What does *abide* mean? He had been listening to Songs of Praise on television. The house was lonely on Sunday evenings. But he had Barbara, no?

'It is so depressing. There is no day here. '

But it was good to have singing in the house and the

words were on the screen for him to follow. But what did *abide* mean? Abide, abode, abode. *I have abode here for 20 years.* In Scots, of course, *bide* was still the normal word to use. *Where do you bide?*

'It's archaic,' she said 'though it's still used in phrases like *You must abide by the law.* There's even an adjective - *law-abiding*.' Ah yes, here everybody was abiding by the law..... .

'Today I want to do the Past with you,' she interrupted. She'd no wish today to be waylaid with talk about the differences between the French and the British ways of life. She hoped he had noticed the slight but meaningful emphasis she'd put on the word *Past*. She'd keep a certain distance from him from now on. Enslaved to a man? Losing sleep like Kirsty? Reduced to walking down one long dark corridor of disappointment, only occasionally illuminated by a window? No, that wasn't for her, she was free, she was her own mistress.

'The problem for French people is that you only use one past tense. In English we have two tenses. Sometimes we use the simple past - *I saw*- and sometimes the tense known as the Present Perfect - *I have seen.* ' The Present Perfect. What did *Perfect* mean? How about a Present Imperfect?

'The Present Perfect is really a present tense. We use it if we are talking about something that started some time in the past and is still continuing into the present. We always use it after *since*. For example *I have lived in Aberdeen since 1985* but *I lived in Paris for 5 years.*

She put up another example on the board. She was glad she was in her Russian army dress, stylish but not too fitted. She put one hand in her pocket, like Professor Werther used to do, as she wrote *Since I got up this morning I have drunk 3 cups of coffee.*

'This morning is still continuing. In fact it is still only half past eight.' Outside the sky was now a fondant pink. 'But this afternoon when this morning has become the past I will say *This morning I drank six cups of coffee.*'

'Tell me what you have done since you got up this morning. How many cups of coffee have you drunk for example?' With Barbara sitting with you at the breakfast table?

'I have drunk two cups of coffee at 7 o'clock.'

'Ah no! If you mention the time in the past you use a past tense. So you would say *At 7 o'clock I drank two cups of coffee.* It's only if you are talking about a period of time up to *now* that you use the Present Perfect: *So far this morning I have drunk two cups of coffee.* In the same way you might say *I have never been to China* because you are still alive, the period of your life is not yet at an end. If you were talking about General de Gaulle on the other hand you would say *General de Gaulle never went to China* because General de Gaulle is dead.

'He was a big man,' said Thierry.

'Do you mean *big* or *great*?' The French had only the one word - *grand* - for both. Of course he meant that de Gaulle was great, though of course he was also big. She might have guessed that he would be a Gaullist. She wondered what he'd done in '68. Had he taken part in student demonstrations? Probably not, so it wouldn't have worked. How could she possibly have lived the rest of her life with someone not capable of running down the Boulevard St Michel with a paving stone in their hand? Not that she was in favour of violence, but the gesture.

Should she embark on the other use of the Present Perfect tense? Did she want to leave him in an even greater muddle than he was in now? Why not? There was still a quarter of an hour to go.

'It's true though that the present perfect can sometimes be used for an action that is not continuing into the present. For example if I'd lost my car keys I would say *I have lost my car keys* and not *I lost my car keys*. Why do you think that is so?'

'It is because you are not thinking on the same side of the head. Here the pepper pot has three holes and the salt pot has only one. In France it is the contrary. We have one hole for the pepper and three holes for the salt.' Definitive evidence for why the two countries would never be able to get on.

'So we'll never agree,' she said.

'But it is good to discuss,' he said. 'I enjoy to discuss with you.' He looked at her long and was it tenderly? 'Are you meeting me for a drink one evening this week? Or dinner? We are having dinner together - Saturday, for example?' Planned future activity. But what about Barbara? Was he a philanderer - or two-timing as Annie would say? She wasn't going to be taken in by him again.

'That would be very nice,' she said 'but I'm not sure if I'm free. I'll phone you.'

Laurent was waiting outside the door as she came back down the corridor with her mug of coffee. Nice tie in a pattern of dark purples and reds and greens. She'd got delayed, talking to Pete about his Japanese business men who were now in the last week of their course. Did Laurent want a cup of coffee? No, he didn't. What he wanted was for her to explain the Conditional in English. Ah, the Conditional.

'Well, there are three main ways of expressing the conditional in English.'

A recent book dismissed this analysis as simplistic. The English Conditional could not be reduced to three. It was more complicated than that.

'There are three main ways of expressing the conditional in English,' she repeated. 'Two of them refer to the present and the future. Can you see a difference between them?' She got up and stood at the board.

If you leave now you will catch the train, she wrote up.

'Now, what is the difference between that and this sentence?' Underneath she wrote up

If you left now you would catch the train.

Laurent could not see any difference between the two sentences. And yet there was a difference, she assured him.

'If you leave me for this woman I will refuse ever to see you again, 'she'd said to Bob.

'In which of them would you be less likely to leave?' she prompted. Ah yes, the second sentence was less factual. If I left now I would catch the train but I'll probably stay. To use *left* instead of *leave* put the statement further into the realm of speculation and hypothesis.

'If you left me for this woman I would refuse ever to see you again.' She'd not said that because she and Bob had rapidly moved from the realm of speculation and hypothesis. Had they ever inhabited that realm anyway? Could all that screaming and sobbing and door slamming have been described as a realm of hypothesis?

Banging and stamping and roars of laughter from next door. Pete had worked wonders on his Japanese businessmen over the weeks he'd been teaching them. They were probably engaged on a performance session - matching words to actions, giving expression to their emotions. This involved students standing on chairs and jumping off tables and dancing and talking about themselves, their feelings, their memories.

'And the third conditional is the Past Conditional. It is often called the Impossible Conditional because it is about the past and can't be changed. For example

If I had left then I would have caught the train

'But you didn't leave then so you didn't catch the train.' She asked him to express a regret about the past. Pete would have begun by giving an example from his own life like 'If my wife hadn't become a lesbian she would never have left me.'

'Yesterday evening if I had tied my flies properly I would have been happy,' he said.

'Your flies? Tied? You mean if you'd *done up* your flies.'

'No, *tie*. I am going every week to learn how to tie flies.'

Ah, fishing again. But he had to be careful, she told him, because he could be misunderstood. Did he know the other meaning of *flies*? The zip in the front of his trousers? Or did he have buttons? Buttons were old-fashioned but they were also fashionable at the moment. Stephen had buttons, Kirsty had told her. Kirsty found buttons on flies sexy, she liked reaching across when she was in the car with Stephen and slowly unbuttoning his flies. Much better than a zip that got stuck or that your fingers got caught in - or that Stephen's willy got mixed up with, Tess had thought but not been bold enough to say. What had she got against Stephen's penis? And why had she used that particular word that she'd never ever uttered in her life?

'You do up your flies if they are undone. So ....' She wrote up on the board *If my flies are undone I will do them up* and then handed the green pen over to Laurent.

'Now change the sentence into the second and third conditionals.'

If my flies were undone I would do them up

Yesterday if my flies had been undone I would have done them up.

He turned round from the board and caught her looking at his crotch.

'Are my flies undone?' he asked, feeling with his hand. Roars of laughter from next door but for once she felt she had the edge on Pete.

'No, no,' she said, still not sure whether it was a zip or buttons she'd seen.

Chapter 22

She was about to phone Thierry and tell him she'd be delighted to accept his invitation to dinner on Saturday when Denis arrived. And then the multiple choice grammar test. Among the pot-pourri of items: *He dances well: a) in spite his limp b) in spite of his limp c) in spite he is limping.*

'What means *limping*?' he'd asked.

She demonstrated by limping towards the door, she was in a frisky mood this morning. Ah, that was like Barbara, the Polish geologist in his office. 'She is dancing very well - in spite she is limping.'

'Is it a permanent characteristic? In which case it should be *in spite of the fact that she limps*, not *is limping*. She limps, she is a woman with a limp.' And she speaks in a funny voice and wears nasty coloured blouses. But how did he know that she danced well?

'She dances well? You have seen her dancing?'

Yes, they had had a small party in the Exploration Department for somebody who was leaving. Was it Barbara who was leaving? No, but she would be leaving soon.

'And Thierry is dancing very well too.'

'Really?'

'Yes. What means *a dark horse*?' The next day one of the secretaries had said to Thierry that he was a dark horse. Tess explained that it meant he'd an unexpected side to him. Nobody had thought that he would be such a good dancer. The widower Thierry and limping Barbara.

'Okay, so *he dances well but he is not dancing at the moment* and *she limps but she is not limping at the moment.*' How did she know? It was ten o'clock on Tuesday morning but maybe they'd both taken the day off and were at this very moment dancing/limping around his bedroom to Salsa music. She would phone him back to say that she would not be free on Saturday after all.

'In the same way you would say *I speak Spanish though I am speaking English at the moment* because you are stating a fact. Are you speaking Spanish?'

'Yes, I do,' he said

'No, you're not.' she said, perhaps a little too sharply. 'You know, Denis, I think your English is improving,' she added.

The next morning, as she was filing her nails, the phone rang.

'That will be Jean Louis cancelling,' she thought, picking up the receiver. It was Thierry.

'Tess, I am very very sorry but I must go in Paris immediately. My father is die. I am afraid I will not be able to see you on Saturday evening.'

She murmured her sympathy. Was it very sudden? Her own father had died suddenly of a heart attack just about the time Annie was born. Yes, the end was sudden.

'But he is dead for me since many years,' he added. What did that mean?

'So I'll see you when you get back,' she said after a pause, in a voice promising tenderness. The phone rang again and this time it was Jean-Louis.

'I will not assist your English lesson this morning.' No apology, no excuse. Would he be able to come tomorrow, she asked him, looking at the blank page in her diary. Yes, that would be all right. Outside in the corridor she passed Franck on his way home.

'Gutbye, Tess,' he said. He'd got more friendly since Hilary and herself had bumped into him at the university the other week. They'd discovered he was writing a thesis on Byron. That was what had drawn him to Aberdeen in the first place. Bryon had lived and gone to school in Aberdeen till he was about eight.

On the drive back to Kineldie she was stuck behind a lorry piled high with turnips golden in the sunshine. It was a beautiful afternoon - pale blue north eastern skies, the bracken along the roadside fiery after the rain, the tops of the pine trees swaying indolently in the wind. Sometimes it was warmer in November than in July up here. She would suggest a walk in the woods with Thierry on his return. No greater solace than woodland paths with the sunlight glancing off the slender trunks of the birch trees.

Kirsty got in at ten, just as Tess was finishing typing out a recipe for Shepherd's pie with plenty of phrasal verbs in it that she would work through with Jean Louis next day. *Starry-eyed*, yes, I suppose there is such a thing, thought Tess looking at Kirsty as she came into the room. It had been fantastic. For once Stephen hadn't had to get back home for six. Cynthia had a meeting so they'd been able to have a meal together.

'I think I'll have an early night,' she said, stretching and turning towards the door. There were twigs stuck to her blouse.

'Me too,' said Tess.

I hope I don't wake up at five like last night, she thought as, an hour later, she put a mark in Dante's *Inferno* and switched the light out.

Just after midnight she was woken by a banging at the front door. A policeman to tell her that Annie had had an accident? She went trembling to the window to look out. At the door stood Stephen with his wife beside him. Tess stuck her head out the window.

'Is Kirsty there?' Stephen called up. His upturned face looked haggard in the moonlight.

'Yes, but she's asleep.'

'Wake her up. Tell her to come down here. We want to talk to her,' Cynthia shouted up.

Tess couldn't imagine anything Kirsty would want less than to be woken up in order to go down the stairs in the middle of the night to talk to Stephen in the company of his wife.

'Can't it wait till morning?' she asked.

'It most certainly can NOT.' Fury in Cynthia's voice.

'Oh, my God!' Kirsty had come into the room. She was struggling into a coat. 'Why did you tell them I was here,' she hissed.

A moment later Tess heard the door opening and

Cynthia's voice. She didn't need to strain her ears to hear the words.

'Bitch. You bitch. How dare you think you can mess around with my husband. How dare you think he would ever leave me for you. Tell her, Stephen. Tell her that you have no interest in her whatsoever - except for an easy fuck now and again. Tell her. Say it. Say that you don't love her, that you never have, and that you don't ever want to see her again. Go on. Say it. Tell her what you told me just now in the kitchen.'

And then Stephen's voice, a mutter...

'I ....'

'Go on'

'I'm sorry, we mustn't meet again, Kirsty.'

'Tell her. Tell her you don't love her. Tell her you have no interest in her beyond a fuck to remind you of when you were a spotty adolescent on your first date. Say it.

'I don't love you Kirsty. We'll have to stop seeing each other.'

'So that's an end to it. Please do not think of speaking to my husband ever again, do you hear?'

From the window Tess could see Cynthia catching Stephen by the arm and marching him towards the car. Tess wondered if he would look back at Kirsty whom she sensed was still standing in the doorway watching them, but he got into the passenger's seat with his head down. The tyres skidded on the gravel and they were gone. Silence. In the nearby woods the hoot of an owl.

Kirsty came back into the room, followed by Trotsky hoping a second supper might be in the offing. Tess hardly dared to look at her.

'Did you see her? Did you hear her? I thought she was going to attack me with her scarlet nails. And I'd have hit her with the spade - it was beside the door. And Stephen would have run away. He was shaking in his shoes, he was like a petrified rabbit. 'Say, say, you don't love her. You love only me.' Well she can have him. She's welcome to him. Good riddance to him. Let's drink a large glass of whisky to the future of Stephen and Cynthia in their ugly bungalow with their vile furniture and their mustard carpet and their boring lives. He was like a little circus flea. No, not a circus flea, a circus flea would have more spirit than him. Where's the whisky?'

In the end they settled for tea and a packet of digestive biscuits.

'Say it, say it, tell her you do not love her.' The words were still ringing in Tess's ears the next morning as she drove in from Kineldie. Kirsty had stayed behind. She had no teaching that morning. Tess wondered if she wasn't secretly hoping Stephen would phone her, or even come out to the cottage. But no, he had looked so pathetic standing next to Cynthia in the moonlight. The daring and carefree lover was lost for ever as far as Kirsty was concerned, Tess was sure of that.

Jean Louis was already there in his dogstooth jacket when she arrived at nine.

'Let's go on with phrasal verbs,' she said immediately, being in no mood for idle talk this morning. She passed him a recipe for marmalade that she'd made up at the weekend and told him to read it while she looked out of the window at the sea. A leaden grey this morning, barely distinguishable from the sky which was almost down upon it. Soon the horizon would be completely blotted out, the distinction between the two erased.

On the whole Jean Louis, like all the French, had a very low opinion of any meal which wasn't French, so he'd surprised her last week by praising 'your afternoon tea.' He'd stopped in a small village the previous weekend and they'd had afternoon tea and it had been very nice.

'A pot of tea and scones and marmalade. It was very good. Better than on British Airways.' On a recent flight they'd been given *clotted cream* with their scones, which he didn't like the sound of, the word *clot* reminding him of blood clots.

'Jam, not marmalade. You have marmalade for breakfast and at any other time what you eat is jam. At breakfast it is always marmalade and at tea time it's jam.'

The combination of scones and marmalade was faintly disgusting to her. Of course in France there was no tradition of eating marmalade, only orange jam made with sweet oranges. She was quite pleased with this recipe for marmalade, especially the opening paragraph in which she'd managed to introduce no less than six phrasal verbs.

*You only **come across** Seville oranges in the shops in the month of January so January is **given over** to the making of marmalade for the whole year. Recipes for marmalade are **passed on** from one generation to another. Sometimes brothers and sisters even **fall out** about how exactly their mother and grandmother used to make marmalade. Sometimes they never **make up** their quarrel and **end up** never speaking to each other again.*

She'd blanked out the phrasal verbs and she now wrote these up on the board and asked him to choose the right one to fill each blank.

'I'll leave you to do that by yourself,' she said, trying to make it sound as if that was the very best thing for him rather than for her. She disappeared out the door and made her way to Hilary's room. Tess knew she had a free morning.

'I'm trying to find limericks I can do with my class to improve their pronunciation. What do you think of this one, Tess?' she asked.

There was a young lady of Spain
who liked to make love now and again
not "now and again"
but now! and again! and again! and again! and again!

'Do you think they might be shocked by that?' Hilary the dedicated bohemian always became embarrassed and secretive on the subject of sex. Very pre the 1990s.

'I'm sure they'll love that,' said Tess, not wanting to seem pre-1990s herself.

'Let's go and see a film on Saturday evening.' She, Kirsty and Hilary - maybe the three of them could go clubbing as well afterwards.

She returned to her room and to Jean Louis and his dogstooth jacket. He was sitting studying the map of France she had up on the wall. It had obviously not taken him long to do the exercise. She looked at what he had written.

*You only **end up** Seville oranges in the shops in the month of January so January is **giving over** to the making of marmalade for the whole year. Recipes for marmalade are **coming across** from one generation to another. Sometimes brothers and sisters even **make up** about how exactly their mother and grandmother used to make marmalade. Sometimes they never **fall out** their quarrel and **pass on** never speaking to each other again.*

'Maybe if I put a rough equivalent in meaning beside each phrasal verb,' said Tess, which is what she should have done in the first place. She wrote *quarrel* beside *fall out* and *encounter* beside *come across*.

She looked out of the window while he redid the exercise. The sea and the sky were now one. This time he managed to fill in all the blanks correctly, but didn't *make up* mean *invent*? Yes, indeed, in fact *make up* had several meanings. Did he not remember? They had done this last time.

She went over again the different meanings of *make up*, like a detective taking a witness over the route of a crime, hoping this would stir their memory. You could make up your face, you could make up a sum of money, you could make up a mixture, you could make up a quarrel. Could she ever make up her quarrel with Fergus? Had they actually quarrelled? And yes, you could make up or invent a story, like settling down in a *manoir* for the rest of your life.

'Not only does English have over 3000 phrasal verbs but many of them have several meanings. So.' She gave Jean Louis a smile, or was it a baring of teeth?

'But of course you don't need to know them all,' she added reassuringly.

She called in at the auction on her way home. It was viewing day. It would be much cheaper if she could pick a mirror up there rather than from Thierry's antique man. A large old one in a gilt frame was what she was after, to put over the mantle-piece in her bedroom.

The usual crowd of shabbily dressed dealers were there, opening drawers, turning over plates, rummaging through pictures stacked against the walls, standing back to look at wardrobes, coffee tables, dining tables, bedside tables, sets of chairs, saggy sofas, poking in large cardboard boxes, rooting around among copper vases and brass jugs and cushion covers and broken table lamps. Tomorrow at the auction the auctioneer would be calling out "Who will bid me £50?..... £40?..... £30?..... £20? £20? £20 for the lot!" The hammer would come down. The possessions of a lifetime put into cardboard boxes and sold for £20. Going ...going .... gone! Would Thierry's father's possessions go like that? Probably not. They would remain in the manoir, passed on to the next generation and the generation after that.

The mirrors - and there were several of them of different shapes and sizes - were all in curly gilt frames - B and Q circa ten years ago. An enormous oil painting on one wall, painted maybe by the same person as had owned the mirrors - a small orange boat set against a great expanse of peacock blue. She imagined it on the wall opposite one of the mirrors, that way you'd be able to see the picture looking in both directions. There was nothing there that she would be interested in bidding for. How long was Thierry going to be away for?

Chapter 23

Thierry was already there waiting for her when she arrived at the Institute on Monday morning at eight. He'd phoned her at Kineldie late Sunday afternoon as soon as he'd got in from Paris. She surprised herself by putting her arms around him and they stood there for several seconds without saying anything.

'. "I was ill but now I am hill",' he began, as he sat down with his battered brief case in front of him on the table.

'Sorry?'

'Ah no, I was ill but now I am hilled. What means hilled?'

He'd been listening to Songs of Praise again. Sunday evening in the winter in Aberdeen when it got dark at four was a lonely time for him.

'Especially when you've just got back from your father's funeral,' thought Tess. Had Barbara not been at the airport to meet him? She could have suggested coming round to his house when he'd phoned yesterday, maybe that was what he'd been hoping.

'Healed,' she said. 'I was ill but now I am healed.' She explained *healed*. Was he healed so soon after his father's death?

'Were you very close to your father?' she asked, and for the next hour she sat and listened as he talked about his parents, his childhood and their holidays on the white sandy beaches of the Atlantic and how his father who was a military historian made the most perfect sand castles with moats and battlements and *machicoulis* and then, just after Thierry got his first job, his father had begun to go - how did you say that in English - *gaga*?

'Away with the fairies,' said Tess. 'That's what people say.' It certainly sounded much nicer than *senile*. Would he suggest meeting this coming Saturday?

'I am sorry it will not be possible to meet this Saturday either,' he said. 'On Friday I am returning to Paris. I have many businesses to do. I am sorry.' He looked across at her.

'I'm sorry too, but maybe the following Saturday,' she said. Or the Saturday after that? Or after that?

'The trouble is we are eating too much,' said Vincent. Somehow the conversation had got onto global warming.

'How doos dhat affect de envoironment?' she asked. She'd decided to practice her Irish accent today on Vincent. He launched into an explanation. It was several minutes before she realised he was talking about heating not eating.

'People use far too much water. People are wasteful when they are taking a shower.'

She agreed. People nowadays seemed to have a shower every day, sometimes twice a day. This wasn't necessary in a climate like Scotland's. She had grown up with a bath a week. In the old days most people didn't even have a bath in the house. Her memory of France in the old days was of the smell of eau de cologne. They never washed themselves in France, was what they said about them in England, just slapped eau de cologne on. He agreed that one shower a day was quite enough.

'And as for hair washing, it's the same,' she said. She had dropped the accent as she warmed to the topic. 'People used to wash their hair once a week at the very most. Now it's every day. It's absurd to wash your hair every day. It's just making the shampoo manufacturers rich. They sell you shampoo and then they sell you expensive conditioner which will, they claim, put back into the hair the goodness which washing it daily with their shampoo has taken out.' But here he disagreed.

'I am not agreed. My wife has very beautiful hairs and she is washing them every day. She explain me why.'

Their heart-to-heart about the way other people were destroying the environment by their obsession with cleanliness came to an abrupt end. Now he was probably thinking that it was no wonder her hair was such a mess, washing it only once a week. His own hair was a fluffy well-washed light brown.

'You are still over-using the present continuous,' she told

him. *Your wife washes her hair every day,* not *she is washing.* So, your wife washes her hair every day. Is she washing her hair at the moment?'

As she asked the question she remembered that his wife and children had gone back to Bordeaux as a prelude to his departure for Angola next month. A good question then. What could his wife be doing at the moment, mid-morning in Bordeaux with the children at school? Tess imagined her in a purple bathrobe and fluffy mules, opening the door to some lithe, dark-haired, out-of-work actor.

'She is doing the homework and the shopping.' Or so you hope.

'And you. Are you speaking French?'

'Yes, of course I am speaking French.' He looked at her as if he thought she was daft.

'Oh, I thought what you were speaking was English.' Big joke. She'd made it countless times and was tired of it except that it always reminded her of the scene in *Gentlemen Prefer Blondes* when the two blondes in their Paris hotel get a visit from two Frenchmen. 'We don't speak French. We don't understand a word,' they kept saying, until it suddenly dawned on them that what the men were trying to speak was English.

'Do you have any written work for me today?' she asked.

'Perfect,' she beamed as she came to the end of checking through the three page report. There was still ten minutes to go.

'Now read it out, Vincent. 'Remember what I told you. It's okay to say *t* instead of *th - tirteen-and-tree-eights.'*

Tomorrow she would be seeing Thierry for his lesson. She wouldn't even try to teach him anything, they would go on talking like last time, about his father, maybe about his wife. And maybe she'd talk about Bob, about how that had been a sort of death too.

Vincent was into the third paragraph of his drilling report. *Holy water,* he was reading out.

'Holy water? Oh, no. *Oily* water. There is a difference, you know, between holy water and oily water.'

'Not for *Termoil* there isn't,' said Vincent.

She really would miss him when he went. When would that be exactly? Would he still be there next week? Possibly. She'd put his name down anyway.

She wandered down the corridor, putting her ear to each of the classroom doors as she went. Maggie was teaching her 'O' grade Italian class - *Yes, very good Moira. And now can anybody tell me ..... .* Pete was playing *It's been a hard day's night* to his Japanese businessmen. Tess imagined them sitting there nodding their heads. Franck seemed to be reading out a passage from Die Spiegel in a very loud voice. Kirsty in Room 5 sounded as if she was haranguing her class - Vraiment, vous etes absolumment ..... . In Room 2a Hilary was explaining *Ode to a Nightingale*. Why did Tess have to be spending her time explaining how *you raise prices* but *prices rise* and *you raise questions* but *questions arise* when she could be reading Keats? Maybe tomorrow she would do a poem with Thierry.

But the next day, as he settled down opposite her, he made an announcement which straight away made the poem she was about to share with him irrelevant. He was leaving Aberdeen.

He explained. His sister who looked after his daughter and son in Paris was having to return to the manoir because of their father's death so his children needed him back in Paris and the oil company had accepted to move him back there so he was leaving for good before Christmas.

'But I will miss you,' he said.

'I'll miss you too.'

'Oh and I have a question. What is the difference between *surprised* and a*stonished?*'

She explained that it was a question of degree. She was surprised to hear that he was returning to Paris, and even astonished. Not to say astounded, dumbfounded, gobsmacked.

'I'd be *surprised* if you weren't looking forward to going back to France. I'd be *astonished* if you wanted to stay here

144

and become British.'

'Oh no, I have nothing against the British. Only they do not use the same side of the head as we.'

'Yes, yes, you have already told me about the pepper pot.' In a few weeks he would walk out of her life for ever with a brief peck on the cheek.

He wanted to know how to end letters. He was writing to the bank to close his account. Would Tess help him to write the letter, how would he end it?

'How about *Cheers* or *Yours*?' he asked. (How do you end a relationship, how do you walk out on someone?) 'And how you say *Meilleurs souvenirs*? You do not have *Best memories*? And *Amicalement*. You cannot say *Friendly*?

'Yes, we have *hugs*. But mostly we just say *Love*, but not when writing to the bank manager. For the bank manager you end the letter *Yours faithfully*.'

'I'm writing to say him I am leaving the bank, I am closing my account, and I am never returning and I write *Your faithfully*?' He found this a nice example of British hypocrisy. (Would it be any more appropriate for him to end a letter to her with *Your faithfully*?)

'But what about all those long meaningless French endings assuring the recipient of *sentiments distingués* and *hommages respectueux*?'

He shook his head and was silent.

'Before you leave you really must visit the old part of the town.' In her mind she was beginning to form an invitation. 'You complain about the greyness of Aberdeen but Old Aberdeen is all pink granite and lovely little 18th century cottages and splendid mansions and a 16th century chapel and an impressive library. I could show you round it one week-end before you go.' The brief amount of time left to them was making her bold. She would suggest visiting Old Aberdeen once he'd finished writing his letter to the bank.

He was already folding up the sheet of paper on which he'd scribbled his farewell to the Bank of Scotland.

'It would be a good idea if you wrote it up on the board,' she said, 'to make sure you've got it right.' She was becoming the school marm and he the little boy, hitching up his brown corduroys and writing carefully in a round hand.

'You've got the wrong punctuation.'

He rubbed out the full stop and replaced it with a comma.

'There's something wrong with the way you've spelt *writing* And the *y* of *Yours* should be a capital letter and you've forgotten the *s*.' Lash, lash. She'd turned from school marm into Madame Whiplash.

'Okay. That's fine. Now you can copy it down and that will be your letter all ready to copy out when you get home.'

'*Copy out ....copy down* ..... English is an impossible language,' he muttered as he sat down.

'Oi mustH show you roundH de old tHown before you go,' she said, echoing her mother's tone of voice. She explained the charms of Old Aberdeen.

'Oh no, I am sorry but I will have no time,' he said. He had far too much to do what with writing letters and packing.

'How single-minded he is,' she thought. Or how little interested in her. He seemed to need days for what she would fit in between two cups of coffee.

She picked up *Making your Mark at Meetings*, opened it at *The Language of Persuasion* and began playfully to read out the phrases:

Have you taken into account the regret you might experience? Has it occurred to you that .... Wouldn't it be a good idea to ...... I wonder if you've considered .....

It was difficult to go on in this flirtatious manner. She stopped and looked up. He was amused but adamant. There would be no time - there wouldn't even be time for another lesson.

'But when you are in Paris - because you are coming in Paris, no? - you must come in Versailles.' His 17th century flat in Versailles full of wooden armchairs and a Scottish grandfather clock.

'I would love to visit your flat and see your grandfather clock,' she said. She would never go there, this was goodbye for ever. 'And Versailles, especially the *parc*,' she added.

'Oh no, it is not nice compared to your parks here.'

146

'Ah, yes, the one thing about Scotland that you like,' she said. No, no. There were a lot of things he liked about Scotland.

'Your lovely cottage,' he said. 'And you in it,' he seemed to be saying now with his eyes. And then the countryside was beautiful, and the gardens were delightful. The only thing was he was very sorry he had not visited the west coast.

'But it is lonely visiting these places by myself.'

I would gladly have gone with you, she thought, only now it is too late, too late even for a tour of the old town. She glanced at her diary. Jean Louis at eleven o'clock.

'Goodbye.' She opened the door for Thierry and waited as he got into his rain coat. As they embraced she remembered their long embrace of the previous week. Ah yes, he would give her his address in Paris and he was waiting her visit.

'Goodbye,' he said again, touching her on the arm. She stood and watched him hurrying away down the corridor. Would she ever visit him in Paris? What would be the point? Was she not simply his charming English teacher who had been so nice and patient with him?

Chapter 24

Jean Louis had a question. *To let someone down,* what did that mean?

'It means *to disappoint*.' Fergus

'Oh, it actually means *to disappoint*, it is exactly the same?

'No, not exactly the same, but they are more or less the same sometimes.' She was beginning to remember she'd been awake since five. She'd woken up suddenly from a dream she'd been having about Thierry in which he'd gone off without even saying goodbye. It was only when she saw him arriving at eight this morning that the unhappiness and alarm caused by the dream had disappeared.

And *like so*. She had told him that it wasn't good English.

'But I have heard *like so* because every time I am listening and repeating what people are saying. That is why I am doing so little mistakes. On the plane the air hostess when she is demonstrating the life jacket she is saying "and I tie a knot like so.'

She'd intended doing another recipe with him - Shepherd's Pie this time, maybe - but she hadn't finished making up the exercise yet. She'd do that this evening.

'Next week we'll do another recipe for a delicious meal with beef,' she said. Or was it lamb you made Shepherd's Pie with? Surely more appropriate. But no, next week and the week after he would be on a course, and then it would be Christmas, he pointed out.

'Revision, then,' she said. 'Let's do some revision.'

'So, I'll see you after Christmas,' she said as he struggled with the door knob an hour later.

Christmas. She must ring Annie to see if she would come up to Kineldie for a change. Her sudden decision, after the lunch at *Termoil*, to go to Petersburg had been foiled when she'd discovered the difficulty of getting a visa. She'd phoned the Russian Embassy and listened to a long slow message on the answer machine, preceded by the warning that the phone call was costing £1 per minute. Several minutes later she'd heard enough to realise the impossibility of obtaining a visa in time. In any case, hadn't she resolved to end her relationship with Fergus?

Kirsty was taking her mother to a hotel in the Borders. Last year they'd spent Christmas at her mother's house, just round the corner from where Stephen lived. She didn't want a repeat of that.

'We were sitting eating chicken that tasted of old fish and my Mum was forcing herself to drink the wine I'd brought and wishing it was Iron Bru. And he was across the road with Cynthia and his two kids eating goose and sipping Chateau Lafitte.'

Wisps of clouds in a blue sky. Towards the sea what looked like a range of mountains - dark tops appearing above mist on the horizon. A moment later and the mist had cleared and the chain of mountains had disintegrated. It was Vincent's last lesson. He was going to Paris next week and then to Angola after Christmas. The phone rang. It was him.

'I will not go to see you this morning and I will leave on Friday to France.'

So bye bye Vincent, and good luck in Angola. 'I really enjoyed my English lessons with you' would have been nice. Or even just 'Thank you for teaching me.'

She thought of the nicest compliment she'd ever been paid - several years ago now. She'd been sitting there listening to this engineer talking about the problems of gas transportation from far out in the North Sea to the Gas Terminal north of Aberdeen, thinking that in half an hour he was going to walk out of her life for ever and she could hardly wait. She was bored, bored, she had rarely been so bored.

At last it was time.

'Goodbye and thank you for teaching me,' he said as they shook hands. And then 'With you I have never been bored, never. That is one thing I can say of your lessons. I have never been bored.'

Did Vincent want her to send him the copy of the drilling report he'd left with her to check? She had it in front of her. She'd been reading it aloud, using it to practise her Irish accent. No, it didn't matter. He had already given the report to his boss.

The phone again. This time Thierry. Her heart leapt in spite of herself. Maybe he had been overcome by the sadness of not seeing her again before his departure.

'Tess, let's meet for a drink before I go,' was he about to say?

'Tess, how do you say *chevreuil* in English?' he asked. He wanted to take some back to France for Christmas. And where was the best place to buy it? She told him the English word was *venison*. But was that the male or the female?

'I don't think we make a distinction,' she said. Big laugh on the other end of the phone. He thought this was very British. Would he have time after all to come for another lesson before he left for France? No harm in asking.

'No, I am sorry but I prefer not coming.' (Of course not.) 'I have so much works because as I said you I am leaving in a hurry. But I am waiting your visit in Paris. In January? You will come in January?'

'Maybe,' she said. She could always contact Jennifer and fix up to go over and stay with her, but she'd prefer February, the most depressing month of the year for her. February would be a good month. She remembered sitting in the metro station at Montparnasse with Marc one February, waiting for the last train back to her flat.

'Are you glad you met me?' he'd asked her, the answer obvious but he wanted to hear it. 'Oh, yes,' she'd said, 'February is usually such a dull month.' *Si ennuyeux*. He'd found this very funny.

She got her makeup bag out of her handbag. In it a little tube of beige foundation cream - a free sample she'd picked up somewhere. She dotted it over her face and gently stroked it in with light upward movements as they said you should. If anything the effect was to emphasise the wrinkles she thought, as she looked at herself in the mirror. She aimed the bottle at the bin in the corner of the room and managed to get it in first time.

A knock on the door. Maggie, looking lovely in a pale grey suit. Did Tess want to come over on Christmas Day? No, that was very kind of her but she was going down to London. That's nice. Well, yes and no.

'It will be nice to be with Annie, won't it?' said Maggie.

Yes, it would be very nice to be with Annie but she wasn't at all looking forward to going down to London. With Fergus not there she'd tried her best to persuade Annie to come up to Kineldie. But Annie was trying to make her way as an interior designer. She couldn't be taking days off, coming up to Scotland to sit around in Kineldie, helping to keep the fire going, having to walk half a mile down to the village in an icy wind to buy a paper because Tess disapproved of taking the car, and fending off suggestions to look up Karen - 'you used to be such good friends when you were at school.'

She hadn't actually said all this to Tess. All she'd actually said, in response to Tess's invitation to spend Christmas in Kineldie, was 'Oh Mum!'

'You're looking wonderful today, Tess,' said Maggie.

'Am I? It must be because for once I'm wearing lipstick.'

'No, it's your skin.' Tess looked across at the bin. Maybe she should retrieve that tube and make a note of what it was and go out and buy a big pot of the stuff, to hell with the expense.

'Let's go into town and go round the shops. And we could have lunch in Michie's.'

Tess loved it there. The other morning she had sat there for an hour over a pot of coffee wondering what the two elderly ladies across from her were finding to talk about. Beautifully groomed - lipstick, nail varnish and fresh-from-the-hairdresser's hair - and both dressed in their Pringle sweaters and tartan skirts, one in shades of orange and brown, the other in refined shades of green, and with jewelled rings on their fingers, as well as the marriage band, of course, and expensive watches. All she could catch were their *Aahs* and

Ooohhhs and *Oh no-s* as they swayed towards each other, waved their hands about, laughed.

The phone again just as they were leaving the room. Laurent. He wouldn't be there either next week

'Because I am going in holidays next Wednesday.' Oh, well. Time for her to do her Christmas shopping and make a Christmas cake and prepare herself for London. Also she'd promised to make a Scottish dish for the foreign students at the university. It was the last time she would be seeing them as a group. Next term they would come to see her individually with the essays they were writing.

The plan was for them each to make a typical dish. Mr Sakura had promised seaweed rolls. 'Where can I buy dried tangle?' he'd asked her last week. And Asi from Thailand wanted to make a stew but for it she needed a pound of buffalo meat and half a pound of clotted blood. Where could she find that in Aberdeen?

'Oh, by the way, Maggie, when you buy venison, is it stag meat or deer meat that you buy?' Tess asked as they left the Institute. Maybe she could bring a chunk of venison down to London for herself and Annie now that Annie was no longer vegetarian. Stag or deer, she was sure Annie wouldn't mind which.

Chapter 25

The plane was late arriving back in Aberdeen. There had been an incident as the passengers were getting on. An oil worker had slapped the air stewardess's bottom as she'd led them out to the plane and she'd called the police in. Take-off was delayed while the oil worker was called to the front of the plane and cautioned by the police officer.

'It was probably because she has *EasyGo* written in large letters across her back,' the Pakistani sitting next to Tess explained to her. 'We men, we do not mean any harm. It is just in good fun. It is because it is Christmas time.'

Christmas time. Good fun. How often did the two go together? In fact it hadn't been as bad as she'd feared. It was the coming back to Aberdeen that was the hard part. Annie had finished with her boyfriend Robert at the beginning of December so it was just the two of them in Annie's minimalist flat with the wavy chairs and funny lamps.

They'd gone on Christmas afternoon to have tea with Fergus's mum in the little house in Vauxhall where she'd been born. All the time Fergus was growing up his mum had been a cleaner in the Houses of Parliament across the river. She used to arrive home often with the leftovers from functions held there - 'government grub', Fergus used to call it. Tess sat there eating mince pies and listening to her talking about Fergus and reading the postcards he'd sent her. He was never a one for writing letters, she told them. Tell me about it, thought Tess.

'You know Samuel Johnson was known as a man of letters? Well, I think I'm a man of postcards,' he'd said once to her.

And then the phone had rung and it was him.

'Tess is here. Do you want to have a word with her?' his mum had asked him after a few minutes.

It was only the second time Tess had heard his voice since he'd left. He wasn't a man of phone calls either. He told her he'd been trying to get through to her at Annie's.

'I'll try to ring you again this evening,' he'd said but the only phone call that evening had been for Annie.

They'd spent the evening looking at videos of old Charlie Chaplin and Buster Keaton films. At one moment, while Annie was in the kitchen cutting up slabs of the Christmas cake Tess had brought with her from Aberdeen, Tess had turned face down the large Christmas card *To dearest Annie from Bob, Liz and Linda with all our love and hope to see you soon!* sitting prominently on the mantlepiece. It had been bugging her since her arrival. How much did Annie like having a baby half sister? How often did she see them? Tess never asked and Annie never said.

The next day they'd gone to the sales in Oxford St. and Annie had bought a slippery midnight blue dress and talked Tess into a long grey raincoat and a jaunty black hat.

'You look great, Mum, you look like a concussed actress who's trying to find her way back onto the stage.'

It was seven o'clock before she got to Pam's shop to pick up some milk and bread and thank her for feeding Trotsky. Colonel Forbes was there in his tweeds, clutching a bottle of whisky. *He* looks like a drunken farmer trying to find his way back onto his tractor, Tess thought.

'Did you have a good Christmas, Tess?' he boomed.

'Yes thank you.' You've got a bit of ham stuck in your moustache, she wanted to say. 'And you?' she asked.

Pam and herself stood while he launched into a blow-by-blow account of their day, how they'd had their two sons and their families for Christmas lunch and how they'd had turkey this year because last year they'd had a goose - a large goose, it had maybe weighed ten, no maybe eleven pounds, but still only just enough to go round and then you know what it's like, the next day if it's turkey there is plenty of left-overs and you can rustle up a meal but with goose there's nothing left the next day and you've got to think of something else and his wife Morag had been obliged to set to again and well, you know what it's like, they weren't in their first youth. But the grandchildren - there's Anthony - he's six now would you believe it - he's a little rascal......

Why are some people, thought Tess, mostly men it must

be admitted, so inept when it comes to conversation? Why does this man stand there assuming that his function is to entertain us and our function to stand there listening, nodding and saying *Mmm* and *Oh* and *Really?* and *Yes, I know* and *How interesting*? Men were like the nuts in a bag of Muesli when it came to conversation in mixed company if the women didn't watch out. They always somehow worked their way to the top, vying with each other for attention. 'Look at me!'

And no glory attached to listening, of course. except, if you were good at it, when it won you the reputation for being charming. He'd probably go back home and tell his wife that at the shop he'd run into that charming lady who lives in Kineldie. Pam wouldn't be a charming lady, of course, she'd just be the very pleasant and obliging woman in the shop.

'I must be going,' Tess cut in, before he could get started on the exploits of the grandchildren. 'It may be quite difficult getting up the track to the house.' Outside it was beginning to snow. On the mat when she got in a letter from Thierry thanking her again for her 'patience' with him and saying that he was going to be away on business most of January but in February he'd be back in Paris.

Thick snow still, several days later when she and Kirsty set out very early from Kineldie and drove gingerly at ten miles an hour down to the main road, praying they wouldn't meet another car coming the other way. At least the car had started.

Once on the main road they were able to drive at normal speed so they reached Aberdeen well before they needed to.

'We could go for a walk in Hazlehead Park. We've plenty of time,' said Kirsty. Tess was surprised. Hazlehead Park was where the memorial was to the hundred and sixty seven men who had died the night the Piper Alpha oil platform had exploded, one hundred and twenty miles off-shore of Aberdeen. Kirsty had never wanted to visit it up to now. Her brother had been one of the men.

It was a lovely sunny morning, the winter-flowering

rhododendrons emerging bright red from their ruffs of snow and crows flying low over the unfamiliar white ground. They walked past the little zoo where Tess used to bring Annie to see the seals, to the rose garden. In the centre of it a statue in bronze of three oil workers, strong, helmeted - and the names of all those who had died that night inscribed on the plinth in gold. They found Angus's name, half way down the second column. There were tears in Kirsty's eyes. They stood there in silence for what seemed to Tess like a very long time. She wandered over to read the names of the roses which had been planted at each corner of the statue: *Remember Me   Our Love Sweetheart   Wishing*

'Okay, let's go. You must be getting cold,' Kirsty said at last, and they walked quickly back to the car.

At the entrance to the Institute they met Pete. It was the first time they'd seen him in the New Year. New Year was one of the rare occasions when Scots shook hands. Or kissed. Pete leapt towards them, his arms outstretched and to Tess's surprise Kirsty fell into them.

'Oh Pete, I'm so sorry. I let you down before Christmas. I said I would come round and look at your computer.'

Pete's computer was still paralysed but if Kirsty had the time this week. Yes, yes, she would go back with him to his house this afternoon. Pete's face was shiny with delight. That's nice, thought Tess.

Arriving in her room, she opened her new desk diary, a dark green cover to it this year, the pages inside almost blank except for the few faithfuls - Laurent, Denis, Jean Louis. Dominique would soon be leaving. And no Thierry.

The sea streaked with silver. Jean Louis arrived on the dot of eleven - an acid yellow tie with green frogs jumping around on it. A Christmas present? And his cream and black dogtooth tweed jacket. How can he expect me to sit for an hour and look at that? she thought. Maybe she'd set him some work and then she could go away and chat with Pete.

He wanted to know what *stroll* meant.

' "I'm going for a stroll over to the warehouse," they say

at work. What means *stroll*?' Stroll means walking in a leisurely fashion.

'Then if they're at work they should not stroll,' he said.

And expressions for different sorts of light. He was confused. There was *gleam* and *glisten* and *glare*. They all began with *gl*. (Did *gl* have a meaning?)

'And also *glow*,' she said, thinking of the warm glow there used to be on Kirsty's cheeks when she came in after seeing Stephen. 'You could say there is a glow in the sky at the moment.' Or was it just at night you got a glow?

'Yes, it is a better weather today.'

'And then there are glow worms.' She wrote the word up on the board. What was *glow worm* in French? She passed him the dictionary.

'Ah yes, *vers luisant*. And then there are tape worms,' he said as his eye travelled down the page.

He'd had tape worms once and had been obliged to have a - he opened the dictionary again - a stool analysis. Which was negative.

'Good,' said Tess. Yes, but it was because he should have sent fresh stools and taken medicine beforehand so that the worms were not sticking to the stomach.

Was it the moment to introduce the recipe for Shepherd's Pie? Maybe *Scones in a Hurry* would be easier on the stomach. In any case she'd never got round to checking out what sort of meat went into Shepherd's Pie. Was it really beef?

'You remember the phrasal verbs we did before Christmas in the recipe for marmalade?' He had only the vaguest memory. He had been away on an expensive computer course since then. The teacher had kept asking them "Is what I am doing with you okay?" But she was the teacher, she should have known.

'Yes, well, here is a recipe for something called *scones*.'

This time she gave him the opening paragraph of the recipe to look at first with the phrasal verbs in bold.

*If people **drop in** on you one afternoon and you have **run out** of cakes or biscuits, you can always **turn out** these scones* *in not much more than 10 minutes. They are simple but should not be **looked down on**. All the best hotels have scones on the menu for afternoon tea. So why not **try them out**? If you don't have a rolling pin you can **get away with** using a bottle to **roll out** the dough.*

'Try to guess the meanings of the phrasal verbs. I've marked them in bold,' she told him. She hesitated. 'I'll be back in a moment,' she said.

Out in the corridor she met Pete who had that week started on an intensive course for Hungarian teachers. He was carrying a plastic bag and was in a state of some excitement.

'Look inside,' he said. She peered in at an unlikely collection of objects. He'd got the students out of the classroom - "Imagine this is a fire drill. Leave everything behind, no time to put on coats or collect bags, just go downstairs quickly but calmly. No, Attila, don't take your mobile phone, leave it on your desk, it's not going to walk. Hurry up Illona. Come on Csilla."

He'd then gone round throwing gloves, hats, scarves, books, Attila's mobile phone into the bag.

'They'll be back up in a minute and then they'll have to tell me what they're missing. You don't want to help me?'

As he spoke the first of the class started appearing at the end of the corridor, hunched up, shivering, sullen.

'I'm in the middle of teaching someone,' said Tess, trying to put a regretful note into her voice. Jean Louis had suddenly become a highly desirable person to return to.

'What's the difference between a lottery and a ramble?' he asked her as she came through the door.

'You mean *raffle*,' she said. What was the relevance of this to *Scones in a Hurry*? 'A ramble is like a stroll. A raffle is a ..... ' She started hunting for the word in the dictionary. 'Anyway a lottery is *une loterie*.' Or was it *un loterie*? She waited for him to correct her. She found *raffle*. That was *loterie* too in French.

Angry Hungarian voices began to be heard the other side of the wall with Pete trying gallantly to override them.

'What sort of scarf? You'll have to describe it exactly Istvan. What is it made of? What colour is it? I am sorry there is no scarf answering that description in my bag.'

'Istvan thinks I've stolen his scarf,' Pete told Tess later in the coffee room. And they were now saying they wanted to do grammar exercises for the rest of the time they were here because they would have an exam when they got back to Hungary.

'Two weeks of Happy Grammar,' said Pete, taking the book out of his brief case. 'p. 71,' he announced, opening the book. *Exercise 105: - Put into the Past Tense 1. You cut your face 2. Her dog bites him 3 The servant sweeps the room.*

I suppose we could act out each of the sentences. I could put some red ink on my face to look as if I've cut it. Csilla could be Illona's dog and she could get to bite Attila who I think she fancies anyway. And Tibor who claims to be a member of the wealthy Esterhazy family could be the servant sweeping the room.

'You'd be better doing it as a written exercise,' said Stephen who'd come in unnoticed. Tess had hardly seen him since that appearance in the moonlight. He'd have been better doing *that* as a written exercise too, she thought.

Dominique was late. Tess went down the corridor to get herself a cup of coffee. She found Maggie there. Maggie was planning a holiday in Florence. Tess had been there, no? Maggie didn't know Florence, she'd always gone south - to Genoa, Naples, Sicily.

'It's years since I was in Florence,' said Tess. It was after Marc's death and before she met Bob. And the only thing she had any clear memory of was that boy on the scooter who'd driven her to the outskirts of the city to a hillside to visit some chapel there, his one intention being to bed her. Gino. 'You were meant for love,' he'd whispered but she'd sent him away, immersing herself in Ruskin's *Mornings in Florence*, getting up at dawn as he instructed to admire the new day's sun shining on Giotto's frescoes in Santa Croce.

161

Back in her room the sun was streaming in. This was really a very pleasant job, particularly when the student didn't turn up. A read of the paper and then a look in at the auction room before driving home. She was about to leave when Dominique appeared in the doorway, all apologies - plane late from Paris, re-routed via Birmingham, terribly sorry.

'There is cow in Paris at the moment.'

'A herd of cattle wandering down the Champs Elysees?'

'No, cow-o.'

'Ah, chaos.' The metro was on strike. He had bought a "funny" book in the airport full of unfunny disinformation about Scotland. One mildly amusing cartoon of a woman on a chair and a mouse on the floor with the caption - *wee, sleeket, cowran, tim'rous beastie*. What did that mean?

Dominique was the man who'd bought Burns' *Poems and Songs* for his wife. He 'd told Tess he was very much in love with his wife who was a very beautiful woman of aristocratic Polish origin.

'Is she really beautiful?' Tess had asked his secretary whom she'd happened to meet one Saturday in John Lewis's.

'Well, beauty is in the eye of the beholder,' the secretary had said, looking hard at Tess.

Tess told him that the quotation came from the poem *To A Mouse, On turning her up in her Nest, with the Plough, November, 1785*. Yes, but what did it mean? Well *wee* was *little* and *timerous* was like *timid* and *cowering* - she told him to look that one up for himself while she reached for her own copy of Burns' *Poems and Songs* to check what *sleeket* meant.

Would her command of Scots allow her to read the poem aloud? She thought not. Instead she paraphrased the story of the mouse that had carefully built its nest against the winter winds only to have it destroyed by the ploughman ploughing his field. *The best laid schemes o' Mice an' Men .... .* Was it better not to have any plans at all, like her at the moment?

162

Chapter 26

The wind whimpering and whining away outside, like a lost child, a streak of the softest of blues narrowing as clouds billowed towards each other. Tess had been waylaid by Hilary in the car park, huddled in the old tweed Crombie coat she'd bought for £5 in Oxfam. Cecil had gone into a Drying Out place and she was off up to bring him some books to read. Denis arrived as she was trying to find a way of sticking up the new calendar. It was one Annie had given her of paintings of languid Victorian women.

'Asshole,' he said as he came through the door. Pardon me?

'I thought it was a rude word but they was using it all the time in the meeting yesterday. They was all the time saying everything was too much asshole.'

'Ah, hassle,' said Tess. 'Too much hassle. The word begins with an *h* and the stress is on the first element. Listen:

hassle - asshole hassle - asshole hassle -

A perfunctory knock on the door and Stephen's head appeared round it. *asshole*, she finished.

'Sorry to interrupt but I need to know your hours for December,' he said. Had he heard? Probably, but then it wouldn't occur to him that the word might be directed at him. Funny word to be calling her student, though. Maybe Tess wasn't quite the sort of person they wanted teaching at the Institute.

But what did *hassle* mean? Denis had never heard the word before. And then there was another word he wanted to ask about.

'What means *grumble*?'

It's what the French do all the time, she was tempted to say, only he might then think that it was a slang word for making love as Frenchmen, according to the British, were supposed to be in a permanently amorous state. ('I will like to grumble with you'). Was Thierry in a permanently amorous state over there in Paris? There had been another card from him yesterday, saying again how he was busy but he'd be free to receive her in February.

'Have you heard from Thierry?' she asked him. And then 'And did somebody tell me Barbara has moved to Paris too?'

Denis gave a big laugh. No, thank goodness Barbara has gone back to Warsaw.

'It was my fault, I am stupeed,' he said. 'I have met 'er at a conference in Cracow last year and she, how you say, has fall in love with me. So she came 'ere. But I am a married man with a little baby. It is very embarrassant and Thierry is very nice, 'e promised me he would keep 'er away from me.'

'Which he managed to do?'

'Yes, but he was finding her borring, borring but poor Thierry he was very kind.'

'I see,' said Tess. She looked at her watch. After midday in Paris now, a good time to ring. Jennifer would soon be sitting down with Bertrand to have lunch in their airy dining room looking out on the Boulevard Raspail. Every day for the last twenty five years Jennifer would have sat down at 12.30 to have lunch with Bertrand. She could phone from Hilary's room once she'd got rid of Denis.

Could she explain him words like *bloke*, *chap*, *fella* and *guy*, he asked her now. Would Tess use a word like *guy*?

'I am a gauge,' she thought. If someone as old as me uses *guy* then it must be an okay word.

'Yes, but I usually say *feller*,' she said 'I say - *I met this feller* ... . Met this feller? Would she ever again be able to say that - with a feeling of suppressed excitement? The dream she'd had the other night came back to her. She'd been sitting in a high-ceilinged room in a castle all by herself and then this man, young, dark, foreign-looking, had crept into the room, followed by a girl in a pink satin ball gown, a red carnation in her black hair. 'Come with me,' he'd whispered to her, opening a secret door in one of the bookcases that lined the walls. And Tess as she'd watched had been overcome by sadness that never again would any man ever whisper to her 'Come with me.'

164

But maybe that wasn't true. Thierry was asking her to come to Paris, Thierry was asking her to come to stay with him in Burgundy in the summer.

But what if she arrived there and found she was in the middle of a different story, found that the tender look in his eye was just for 'my dear eengleesh teeshair who has been so patientful with me and now I would like to present you my fiancée, Colette'? Would she then make the best of it? Set to, baking Irish Soda bread as her contribution to the elaborate catering? Or maybe, at their request, explain the uses of the Present Perfect in English? No, she'd have to make quite sure there was no Colette in his life before she set out for Burgundy.

And what words, Denis was now asking, were there you could use instead of *girl*?

'Well, there's always *woman*,' said Tess rather sharply. Why did people avoid that word as if there was something insulting about it? People didn't have a problem with *man*. She could think of no words like *bloke, chap* and *fella* that people used instead of *woman*. Women were *girls*. Or *ladies* if they were really past it sexually. In Lancashire a woman was addressed as *duck* when she wasn't *luv* and in Glasgow she was *hen* but you wouldn't say 'I met this duck/luv/hen yesterday evening.' There was *lass* or *lassie* in Scotland, of course and at the Burns Supper there would be an *Address to the Lassies*. She should maybe explain that to him, but the hour was up.

Hilary's room - smell of tobacco, and a copy of Yeats's *Selected Poems* open on her desk. Tess glanced down at it - '*Had I the heaven's embroidered cloth ...*' Hilary was probably using this to teach the Conditional. *Had I the heaven's embroidered cloth, Thierry, I would ....*

'Allo?' Jennifer's English accent immediately recognisable on the other end of the phone.

'Tess, how nice to hear from you. We were just in the middle of lunch ... ' She'd be delighted to see Tess for as long as she wanted to stay.

'I'll phone Thierry this evening to tell him I'm coming,'

Tess decided as she walked back to her room.

She was glad she was going to be having lunch with Maggie. She needed to talk and Maggie was the best listener she knew. Maggie suffered from a chronic ache in her neck that had been diagnosed as arthritis but Tess privately thought it was more likely to be repetitive strain injury from nodding while people told her all about their troubles.

Well, she would be doing the same thing, talking things over with her. Was she telling herself the wrong story about Thierry? There had been that letter from him on her return from London, saying again how pleased he would be to see her in Paris. And the talk over the phone yesterday evening when she'd told him she was coming to Paris to see Jennifer. Was she starting on a journey that would lead to a declaration: *I want to carry you away from Aberdeen where everything is grey - the granite, the sea, the skies, the people - to a place where life is joyful?* Or was she, in the words of Belinda Chimey, trying to turn lust into love? Where was Fergus now? What was he doing? What was he thinking?

'The cake shops here, they are so boring! Water is not coming in the mouth when I look at cake shops 'ere. In France the cake shops are so beautiful,' Jean Louis was saying. She looked at her watch, twenty more minutes still to go. The phone rang. It was Fergus.

'Hello, Tess, I'm in someone's house in some town by the Danube and they said I could use their phone. How are you? Did you get my cards? I sent you one from ....'. The line went dead. She wanted to cry. A town by the Danube. She replaced the receiver.

'I don't agree,' she said. 'I love Scottish cake shops with their rows of cream buns and currant scones and muffins and rolls and pancakes and jammy biscuits and cakes with pink icing and cakes with mint green icing and gingerbread with white icing.' Why didn't the phone ring again? Why couldn't Fergus learn to use a public phone? It couldn't be that difficult to phone from Eastern Europe - other people managed it - if he really wanted to talk to her. This morning he had at least tried, but why wasn't he trying again?

'French cakes might look nicer, more artistic,' she continued, 'but who wants to eat a work of art?' Ring phone, ring. 'A lot of those cakes that look so beautiful, when you eat them they taste just like shaving soap mixed with vanilla. They're all mouth and no trousers! She felt like a soldier with a machine gun – Jean Louis should be slumped over his desk by now.

'Mouse in the trousers?'

'No *mouth*. To pronounce *th* the tongue is just visible between the teeth.'

She opened the filing cabinet and extracted her handout on *th*, dated *1995* in the top right hand corner. She'd meant to re-do it, changing the date to 2005. Why can't you ring again, phone?

'Let's practise hearing the difference between s and *th*,' she said. 'Listen.'

She read out the book titles slowly:

A	B
Sudden Comfort	*Southern Comfort*
Delight Came Slowly	*The Light Came Slowly*
Disagreement with Europe	*This Agreement with Europe*
Departed Friends	*They Parted Friends*

'Now tell me which book title I'm reading out: A or B.' The phone remained silent.

They were meeting in Susie's, a little vegetarian restaurant in a back street in town where they'd be able to talk without fear of being overheard or interrupted. How would she begin? Maggie, I'm going to Paris next week. I've fixed up to have lunch with Thierry. You remember Thierry? The widower with the hole in his jumper? I think I might try and get off with him, Tess would confess. No, she wouldn't say that, not to Maggie. Has he actually shown signs that he fancied you? Maggie wouldn't ask that either. Maggie would be interested in the possibility of a serious relationship, not of the Sir Galahad on a white charger variety, more of the serious commitment between two consenting adults sort. That's why she'd had reservations about Fergus when she'd met him last summer. What were the words she'd used to describe him? Weird?

'But I like weird people,' Tess had said.

But not so weird that he could rush off like that for six months. Hearing his voice just now her urge had been to take the first plane to Eastern Europe to join him on the Danube, but then 'Don't be stupid. One aborted phone call on a Tuesday morning from a town on the Danube - only the second phone call he's made to you since he left - and you're ready to rush across Europe.' What would they have said to each other anyway, if the phone had gone again?

There was something a bit grubby about Susie's that went along with its cheerful decor - bright yellow oilskin tablecloths, with splashes of indeterminate red flowers on them, that nobody got round to wiping between customers, paper lampshades, odd chairs, a large mahogany mirror propped up against the wall. Maybe I should have suggested Michie's, thought Tess, standing at the counter beside Maggie in her black leather coat with her red lipstick and matching red nail varnish.

They settled down with their spinach pie and two salads and glasses of water. Across from them an old man and a young girl - his granddaughter? She was talking to him in a very loud voice in the local language, Doric, which Tess still had difficulty understanding. Were they having a violent quarrel or was he just very deaf?

'So will you be seeing Thierry when you're in France?' Maggie began. The perfect opening, like a gentle serve. How wonderful that Maggie actually remembered Thierry and even seemed to think it natural that they should meet. She would as gently pat the ball back and Maggie would return it, a little spin on it perhaps but not too much, enough to start her thinking out what she really wanted.

'I'm very sorry but there are no free tables. Do you mind

168

if I join you?' It was Stephen's secretary, Eileen, with her cup of coffee and a tea plate with a square of gingerbread on it and a rectangle of butter wrapped in gold paper.

'Of course', said Maggie, making room. 'How are you? We haven't had a chance to chat for ages. You were off with flu, weren't you? Are you feeling all right now? You're looking a bit pale still.'

Eileen was feeling much better only she had her parents-in-law and Derek's brother and his wife Sandra and their daughter Mairi coming for a meal on Sunday. Eileen had a very quiet voice and Tess had to strain her ears to hear her. What was Derek's brother called, and who was Derek anyway? Presumably Eileen's husband. The young girl at the next table was still shouting at her grandfather, making it even more difficult to follow what Eileen was saying.

She didn't know what to give them, she was explaining to Maggie. She'd probably make a stew for the main course but it was the pudding that was bothering her. Maggie suggested a trifle - it would be easy and she could make it the day before and have it all ready in the fridge and most people liked trifle and she could give her a recipe for a super one if she didn't have one already but she had the Delia Smith *Complete Cookery Course*, didn't she? and there was a recipe for a trifle in that that Maggie herself had made and it had turned out fine. But had she enough plates for all that many people?

As she talked Eileen was carefully cutting her gingerbread into segments and putting a little smear of butter onto each one and popping it into her mouth.

'Well I've got five dinner plates. I had six only I broke one. But I've only got ...... pudding bowls.'

Tess didn't catch how many pudding bowls. Should she interrupt? Did she care how many pudding bowls Eileen had or hadn't to serve the trifle in for Derek and Sandra and Mairi and whoever the others were? In any case Eileen's face was turned all the time towards Maggie, as if Tess wasn't part of the conversation at all. She decided to make an effort.

'How many pudding bowls?' she asked.

'Four', said Eileen, turning her head briefly to look at Tess before turning back to Maggie.

'But I could always .....' The rest of her sentence was lost to Tess as the grandfather and granddaughter made a noisy exit.

'Oh that's a good idea,' exclaimed Maggie, 'and yes, then you wouldn't have to bother with washing up and you can get some very nice ones in what's the name of that little shop just down from John Lewis's - you know, the one that sells everything? Shall we get some coffee, Tess?'

'I'll have another cup if you're having one,' said Eileen who had now got to the end of her gingerbread.

'I don't think I will,' said Tess, 'I'd better get back. I've things to clear up.'

'Tess is off to Paris on holiday, lucky thing,' Maggie explained to Eileen. 'How long are you going for, Tess?' she asked.

'Oh just for a few days,' said Tess. Or a few weeks, or a few months, or a few years, or the rest of my life.

They made their way back to the Institute. It had begun to rain and all three of them were trying to fit under Maggie's umbrella.

'I actually don't mind getting wet,' said Tess, giving up. This was true, she liked the rain.

'Have a good holiday,' said Eileen as they parted in the entrance to the Institute.

'Take care if I don't see you again before you go,' said Maggie, giving her a long hug. What help would it have been talking to Maggie anyway? She should know her own mind at her age, surely, and Maggie couldn't possibly know what was going on in Thierry's. Could Tess?

Chapter 27

Would he be wearing his green pullover with the hole? She'd thought she was early but now she was beginning to worry that she'd be late. There were five more stations to go on the metro out to where he worked at La Défense and it was almost one o'clock.

She was still recovering from yesterday. The plane from Aberdeen had been at six fifty in the morning so she'd had to get up at five. Kirsty had driven her to the airport.

'You'll arrive in time to have lunch with us,' Jennifer had said.

'Well no, there are a few things I have to do in Paris first,' Tess had said. Like sitting in a cafe drinking a *ballon of vin rouge* and biting into a *sandwich gruyère* and wondering what all the other people could be doing there, talking animatedly, and not having to make conversation herself. In the afternoon she'd gone to the *Musée D'Orsay* and ended up slumped on an uncomfortable leather bench contemplating a Van Gogh painting of two peasants asleep under a haystack in the sunshine.

And then in the evening Jennifer and Bertrand had had people to dinner and they had sat until midnight discussing *le problème de l'eau* in the world - the shortage of water. 'But not in Scotland, Tess' someone had said facetiously. No shortage of water there. 'What do you think of Cameela and Prince Sharle?' someone else had asked her at one in the morning.

'Excusez moi de vous déranger messieurs dames ...' A voice asking for passengers' *compréhension*. 'I am unemployed. If any of you can tell me where I can find work I would be grateful but meanwhile I am hungry, I have nowhere to live ...'.

Like the rest of the passengers Tess looked into the middle distance as the voice moved down through the compartment. She felt shame. Maybe on her way back into the city she would have a euro or two ready to drop into the outstretched hand.

'Ah, le chapeau!' he greeted her. She had been unsure about the hat. Annie had said she looked like the Queen in Alice in Wonderland in it, it was so big, so she'd made it smaller just before leaving for Paris with a few tucks here and there. She took it off now to reveal her newly hennaed hair.

'A modest little French restaurant or a Chinese?' he asked. He was wearing what looked like a brand new dark blue swing back coat but peeping out from the coat a green pullover.

'How nice to see you. I am so very pleased you are here.' He walked quickly, negotiating the pedestrian crossings with élan as he asked her for news of Aberdeen and she had a job keeping up with him. They had been out in the open together so little in Aberdeen. Also this was the first time they were speaking in French.

'We'll speak in English,' she'd said when they met. While they spoke in English she was still in control, she the teacher, he the student but after a few words he'd gone into French.

A little restaurant with pink check tablecloths in a quiet street with hardly anybody else there. A table for two and a hand written menu. He'd taken off his coat. A green pullover but a new one. No hole. She chose *crudités*, he *pâté*. Hers came - a big plateful of tomatoes and cucumbers and grated carrots and olives. His was a small slice of pâté in the middle of a large plate.

'Have some of my cucumber and tomatoes,' she said. 'I have far too much here and you have none.'

'Non, non,' he said. Had she been bold to suggest it? Was it only with family and close friends - lovers - that you swopped food? Maybe he just didn't like salad.

'You're just back from Indonesia,' she said, casting her mind about for something to talk about. As she spoke she realised that that was a topic she should maybe be avoiding - a repressive government, and the position of someone like him there as a representative of a western oil company. She didn't want to discover he held views which in other circumstances would have turned her off him completely. In

172

other circumstances ... How reactionary did a prospective lover have to be before she would find him totally undesirable?

'Do you know the States well?' she asked. 'I was wondering about going there.' Now that was a safer topic. But impersonal - he talked for longer than she would have liked about New Hampshire and Arizona.

'How are your children, by the way? How are they getting on?'

His daughter was at a weekly boarding school run by nuns and quite strict, too strict for her liking but not a bad thing. The half carafe of wine was still almost full. He'd poured just a small glass for each of them when the waitress came with their main course - escalopes in a green peppercorn sauce and pasta - and her glass had been empty for some time. Could she reach out and help herself? She raised her glass of water to her lips slowly, hoping he would take the hint. He was still talking about his children. His son was preparing an exam to gain entry to one of France's prestigious Grandes Ecoles.

'How old were they when they lost their mother?' she asked. How long had he been a widower?

'Six and four', he answered. Thirteen years.

'Et tu t'entends bien avec eux?' You get on okay with them? She'd used the *tu* form - like catching hold of his hand across the table. Rapidly she followed it with a *vous*, to show it had been a mistake. Nothing to be read into it, or everything. She wished he'd pour more wine.

'And the grandfather clock you bought in Aberdeen?' she asked.

'It is still going,' he told her. But she must come and visit him in his apartment in Versailles while she was here and he'd show it to her. What about Saturday? Yes, that was certainly a possibility. She could come out with the friend she was staying with. (Or maybe she would turn up alone.) But they would see each other before that, surely - he was sorry he could not take time off work to be with her this afternoon, but what about this evening? He watched her pulling on her hat. He was now using the 'tu' form. Yes, yes, that would be good. Where would she like to eat?

'There's a restaurant in the Latin Quarter called the Balzar,' she suggested.

They walked briskly back through the rain to the entrance to the metro. But he hadn't had a cigarette, all the time they'd been together. He'd given up in the New Year, he told her. She held out her hand.

'Until this evening, then,'

'Je crois qu'on peut s'embrasser,' he said.

'Yes,' she said. By all means

They kissed, first on one cheek and then on the other, a slight brushing in his case, in hers something more positive, a firm planting of her lips on his rough cheek. Had he got more than he'd bargained for, she wondered, sitting in the train. Had she seemed too ardent? Or maybe too businesslike, perfunctory even? 'The way you kiss reminds me of the woman in the supermarket with that gadget for sticking prices on things,' Annie had said one Hogmanay when Tess had gone round planting kisses here and there. No, surely it hadn't seemed like that to him.

In the metro going back into the centre of Paris the same appeal, this time a woman's voice.

'Bonjour Messieurs Dames, I am out of work, I have nowhere to live...'.

A woman with large sad eyes walked down the corridor pushing gently past people. One man across from Tess dropped a coin discreetly into her tin can. Tess hunted in her pockets for the two euro piece she had taken out of her purse along with her metro ticket, found it too late, just as the woman reached the end of the compartment.

'I used to come here a lot when I lived in Paris,' she said. Why had she wanted to come back? Not a hundred yards away from here was where it had happened.

'My taileurr eez reesh' and then the thud and Marc flying through the air, people exclaiming - 'Oh Mon Dieu' - the scream of the ambulance arriving.

174

'The place where I worked was just round the corner. But this is the first time I've ever eaten here.' They could never have afforded to eat here in the Balzar, the teachers from the English Language Centre round the corner. They used to sit there mid-morning with their coffees, or in the early evening with their glasses of white wine, marking dictations, preparing classes, hardly aware that the main life of the Balzar happened after they'd all hurried off to teach.

The place hadn't changed. There were still the same heavy wooden tables and seats, the same mirrors around the walls, the same waiters also you might have thought, in their black trousers and waistcoats, with their long white aprons. And the same people sitting at the tables, silver-haired and eloquent professors from the Sorbonne, women all looking like Simone de Beauvoir with earnest expressions on their strong faces.

A white starched table cloth, a voluminous white starched napkin spread across her lap, another white napkin encasing golden bread rolls, a large white plate in front of her and now a white bowl brimming with little purple mussels, smelling of white wine and the sea. And Thierry opposite gazing at her. Tess smiled across at him as the waiter filled her glass with wine.

'At last we are here having dinner together,' said Thierry.

'Yes,' said Tess, raising her glass to make contact with his across the table, coming close to shattering both in her joy. He was in what looked like a brand new white shirt under a dark blue jacket. Had he bought it specially on leaving work?

'What sort of day have you had' said Tess 'apart from your lunch with that boring woman?' And what sort of a boring question was that? But he talked happily about his work, his boss, about being back in Paris which he wasn't enjoying. And what about her?

'That's nice,' thought Tess. 'He's asking me about me. Not like Colonel Forbes.'

And as she was by this time onto her third glass of wine she had no difficulty in telling him - not about Marc or

Fergus, but about Kirsty and Pete, Hilary and Cecil, Stephen and the night he'd turned up in Kineldie with Cynthia, and all the time she was wondering at what moment she would ring Jennifer and say - 'Jennifer, I am not coming home this evening.' Jennifer and Bertrand went to bed at ten and it was now half past nine.

Thierry had noticed her glancing down at her watch.

'You are in a hurry to go home?' he asked. Surely he must know that the opposite was the case.

'No, I'm very happy here with you. And besides,' she said, taking up the menu 'I'd like some of their tarte au chocolat.'

'And then I know of a little place along by the Seine where we could have a ….. .' He was interrupted by a clamour coming from the battered brief case at his feet.

'These wretched mobile phones,' he said, pressing the speak button but then his impatient 'Allo' changed to a softer tone.

'Mais non, chérie. Ecoute, chérie …..'

How stupid of her to be imagining that she was becoming the centre of his world. Three people were standing in the door of the restaurant calling to the waiter. Would there be a table for them about eleven thirty? They were off to the cinema. Tess felt the cold air coming in. She hadn't noticed it before. Why had they been given this table so close to the door?

'That was my daughter, Odile,' said Thierry. Ah, his daughter. 'She is in a crisis. She has had a big big quarrel with the nuns in the school and she is sitting in a café wanting me to come and collect her and take her back with me to Versailles. I am sorry, Tess, I am very sorry. I would have liked …' His voice trailed off.

'There'll be another time,' said Tess, reaching forward and laying her hand on his. He caught hold of it and held it tight for several moments.

'I hope so,' he said. 'But tomorrow, you will come out to see me in Versailles, no?'

Chapter 28

Denis was talking about the matrix system.

'What's that?' she asked. She was hazy about matrices. He seemed surprised. Matrix system? Yes, she asked him to explain.

'It is a system where you have a relation between the numbers,' he said, 'For example, it is not like your system of pounds and ounces.'

'Ah, so the decimal system is an example of a matrix ... Oh, sorry, you're talking about the metric system.'

Her mind wasn't on the job. Coming back to Aberdeen had been particularly depressing. She had decided not to go out to see Thierry in Versailles on the Saturday - he would have enough on his mind with his runaway daughter. Instead she'd spent the afternoon shopping with Jennifer. Jennifer's daughter, Claire, was studying drama and needed some material for costumes. They'd gone to a huge emporium on the Boulevard St Denis, at the foot of the Sacre Coeur. Floor upon floor full of roll upon roll of hideous synthetic material.

'It's okay seen from a distance up on the stage,' Jennifer had explained as a surly-looking assistant measured out ten metres of flame coloured bri-nylon and fourteen metres of a khaki flannelette. They can't all be buying material for the stage though, Tess thought, as they pushed their way out through the throng of other women, all burdened with large plastic bags and all looking very pleased with themselves.

'Why I am always doing so much mistakes with my pronunciation?' asked Denis.

'I wouldn't be worrying about your pronunciation, Denis,' Tess said to herself. Tess at Christmas staring down at her battered feet, appalled, and Annie - 'It isn't your feet I'd be worrying about, Mum', suggesting there were far more important bits of herself to be worrying about. She smiled at the memory.

'You see, you are finding me funny but I am peesed euf,' said Denis. 'I am peesed euf. I am here since two years and the other day I call a taxi. "Union Street," I say him and he say straight away "Ah you are a French!" How he know I am a French?' I am peesed euf.'

'But you are a good communicator, Denis,' said Tess, remembering that she had promised to practise vowels with him. But not now, not today, she had nothing prepared. 'You are very good at what has been called *phatic communion*.' She wrote the term up, being careful to cross the t.

'That means being good at talking to people about the weather and their health and asking them where they went for their holidays and things like that. Small talk, social talk. *It's a nice day, isn't it? Yes, it is, isn't it?*, the sort of thing Colonel Forbes could benefit from taking a course in. The phone rang. It was Quentin, sounding unusually excited for Quentin.

'Tess, are you free? I've got some news for you.' Maybe she could leave Denis for a few minutes to have phatic communion with himself. But no, Denis declined the suggestion that he should write out a conversation about the weather with an imaginary other person. He preferred to end the lesson there and hurry back to his office. He had a lot of work at the moment.

'You have a lot on your plate, I suppose.'

'Ah, I will remember that. I have a lot in my plate.'

'Oh, and next time we will do vowels,' she promised, 'to improve your pronunciation.'

Quentin was sitting eating crème caramel.

'Help yourself. Emilio brought it back from the restaurant yesterday evening. He'd made too much.'

'Stephen's leaving,' he announced. 'He just told me this morning. Cynthia's got a job working with the Rockefeller Institute down in Edinburgh so they're leaving Aberdeen.'

'When's he going?' Kirsty would be overjoyed. She hadn't met Stephen face to face since that midnight visitation. She'd tried to see him the following day - to hurl a few insults at him, she'd told Tess - but he'd refused to speak to her, had practically pushed her out of his room.

He'd stay till the summer holidays at the end of June if they really wanted but he'd prefer to go sooner. Did this mean the Institute would close down altogether after that? Quentin was not interested enough in it himself to keep it going. A few months ago Tess would have been disturbed. What would she do? Would she have to sell Kineldie? But now her thoughts had immediately gone to Thierry. Would she join him in Paris, would they get married, live in his manoir for the rest of their lives? But Kirsty and Pete and Hilary and Maggie? What would happen to them?

'Maybe I *will* have some of that,' she said. She spooned a slab of the pudding, dripping with caramel, into her mouth and waited for it to break up and slither down her throat.

'Well we can certainly manage without him as far as the teaching is concerned because he doesn't do any - except for that one Advanced French class and Kirsty can easily take over that.'

It had always riled Kirsty that Stephen kept that class for himself, giving her all the beginners classes and then - when they were still on speaking terms - coming to her to explain obscure words to him.

'But what about the advertising?' Quentin asked. 'I certainly don't feel like traipsing around companies with leaflets trying to talk them into sending their personnel to learn a foreign language at the Institute.'

Quentin was no businessman. He'd happily spend all day sitting at home playing his guitar. And talking to people - he was good at that. Or rather at listening to others talking. At least he was very good at Listener Talk - *Right, I see, Really! Did you? I know ...* But was he really listening? Did he really care about what people were telling him?

'I don't feel like tripping over to Spain, going round companies, persuading them to send their personnel to sunny Aberdeen to learn English.'

Kirsty had volunteered to do that at one time. She'd hoped to coincide with Stephen on a trip to France at Easter to do just that among other things. Tess's second spoonful of the crème caramel wobbled for a second at the entrance to her mouth and then fell sideways, plop onto her pink silk shirt.

'Merde!' she swore in French. How did you say that in

Spanish? She was sure Quentin must have learnt a lot about swearing in Spanish from Emilio.

'I don't mind doing some advertising for the Institute if I go back to France,' Tess said, thinking of Thierry. 'And Maggie's going to Italy at Easter, and surely Emilio knows people with restaurants and things in Spain.'

'Hmm, well … Anyway, I'll tell Stephen he can go as soon as he likes, will I?'

'Yes, as soon as he likes, provided that's very soon.'

There was a mirror in the auction that week just the right size and in the right state of decay. She called in, deciding she'd bid for it. Though if she was going to be in France would she still need it? She could always take it with her, like Thierry had his grandfather clock from Aberdeen. The saggy sofas were all occupied by upturned faces, eyes glued on the auctioneer and the two men holding up the various articles as they came up for auctioning. Tess stood in the crowded doorway.

301: a tray full of china cats; 346: a large Italian red glass table centre; 406: a cardboard box of assorted bits of china. The men delved into the box, each selecting a dainty cup to hold up in his thick fingers. 408: two achettes - Victorian, large enough to hold a whole haunch of venison. Tess was tempted to bid for them but she already had two in a cupboard at home, hardly ever used. When did she ever have a piece of meat large enough to put on an achette? But maybe now in the manoir. They went for £10 for the two of them. The ugly piece of Italian glass fetched £100.

435: a large gilt mirror. 'Who'll bid me £20? - £30? - £40? £50?. A man standing by the wall beyond the sofas - smooth black hair tied back in a long pigtail, his face completely motionless except for the slight flick of the chin answering Tess's clumsily raised hand. She'd meant to stop at £60. £60? - £70? - £80? Who'll bid me £90? Any advance on £80? Tess waited for the chin to move. Going ... going .... gone. The hammer came down. The mirror was hers.

She'd have to come back to collect it later in the day. She

was teaching Dominique at two o'clock and it was almost that now.

'I love the Nature,' Dominique announced. He'd been for a walk with his wife along the old railway track that had originally run from Aberdeen almost to Balmoral. Was that where she'd been with Fergus in that dream last night? The memory of it surfaced with the mention of the countryside. They'd been walking hand in hand feeling very close and then they'd arrived in some sort of building, it must have been a school because they'd gone up the stairs still holding hands, and then Fergus had disappeared into a classroom. She'd wanted to follow him, distressed at how suddenly he'd abandoned her. She'd opened the door and seen him there surrounded by a group of laughing young woman. "Go away, Tess," he'd called to her, not unkindly. And then gently shut the door on her.

'No *the* ' she said mechanically. 'You love Nature, not the Nature.' Though that didn't sound right either. 'In English, abstract nouns don't take a *the* unless they are defined. That is why *the* is called the definite article. You use it when you are being definite, when you are being precise about the particular Nature that you love. For example you could say that you love the nature around Aberdeen.' No that wouldn't do at all, what he loved was the countryside.

She moved onto surer ground. 'Take the word *love*. You can talk about love in general, love undefined. *It's love that makes the world go round. I can't give you anything but love, baby* and what was that Beatles song? *Love, love, love*, not *The love, the love, the love*. But when you become more precise you introduce *the*. *The love that a woman feels for a man makes the world go round. The love that I can give you will make you happy.*

Dominique was listening dutifully. Or was he far away? She didn't care.

'It's the same for plural concrete nouns. Apples, for example. If you are talking about them in a general way you say *I like apples* but when you start talking about particular apples you have to put a *the* in front. *I like apples but I don't like the apples I bought yesterday.'*

She wrote up *Abstract Nouns and Plural Concrete Nouns* in blue and then taking her red pen - *NO <u>THE</u> unless defined.*

'But *singular* concrete nouns are the same as in French.' *Singular concrete nouns* she wrote up, and then, taking her green pen: *always <u>THE</u>.* She waited for him to copy this down. Laughter behind the closed door.

'Singular concrete nouns always have to be preceded by a word like *a* or *the.* You can't say *apple* by itself or *dog* by itself unless of course you are using it as a proper noun. If you had a daughter called *Apple,* for example, or a dog called *Dog* then you'd say *Come here, Apple, come here Dog.* We'll do an exercise on it.' She hunted on her shelf for her battered copy of *English Alive.*

It is pleasant to play game of tennis on summer afternoon ...

She left him to fill in with *a* or *the* where appropriate and went off to get a cup of coffee and eat the sandwich which was curling up inside her cardigan pocket. When she'd got back from the auction Dominique had already been waiting outside her door.

Kirsty and Pete were in the coffee room planning a weekend up near Glen Affric. Suddenly she was back with Bob (totally reliable Bob who'd become totally unreliable Bob with the rapidity of a sandstorm in the Sahara) and Annie. They'd spent many summers in Glen Affric.

'I've fished in every glen in Scotland and this is the most beautiful one,' a fisherman had told them once. It was the end of the day, they were coming back from a bicycle ride and he was by the side of the road counting the number of trout he'd caught - fourteen in a row. They'd hoped he might give them one as they'd offered him one of their sandwiches but he'd packed them all back into his bag.

'You'll love it there,' she told Kirsty and Pete.

'I think it is time,' said Dominique when she at last returned to him.

'Let's just correct what you've written quickly,' she said.

It is pleasant to play game of tennis on summer afternoon ...

She managed to carry the mirror unaided from the auction room out to the car. As she fitted it into the boot she caught sight of herself in it and wondered why she had ever taken it into her head to buy it. If she put it over the mantle piece in the bedroom she'd have to arrange lots of plants in front of it so that she'd catch only a glimpse of her face through the green leaves. She carried it up as soon as she arrived and saw her bed reflected in it. Would Thierry ever lie there with her, listening to the pigeons in the early morning?

Back downstairs she checked her answer machine. There was a message from Bertrand to ring her. Bertrand? Why was Bertrand phoning her? Bertrand never phoned her. She rang him straight away. His voice was distraught on the other end of the phone. Jennifer had died that morning of a cerebral haemorrhage.

Chapter 29

Laurent arrived late. He'd had 'a little accident' on his way to work. The lorry in front of him had hit a swan flying across the road to get to the loch on the other side. The swan had fallen off the roof of his car onto the road, dead.

'Its mate will be sad,' said Tess. 'Swans mate for life.' She thought of Bertrand.

She wrote up on the magi board the first verse of the Stevie Smith poem.

Wan swan on a lake
like a cake of soap.
Why is the swan wan?
He has abandoned hope.

'Listen to me reading it aloud,' said Tess. 'Listen to the vowel sounds. It's very good practice for your vowel sounds. And also notice the use of the present perfect - He *has abandoned* hope and not He *abandoned* hope. The interest is in the present, he is a swan without hope.' Like Bertrand.

Laurent reminded her of Bertrand, the way Bertrand had looked when she and Jennifer had first encountered him, skinny and frizzy-haired, in the university restaurant at the Sorbonne, shovelling lentils into his mouth and looking across at them.

Skinny Bertrand had filled out rapidly after he and Jennifer were married. His gain in weight had kept pace with his rapid rise in the champagne company he got a job with after finishing his law degree. And Jennifer had become a collector of solid gold bracelets with solid gold charms hanging from them, and a buyer of expensive clothes, mostly in Paris but occasionally in London. She'd arrived back once with an orange tweed suit bought in Fenwicks of Bond St.

'Isn't it ghastly, Tess?' Tess could still see her standing there holding it up against herself. 'I can't keep it. It makes me look like a horse.'

Yes, but a race horse all the same, Tess was thinking, whereas, if Jennifer offered to pass it on to her, it would turn her into a carthorse. So she'd have to refuse if Jennifer offered it to her. Or would she? It would be nice to wear something that she hadn't made herself for a change.

'I'll give it to Simone,' Jennifer had said. Simone was Jennifer's sister-in-law, a rather over-powering woman. Oh well, it wouldn't have been wise to have gone round looking like a carthorse.?

Jennifer had in fact realised her mistake almost as soon as she'd bought the suit. She'd rushed back to the shop but they'd refused to give her her money back or even exchange it.

'Madame is old enough to know her own mind,' the shop assistant had told her in the most respectful of voices.

Tess smiled at the memory, caught Laurent's eye, who smiled back. Was he back with Janet? Funny, she'd never been the slightest bit attracted to Bertrand. Just as well since there hadn't been much room for her after that first meeting. Bertrand and Jennifer almost from the start had been a couple, an item. But Laurent was more *fin* than Bertrand, however you'd say that in English. Sensitive? Intelligent? Subtle?

Laurent had copied down the poem and read it out twice. Should she get him to read it a third time?

'Tell me about French funerals, Laurent,' she said. Marc's funeral had been so long ago, and in the east of France. Jennifer's would be in the village where they had their weekend cottage - just outside Paris.

There were speeches at the graveside sometimes, made by close friends. Or the mayor of the commune maybe would say a few words. Or ex-colleagues. Did women make speeches? No, he didn't think so, unless, of course, the mayor was a woman.

'There is no reason why they should not but they do not. I think they should. Why are they always waiting for the men to do everything?'

'Quite right, Laurent.' Women should assert themselves more. It's their own fault if they're treated as objects, regarded as enablers rather than doers, it was her duty to make a speech at Jennifer's funeral.

Jennifer's funeral. Just saying the words struck terror inside her. She had to keep reminding herself that Jennifer was not there any more, that she would never be there any more. If she picked up the phone and dialled the number she'd dialled for the last twenty years there would be no Jennifer on the other end of it, no Jennifer to talk to any more, about their time together in Paris as students, about Marc, about Bob, about Annie, about Fergus.

What would she say at the graveside with them all standing round? How could she possibly find words to encapsulate in a few minutes the whole of Jennifer, even to begin to say what Jennifer had meant to her? And Simone would be there with that look of having just taken a dose of cascara on her face. But she *would* speak, and she'd talk about a Jennifer that the other people there did not know about.

'Let's have a cup of coffee, Laurent.'

From the coffee room they could see seagulls copulating on the roof opposite. The male perched on the female, its great wings arched, flapping. Fifteen seconds of this and then the female's wings began to flap and the male stepped off her.

'So. What have you got planned for the week, Laurent?' Tess asked, turning her back to the window.

The plane was crowded with men in grey suits. She waited in the aisle while one of them fitted his brief case and then his Burberry raincoat and then his umbrella into the overhead locker and at last cleared the way for her.

'Hurry up, hurry up,' the air steward snapped at Tess, seizing her bag. 'You're holding everybody up.'

'Do you talk to everyone as if they were children or senile?' Tess hissed under her breath. She sat glaring at the air steward's profile as she stood chatting to what looked like a Texan oil man - a regular on the route no doubt. Not if they're important looking men in grey suits or handsome Texans, I bet. She got out her pen and started scribbling a letter to *The Manager, British Airways*   *I am writing to protest ...* but then gave up. It wasn't worth the effort. Better try to think out what she would say at Jennifer's funeral.

She had a vivid memory of Jennifer, maybe ten years after her marriage to Bertrand, just before the birth of their fourth child, Claire, a girl at last after three boys. A reception at the George V Hotel in Paris to launch a new pink champagne, magnum bottles on all the low tables and bowls of pink roses and Jennifer collapsing onto a green brocade sofa, glass in hand. 'Oh Bertrand, thank goodness you're in champagne and not in bleaching fluid!'

She could relate this incident and then go on to say that Jennifer had indeed been in champagne all her married life, married to a man she loved and with four lovely kids. That would be neat. Or would it be naff? And would it be true? Had she really been happy and fulfilled, as a full-time *woman of the interior* as Laurent would have said, with an elegant flat in the centre of Paris and an attractive cottage and enchanting garden in the country? And plenty of business trips abroad as Bertrand's spouse - to the States, Japan, South Africa, Argentina - and lots of dining out in expensive restaurants - as Bertrand's spouse? Had she minded just being *Bertrand's spouse*, and the mum of Henri, Jacques, Francois and Claire? But she'd never been *just* that, she'd have protested.

Would her parents be at the funeral, Tess wondered the next day as she travelled out from Paris on the RER. They must be well into their eighties. Outliving their daughter. The thought was shocking. The funeral service was being held in the church in the village where they had their cottage. There was to be a requiem mass. Jennifer had become a catholic. And apparently a very devout one.

'She was at Mass and communion just a few hours before she died so she will have gone straight to heaven,' Bertrand had told Tess on the phone.

Jennifer's parents were the first people she noticed as she entered the church at Rampierre - two frail figures in the front row alongside an elderly man, presumably Bertrand's father, and then Claire, slender in a long black coat and a wide-brimmed black hat. Her mother would have been proud of her. And then her three brothers, all looking like younger versions of Bertrand from the back.

'I always judge men by what they look like from the back," Jennifer had said once, 'particularly the back of their necks.' And then Bertrand himself on the end, motionless, his head bowed.

The priest spoke of Jennifer's exemplary role as a devoted wife and mother - the highest calling for a woman after that of a nun who was of course wedded to Christ - and of how she had fulfilled this role with unselfishness and serenity. He spoke of her work - when her commitments to her family allowed - with the St Vincent de Paul Society, in helping people less fortunate than herself. And he spoke of her *charme* and of her *humour britannique* that had enhanced the life of all who had come into contact with her. He even managed a few words in English for the benefit of Jennifer's parents. *We will miss her, our sharming Engleesh lady.*

There were no speeches at the graveside so the one Tess had prepared so carefully and written out remained in her handbag. Maybe speeches were only appropriate for those who had achieved in the public domain. Jennifer's life was marked by a respectful silence. As the coffin was sprinkled with holy water and then lowered into the ground Tess held tight onto Jennifer's mother's hand. Together then they looked at the wreaths spread out in rows - arum lilies, tulips, daffodils, mimosa. Tess translated the messages for her. Not easy, some of them. Amazing the way some French couldn't compose a sentence that didn't include six abstract nouns and two subjunctives. A simple one from Jeanne, Jennifer's cleaning woman. *We'll laugh again together one day, Jennifer.* Tess wished she could have written that. Instead, on her spray of dark red tulips all she could think of to write was *For best friend Jenny.*

As she sat on the train back to Paris the words that had slipped so easily off the priest's tongue - *wife, mother, primary role, serenity, fulfilment, devotion* - kept coming back to her. Maybe it had suited Jennifer to devote herself to being a full-time wife and mother but to pronounce this as the best calling for all women …

Back in Paris she sat for a long time in the Luxembourg Gardens looking at the children playing in the sand pit by the fountain, a headache brewing. She had drunk three glasses of wine very quickly at the funeral lunch and eaten hardly anything of the buffet of vols au vent and canapés. She must have been a little drunk by the time she left because she'd started to kiss Simone on the cheek as she said goodbye, but Simone had recoiled and proffered a hand. In the France she belonged to, you only kissed close members of the family.

She became aware of a little girl with dark eyes staring at her. Tess struggled to smile at her but couldn't manage it. She got up. She'd told Thierry that she'd phone him after the funeral. There'd be a phone somewhere down the Boulevard St Michel.

Chapter 30

They met in the Café *Le Départ*, opposite the Gare du Luxembourg. Sitting behind the terrace window she watched him arriving, his dark blue coat flowing out behind him in the wind. He ordered a glass of white wine. Tess was already drinking a black coffee. He took off his coat. Underneath an open necked dark blue cotton shirt. She told him about the funeral and a lot about Jennifer and herself as students. And about Marc even and that other funeral.

'At least their children were grown up. The hardest about Hélène's death' - it was the first time he'd mentioned her name - 'was that Guy and Odile were so young at the time. But it will be difficult for him living without Jennifer.

'You know all about that, of course,' said Tess, 'It must have been very difficult for you.' She hesitated. 'It's still difficult for you, no?'

'Oh no. It's eleven years ago. I cannot spend my life in mourning.' He looked at her and smiled and for the first time that day she felt like smiling too.

'I like this Café - *Le Départ* - even if we're not going anywhere,' she said. Except for the one certain final destination. Could she have coped with being alone this evening? The only answer to death, to live life as intensely as possible while you still had the chance.

'But we can't spend the evening here. Where shall we eat?'

'I'm not very hungry and I should change out of these clothes.' She was still wearing her funeral black corduroy suit and white blouse. 'The hotel I'm staying in is just round the corner.'

'I'll wait for you down here among the potted plants,' he said as they pushed open the plate glass door of the hotel.

She hesitated. 'You can come up if you like.'

In the room she got a pair of trousers and a sweater out of her bag. She'd go into the bathroom to change. Thierry had been looking out of the window. He turned and their eyes met and the next moment she had dropped her bundle of clothes and they were in each other's arms.

Next morning they drove out to Versailles together.

'I would like to show you my apartment and introduce you to my daughter, Odile,' Thierry had said as they ate croissants in the tiny breakfast room of the hotel. 'And then tomorrow evening I have been invited ... But you could come along too.' How long was it since she'd ever gone anywhere as part of a couple?

'Oh, but I must show you something.' he said as they arrived in the town. He stopped the car.

'That is the route the National Assembly took in 1789, at the start of our French Revolution. They were being pursued by the army, with more army coming towards them from that direction there.' He pointed to a street at an angle to the first.

'So they turned down this street here.' He started up the engine again and drove down a little side street.

'And then it was here ...' He'd stopped the engine again and this time they got out of the car and Thierry took up a position with his back to a large eighteenth century wooden entrance door. 'It was here at the Jeu de Paume ... How do you say that in English?' Indoor Tennis Court? That didn't sound quite right. 'It was here at the Jeu de Paume that they made their famous declaration.' He raised his voice so that it boomed out, causing passers by to turn and stare. '*Nous sommes ici par la volonté du peuple, nous ne quitterons nos places que par la puissance des baionnettes.*'

We are here by the will of the people. Only bayonets will drive us away. It didn't sound too bad in English either. Sometimes you couldn't quarrel with words, those were exactly the right ones,' thought Tess as they climbed the stone staircase up to his flat. *Nous sommes ici par la volonté du peuple ...*'

Pungent smell on the wide stone staircase. Old buildings, French plumbing or was it someone's Sunday lunch? Not Thierry's she hoped. He had phoned Odile to say that he was on his way and with a friend. Odile came out from her school most Sundays and it was usually she who prepared the meal, he'd explained.

'She will have prepared us something very simple,' he told Tess. There was a broad smile on his face as he let her in and introduced her. Odile was tall and dark like her father but her eyes were different, large and blue, and staring now at Tess, making her feel slightly uncomfortable. Did it show, that she'd spent the night with her father? They must be standing there now before her, looking like a plant that had just been divided into two.

'I must give you a tour of my apartment, Tess, before we eat.'

It was full of curiosities - vases, drums, wall hangings, pictures, chunks of rock - brought back from places he'd worked in as an oil engineer - Indonesia, Thailand, Venezuela, Abu Dhabi ... Tess gazed at the curious wallpaper in the kitchen - geometric designs on a green background. Was it his wife who had chosen it?

'How long have you lived here?' she asked. Fourteen years. They would have bought the flat together a year before she died, chosen the wallpaper together.

'It is a very simple meal, I am not a good cooker,' said Odile as they installed themselves at the table.

A large dish of what the French called *an English plate - une assiette anglaise*. Cold meats, including slices of cold roast beef. Maybe it was because of the roast beef that they called it an English dish. And a bowl of salad. And would she have some wine, produced on his *proprieté?* Ah yes, the manoir - sun on yellow stone and vines stretching up the hillside. Out of the window a grey sky and a view of the back of the chateau over the rooftops. Yes, she would have a glass of wine, just one.

And then the cheese. Next door was a *fromagerie* that produced very good cheeses. Ah, so that was the smell. Odile handed her a camembert for her to cut into. Her first visit to France she'd mistaken the yellow round for a sponge cake and had cut herself a large slice. She'd been unable to eat it, had slipped it into the pocket of her gingham frock and later flushed it down the lavatory. Should she tell them this story now? She decided her French would not be up to it.

'J'aime beaucoup le camembert,' she said. I like camembert.

And then coffee in the salon out of thin white cups, sitting in the armchairs Thierry had bought from the man by the river in Aberdeen, with the grandfather clock ticking in the corner. Suddenly she had a picture of Jennifer, not Jennifer buried deep in the ground, but Jennifer sitting down to lunch with Bertrand at half past midday every day of her married life. Was this the sort of life Tess was planning for herself? She pushed the thought away.

Had Odile liked Aberdeen? She'd spent a week there in November. And what was she thinking of Tess right now? Was she noticing the way Thierry was looking at her, the way their fingers had touched when he'd passed her the coffee cup? Was she wishing Tess would go so that she could have her father to herself?

'Do you like teaching English?' Odile asked her. Tess was surprised by the question.

'Yes, I do,' she said. Did she? Yes, in a way. 'I like language.'

'Ah, languages!' said Thierry.

'No, not languages, just language,' said Tess. What you could do with it. Like a musical instrument. Like a cello.

The grandfather clock struck the hour. She remembered how Thierry had said it had a very nice chime. A bit like an old man wheezing out of metallic lungs.

'How do you say *grandfather clock* in French?' she asked. Odile.

'You just say it's a clock that stands on the floor – une horologe de parquet.'

'Papa, I must go,' she said. 'I hadn't realised it was already five o'clock.'

She turned to Tess and hesitated and then kissed her on the cheek.

'Goodbye, Odile. It was really nice meeting you.'

Would they ever meet again? In Scotland, on the occasion of her marriage to Odile's father? Her mind really was racing on.

'Au revoir, Papa. A la semaine prochaine.' The door banged to and Thierry came back into the room and put his arms around her.

Two hours later they were sitting in Thierry's car, her hand resting on his thigh as they drove towards St. Cloud.

'Tell me about these people that we're going to have dinner with,' she said. Jean Paul was a geophysicist like Thierry, they had been at engineering school together. And his wife, Florence, was a dentist. And then Arnaud would probably be there. He worked with Thierry and Jean Paul. And tiens, his wife Christine was English like Tess.

'I'm only sort of English,' said Tess. Like a whole lot of other people living in Britain. Why did people have to have labels stuck on them? If you're this, you can't be that. It was the fault of the language, like a straitjacket, obliging you to say *English,* like those questionnaires obliging you to tick a), b) or c) when what you wanted to tick was all three or none.

'Well, Breeteesh then,' said Thierry.

Even worse, thought Tess. She couldn't help it, but, for her, British still meant the British Empire. She would definitely have to put on her Irish accent if they were going to be talking in English this evening.

'And Nicole will certainly be there. She is Florence's best friend and she's a geologist. She works in our office too. And she has a husband called Robert who is not Breeteesh. He is American.'

Tess pulled down the sun visor and looked at herself in the mirror. She'd washed her hair in the shower and it still looked like rat's tails. Florence and Nicole would be looking as if they were fresh from the hairdresser's no doubt and in their simple black Yves St Laurent dresses and tasteful jewellery. Tess pulled at the gaps between the buttons on the grey dress she'd thought looked so elegant when she'd stood before the mirror in Kineldie. Good job the bra and knickers underneath were black not scarlet.

Thierry glanced across at her with a smile.

'I am so happy, so lucky' she thought. 'And I mustn't feel guilty. Jennifer wouldn't have wanted me to feel guilty.' She fiddled with the car heater.

'If you turn the fan on I can use it as a hairdryer,' she said. She regularly used this method of drying her hair on her drives in to the Institute from Kineldie. Thierry laughed and ran his hand through her hair.

Chapter 31

Jean Paul and Florence's apartment had a very sumptuous air about it. A heavy ornate mirror over the marble fireplace was filled with the reflection of two elaborate crystal chandeliers and everywhere there were swirling shiny satin curtains in a voluptuous peony pattern, swept up in loops and bows - curtains on the tall windows looking down on the Boulevard, curtains in all the doorways and curtains also as a room divider between where they were sitting now having drinks and the dining area beyond.

'So, you are from Scotland.' Florence had seated herself on the sofa beside Tess with the air of someone determined to find out all about her. Florence, as Tess had feared, was looking exquisite, her short spiky blonde hair going beautifully with her expensive little black dress. The dress was rather on the short side but why not show off your legs if they were as perfect as Florence's? Tess drew in her stomach and hunched her shoulders slightly. Could it be thought daring and sexy to be showing off her underwear? Jean Paul had certainly given her a long look on being introduced.

'So you are Thierry's teacher of English. And is he a good pupil?' he'd said with almost a leer. Thierry had put his arm round her shoulder.

'Tess is the best teacher I never had,' he said. That's what he'd said at that birthday lunch in November. What a different ring the words had now.

Christine said how she could never teach English. She'd tried once and she'd kept being asked questions about the language she couldn't even begin to answer. What was this Present Perfect they were always going on about? She hadn't the foggiest idea.

'It means that the present is perfect,' Tess whispered to herself as she emptied her glass of champagne, her second. Jean Paul was beginning to open a third bottle - a man after her own heart. But 'Non, non, chéri, on va manger, we're just about to eat', Florence intervened, jumping to her feet just as Tess was about to start explaining to her, putting on her best

Irish accent, that, though she lived in Scotland and loved Scotland, she didn't actually come from Scotland. Thierry, and Christine's husband, Arnaud, were standing talking with Nicole.

'I hope they're not going to talk geology the whole evening,' said Christine to Tess as they moved towards the table. There was a slight edge to her voice.

'Is that what they're doing, talking geology?' Tess ventured. It seemed more like flirting to her, which would account for the edge in Christine's voice. Nicole was dumpy, there was no other word for it, not flattered by the dull green clinging two piece she had on and the flat brown shoes. But there was certainly a provocative liveliness about the tilt of her head and the way her straight grey-black hair swung as she turned to look up first at Thierry and then at Arnaud. She also waved her hands around a lot. One of them had come to rest now on Thierry's sleeve as they seated themselves. She had been placed next to him.

'Mon cher Thierry, it is so nice to have you back here with us in Paris,' she said. 'But you have a beautiful country, I believe,' she said politely, gazing across at Tess.

'It is more beautiful than France,' declared Thierry. Everybody looked at him, surprised. 'Because it has Tess in it,' he added. They all looked at Tess and smiled. Yes, Tess would enhance any country, they seemed to be saying.

A plate with a slice of foie gras on it had been set before each of them and Jean Paul was doing the rounds with a bottle of Sauterne - the very best wine to drink with foie gras, he said.

'Oh yes, you'll never believe it, I was eating with some Dutch people the other day and they served a Muscadet with the foie gras,' said Thierry.

'And do you remember,' Nicole called out to Florence, 'the last time we were at the Giberts, and Jean Paul served that wonderful Bordeaux and that woman exclaimed that it tasted just like Beaujolais? No, really.' She shook her head, flicking her hair from side to side. 'She was the one who was trying to say that the Paris police are racist.'

'People who say that the police are racist, they do not know what they are talking about. We need the police with all these foreigners on the streets,' said Christine.

'You're not vegetarian, are you, Tess?' asked Florence.

'Just as well I'm not,' thought Tess as she started eating, overcoming her scruples about foie gras. She was ravenous. Lunch was a long time ago. Thirsty too. She'd almost finished her glass of wine. She hoped Jean Paul would not be slow in coming round with refills. The others seemed to have hardly touched theirs. Nicole's husband, Robert, who was sitting next to her, still had a full glass in front of him.

'I'm not much of a drinker,' he confided to Tess.

'Are you a geologist too?' asked Tess. He didn't look like your typical American - he was small and dark with a sensitive face. But only an American would wear what he was wearing. His slight frame was sewn into a Stewart tartan suit. His grandfather had come from Scotland, he explained, and he'd bought the suit in Edinburgh, which they'd visited last summer.

'No, I'm a gynaecologist up at the American hospital,' he told her.

'Oh,' said Tess. Sitting next to someone who was on such intimate terms with so many women's private parts gave her a funny feeling. How did Nicole feel about having a husband who was fingering other women's vaginas all day long? At the other end of the table she was now holding the attention of both Thierry and Jean Paul. Uproarious laughter.

'Yes, he delivered all four of ours,' said Arnaud. Four children? Christine slender and elegant in her grey trouser suit had four children?

The door opened and a young woman in a brightly coloured apron came in to clear the plates away

'This is Cécile. She's from the Caribbean,' said Florence. Cécile smiled as she walked around the table picking up each plate in turn and taking it over to the side table.

'Which island?' said Tess, not knowing much about the Caribbean.

'Martinique. You know it?' Cécile paused as she was

about to leave the room.

'You can bring in the fish now, Cécile,' Florence interrupted. It was obviously not the done thing to be engaging the maid in conversation.

Cécile reappeared a few moments later, a large oval dish completely occupied by a reclining sea bass decorated with mayonnaise rosettes and with a whole lemon sticking out of its mouth.

'That looks beautiful,' said Robert.

'Yes, people don't eat enough fish,' said Arnaud. 'Christine is going every Tuesday and Friday to our fishmonger's in Neuilly.'

'So you have four children?' said Tess to Christine, helping herself to what she hoped was an acceptable portion of the fish and trying to ignore the animated talk coming from the Nicole end of the table.

'Arnaud wants to make it six,' said Christine, pulling a face. He's one of ten himself.'

'This is a wine from the Loire valley, Tess, especially good with fish,' said Jean Paul.

'None for me, thank you, Jean Paul,' said Robert, putting his hand over his glass. Tess imagined Cécile in the kitchen finishing off Robert's and Christine's almost untouched glasses of Sauterne. Maybe when she appeared later with the cheese course she would be doing a dance.

'You are not a family woman yourself, are you, Tess?' What a delicate way of asking her about her circumstances. Arnaud was beginning to remind her of Bertrand - the contented family man. Only Bertrand was no longer a family man but a widower with all his children gone. Bertrand, she'd meant to phone him. He said he was busy this evening but a brief call … She felt shocked that she could have put aside so completely Jennifer's death and the funeral.

'Not really. But my best friend who was also English like you,' she said, turning to Christine, 'married a Frenchman and she had four children like you. She's dead, though. She died last week. Actually I came over for the funeral, it was yesterday.'

200

A complete silence around the table. Florence gave her a quick smile of sympathy. She knew about the funeral. Suddenly Tess had a desire to tell them all about Jennifer. The speech she'd prepared for the funeral was still in her mind, she had it by heart, she could deliver it now. Jennifer deserved some recognition. She deserved that something should be said in public about her life. She opened her mouth to begin but felt her throat contract and her eyes fill with tears and all she wanted to do was to lay her head on the table and sob.

'Oh God, no, not in front of all these people.' She caught Thierry's eye, smiling uncertainly across at her.

'One thing about living in Scotland, Tess,' Jean Paul's voice boomed at her from where he stood pouring wine into Nicole's glass, 'is that you don't have as many terrorists there, I don't suppose.'

'Ah.' A murmur went round the table, like a wind moving through rushes, a collective sigh. 'Terrorists. Terrorism. Terrible. Terrible.'

'Not like here in France,' said Francoise. 'I am very frightened. All these Arabs that we 'ave living here. I do not trust them, they are outside the law. I am sure that they are supporting the terrorists. Maybe some of them are terrorists themselves. I would not be surprised.'

'Yes, it's true,' said Christine, 'my cleaning lady, she's Algerian. She was telling me that she knows many Arabs who've a lot of sympathy with these terrorists. Her husband says that if a terrorist came to their door he would not necessarily denounce him to the police. It's incredible, isn't it?'

'Yes, every day our son, Henri, comes home with stories about the fights in the playground between the French children and the Muslim children. If they cannot accept our culture and civilisation they should not be living here,' said Arnaud, his shiny face now the same shade of pink as his tie. In the space of minutes he'd changed from the complacent family man into the militant defender of western civilisation.

'Terrorism is a dreadful weapon to use on anyone but that

is not a reason for sticking the label 'terrorist' on someone just because they happen to be Arab,' Tess was about to break in when the door opened and Cécile appeared to clear away the plates and bring on the cheese.

'That was delicious, Florence.'

'Yes, that was superb.'

'Oh, you know, it's not me, it is my fishmonger. My fishmonger is a treasure. I've had him for twenty years. He is a treasure. It is he who prepares everything. Everything. All I do is just carry it home.'

'Anyway, what do you mean by ...' Tess began as they helped themselves to cheese but she was interrupted by Nicole.

'What is this word they are using in English for these people? Eev ....'

'Evil,' said Christine. 'These people are evil, they're bad, they're wicked.'

How could they possibly see everything in black and white like that? They should all the same try to understand what caused people to become terrorists. Nelson Mandela was called a terrorist at one time and whose fault had that been? It wasn't him who was responsible for apartheid.

'They are totally evil and we are totally good. That's nice to know,' said Tess, hoping they would appreciate the sarcasm. Instead Robert gave her a little approving smile and the rest of them nodded their heads. All except Thierry who was busy looking at the label on the bottle Jean Paul was about to pour from.

'Ah, 2005!' said Thierry.

'But it is from your vineyard, Thierry, it's you who gave it to us.'

'I know,' said Thierry, 'and it is the perfect wine to go with this Brie which is also - perfect! Congratulations, Florence, you have a treasure of a cheesemonger too.

'Yes,' said Florence with a laugh. 'The hypermarché.'

'He doesn't want to get involved in this. He wants us all to shut up about evil and terrorism.' Jean Paul was at her elbow, leaning over her, his cheek almost in contact with hers.

'More wine, Tess?' She'd drunk too much already but why not?

'I mean,' she continued, pushing Jean Paul gently away from her, 'you've got to think about what words mean before you stick them on people like … like …' She couldn't find the word. She shouldn't have drunk so much wine. 'All I want to say is that words don't just have simple fixed meanings.'

'I think maybe the word 'war' is a mistake, it is not correct to talk about a 'war on terrorism,' said Thierry, putting down his glass. Ah, he is with me, thought Tess. 'But at the same time,' he continued, speaking slowly so that the whole table turned to listen to him, 'I think we have to attack the possibility of terrorism here in France. There is a danger that we are not doing enough to fight it. And the way to fight it is …,' he paused, 'the way to fight it is by defending our culture and our civilisation.' A murmur of agreement around the table.

'You are right, Thierry. You are absolutely right.'

'And,' he added, raising a finger and catching Robert's eye, 'the Americans are absolutely right to defend themselves against these terrorists who want to destroy our western values.'

'Yes, but there's a danger governments will use the word to justify attacking anyone they don't like in the name of something that sounds good like *western values*. They'll start using the word *Arab* like they used the word *Jew* in Nazi Germany.' Was she going too far?

At the mention of the word *Jew* Tess noticed a slight look of embarrassment on the faces of Arnaud and Florence opposite her.

'Anyway,' Florence cut in,' this is all just words. It's what people think and do that's important, not words.

'You're wrong,' Tess wanted to shout at her. 'What people think and do is influenced by what they say and how they hear language being used.'

'I don't understand what you're getting at, Tess,' said

Robert. 'The people who attacked the World Trade Centre, the people who support them - that's what we mean by terrorists. And they are evil. They had no reason to attack us. And we've started a war on them in the name of Freedom and Democracy. It's going to take a long time but we'll win it. The whole of America is behind this war.'

'And us, too, we're behind you,' said Jean Paul, raising his glass.

'Jean Paul.' Florence gave him a stern look from the other end of the table.

The door opened and Cécile was there again, this time bearing a tarte aux abricots and a silver jug of cream.

'Ah, apricot tart, my favourite,' exclaimed Nicole. 'I am supposed to be watching my figure but I am not going to be able to resist this.'

'Let *me* watch your figure, Nicole, and *you* eat the tart' said Jean Paul, advancing his face as if he hoped she might plant a kiss on it. Christine rolled her eyes at Tess who started to giggle and then she remembered Jennifer and her throat contracted.

'I'm sorry,' she said, getting up from the table. 'Is the bathroom … ?' Florence put her arm round her and led her out into the hallway.

'Tess, we are very happy to have you here with us this evening,' she whispered as she opened the bathroom door for her. She gave Tess's arm a squeeze.

'And I am very happy to be here with you,' said Tess. Was she really? She closed the door and stood against it, the tears still running down her cheeks.

'I'm sorry, Thierry' she said as they drove back to Versailles a short while later. Thierry had jumped to his feet as soon as she'd returned to the table and they'd left immediately.

'No, no,' he said, 'in any case I was glad to make my escape. I was finding Nicole - how you say - a little over ...over...

'Overpowering? Overwhelming?'

Oversexed? Her head was resting on Thierry's shoulder

and they had before them another whole night together. Only her mind kept returning to the argument they'd had.

'I think it's dangerous when people use language like that, when they don't take the trouble to think about what they're saying.' Or when they talk in a loud, slow, impressive voice so that people think that what they're saying must be true.

'Oh, dangerous … '. Tess felt him raising his shoulders in a French shrug. 'It was funny, you know, when you mentioned the word 'Jew'. Robert's mother is Jewish. The 'R' in his name stands for Ruben not Robert but he doesn't like people to know - he prefers his Scottish connection.'

'But you see what I mean, don't you?'

'I think you are too *maniac.*'

'You mean 'fussy'?'

'Yes, fussy. Because you are a language teacher, but I am a scientist and for me the word 'terrorism' and 'terrorist' have precise meanings. And western civilisation has a meaning too.

'Yes, but there's a lot of greed and self interest mixed up with western civilisation, only you don't hear people talking about that. They just talk about defending freedom and democracy because words like that make them feel good but a word's not like the Eiffel Tower. You can't talk about defending civilisation like you'd defend the Eiffel Tower.

'The Eiffel Tower?' He burst out laughing at the idea of anyone wanting to defend the Eiffel Tower and almost missed stopping at the red light.

He was still laughing as they climbed the stone staircase up to the flat.

'Ah words, Tess, words,' he sighed, ruffling her hair. 'You are worrying too much about words because you are a teacher.'

As he put the key in the lock he suddenly bent down to kiss the nape of her neck.

'And because you are a woman,' he murmured.

Chapter 32

Odile would be at the wedding along with her brother, Guy. And Annie, of course. How would Annie get on with her half sister and brother as they would then become? And when would the wedding take place? Early October? That would be a good time - an autumnal feel to the air, the leaves on the turn, and the three women in their elegant suits, the colours of sugared almonds, yes, that would be nice - Tess in lilac, and Annie in a delicate shade of green showing off her auburn hair. Odile would be in pink or maybe a pale cream. Her dark complexion would suit cream. All three of them in outrageous hats, of course, and Thierry tall and distinguished looking in dark grey.

And there they'd be in Fyvie Castle. She'd heard you could hire it for the weekend - no doubt very expensive, but Thierry eager to lavish luxury upon her.

'I want this to be a - how you say – a *stupendous* occasion,' he would say as they lay in each other's arms talking about the day when they would plight their troth. Would she teach him the phrase?

'We will pleat our throats? What does that mean?'

But is this what she really wanted? The certainty, the security of becoming Thierry's wife? Dear Thierry. *Dear Thierry* .... She looked out of the window at the line dividing sea from sky. What could she say? Like a knight on a white charger he'd come into her life, promising to serve her with complete devotion for the rest of her days. That was the message she was getting from his daily phone calls. 'I love you, Tess.' He seemed to be in no doubt. Maybe it was lust masquerading as love but love was the word he used and part of her was being seduced by it.

The phone rang. It was Jean Louis. Could he be fitted in now straight away rather than tomorrow? He turned up in his cream and black check jacket crossed by thin vertical and horizontal yellow lines, a cream shirt underneath and a brilliant red tie.

'What means *lash out*?,' he began by asking.

'It means *to attack, often with the tongue.* For example, *You don't know what you're talking about, you're just saying that*, she lashed out. A lash is actually a whip.'

Jean Louis' eyes lit up. The prostitutes near where he lived in Paris carried lashes. Did she know that? Had she heard of the Faubourg St. Denis? He owned two flats in this district - one of them very old with beans on the ceiling - *beams*, she interposed - as well as a large farm in Normandy. Being chummy with the prostitutes in the district must give a rich man like him quite a thrill, she thought.

'They are very nice, these women, we laugh and joke together, I am knowing them for 20 years.'

A Year in Provence. A Summer in Tuscany. How about *Twenty Years Talking to Learners of English in Aberdeen*? But maybe not for much longer. *Dear Thierry, I want to be back in your apartment making love to you. I want to be there when you come home in the evenings. I'll say 'Look, I've mended the hole in your green pullover' and you'll run your hands through my hair and then later we'll sit out on the terrace with a bottle of wine and talk and talk into the night.*

But would she really want to be sitting all day mending someone's jumper, waiting for them to come home? And what sort of talk would they have?

Other questions - he had a sheet of paper in front of him. What was the difference between *to give up* and *to give in*, between *continue to do* and *continue doing*?

'And you *get round a problem,* but what about *get over* a problem?' He had been on the point of giving up or was it *giving in* English when he discovered all these problems.

Was she giving in? Giving up?

'That's enough for today, Jean Louis.' He'd only been there half an hour.

'I'm sorry,' she said as she stood at the door. 'I'll give you longer next time.' When would that be? Next Monday?

She got into the car and drove to the beach. A gentle wind was blowing from the south and a watery sun was putting a shine on the waves. She started to walk in the direction of the outlet of the River Dee. Talk. She went over in her mind again the talk over the dinner table and afterwards in the car. Thierry had been as bad as the rest of them, worse, because he'd sounded so sure of himself and they'd all listened to him as if he was the Pope speaking ex cathedra. They turned language into a sort of prison, using it like that. If she married Thierry she'd be in permanent conflict with them, trying not to become like them.

'You talk about being civilised when children in Africa are dying because we're making them pay for their water.'

'Oh no, Tess, not that again.'

She found herself in Footdee outside Pete's door. She rang the bell. He was inside, busy trying to find a website on the internet. He'd made a lot of progress. She sat down by the fireplace in the same chair she'd sat in last October talking to Thierry.

'How do you liberate people, Pete?'

'Who are you talking about? The starving people of Africa? The Palestinians? Asylum seekers? The homeless?'

She laughed. 'No, I'm thinking of us well-off westerners, people who're supposed to have some power in the world, people like Thierry who was here that Sunday morning, you remember? I had an argument with him about western civilisation and terrorism and things like that when I was in Paris. He and all these people at this dinner party I went to were talking as if they had name badges on them. *We're from the free world. We're civilised. We're not evil, we're good. You don't share our western values, you're evil, you're not good.* How do you stop people from running along tramlines, not thinking about what they're saying? How can you expect to fight terrorism if you don't even begin to ask why people become terrorists in the first place?'

'I'd put them in one big room and give them all pillows and I'd tell them to go round banging each other with the pillows saying 'You're greedy, you're dishonest, you're ignorant, you're intolerant' and then I'd open the door and they'd find themselves in a big yard.

'And then what?'

'Then I'd pick each of them up in turn on the end of a

crane and I'd dangle them in the air till they cried out: 'I am a terrorist, I am an evil person, I let people die of starvation, I sell arms to countries so that they can commit genocide, I withhold cheap medicines from people dying of Aids.

'But we don't do anything about all this either, except sign a few petitions and go on marches.'

''But at least we're aware of the problems. At least we're using language with circumspection. We're not taking words for granted. Come on Tess, let's have a pillow fight.'

'At least we're not taking words for granted. But where does that get us?' Tess asked herself as she walked back to her car. She'd declined Pete's invitation to have a pillow fight. 'Maybe it just makes us feel good like it makes Thierry feel good to talk about *freedom* and *democracy*.'

It was still light when she got back to Kineldie. The days were getting longer, soon the geese would be departing for Iceland. She put on her wellingtons and followed the path through the bracken from behind the cottage to the top of the hill. She sat for a long time on the large granite stone, looking across at the dark wavy line of hills that ended in the knobbly top of Bennachie, waiting for the warriors to appear on the broken walls of the iron fort. Would she find herself in Thierry's world turning into a sort of warrior, the Boadicea of Bennachie? When what she'd been imagining was sitting on the terrace of his manoir in the sunshine in a floating negligee with a bowl of café au lait and him smiling lovingly across at her? Did she have enough love/lust for him for that? That evening she picked up the unfinished letter: *Dear Thierry* ...

Chapter 33

It was half past nine. Jean Louis appeared in the doorway clutching a copy of *English Without Tears*. He'd discovered it among his books yesterday evening - it had belonged to his mother in law. She stared at its brown cover. Racing back to Paris after an afternoon spent in the *Ile de France* with Marc, lying in the sunshine under birch trees, wondering as she went up the stairs of the English Language Centre two at a time to a crowd of evening class students how on earth she was going to fill the two hours. 'Open your books at p.105 Exercise 8.' Round and round the class of smart-heeled young ladies, each in turn stumbling through a sentence, hesitating, getting prompts from their neighbours while Tess picked birch leaves off the sleeves of her jumper and wondered about twigs stuck to her back.

'Open the book at p.105, Jean Louis.'

The exercise consisted in changing Direct Speech into Indirect Speech, starting out with verbs like *say/tell/explain/cry/urge/warn/inform/grumble* ... and making the necessary changes in the rest of the paragraph.

He said that he had waited for her the day before till nine, Jean Louis began.

He pointed out that he had phoned her at midnight.

(You phoned last night at eleven as I was going to bed. 'Tess, I don't understand.')

He told her that he didn't believe a word she was saying and thought that it would be better if she spoke the truth.

('We were so happy together.')

He cried that that was not the first time she had deceived him and he urged that it would not occur again.

('I love you.')

He shouted at her that it wasn't fair to treat him like this.

(You didn't shout, you just sounded bewildered.)

He informed her that she would pay for what she was doing.

('Please think about it.')

He warned her that she would not get another chance

like this one.

(You won't get another chance like this one. No, he hadn't said that, but that's what he must be thinking. I won't get another chance …)

A message from Dominique on the answer machine to say he'd be late. She'd intended cancelling the lesson but there was no way of contacting him now. She hunted in the mug on her desk full of dried up pens and broken pencils for the brown eyeliner she'd bought one day waiting for her prescription at the chemist's. Maybe it would go some way to hiding the red around the eyes. And now the cheeks. She streaked them with pink and then stroked the colour in, gently, lovingly. Maybe the secret was to be in love with the poor, tired face, to think of the lines as forming a beautiful decorative pattern, like tracery.

Dominique wanted to make one final attempt at improving his pronunciation before leaving. Could he practise once again making a difference between words such as *leave* and *live, heat* and *hit, bean* and *bin, beat* and bit?

Beat and bit. A boy with a permanently running nose who lived in a poky flat at the end of an interminable metro line.

The dog beat zee man

'Not *beat*. *Bit*. Can you hear the difference? *Beat Bit.* '

Each time she'd said *beat* the boy had sniggered into his copybook. As they'd lain in bed that evening in her attic room looking out at a sliver of a moon, Marc had told her that *bitte* was a slang word for penis.

It was that evening they'd noticed the blind had gone from the window, disappeared mysteriously, blown away in the wind. After that they spent long hours looking out at the Paris sky, at tortuous clouds moving across the moon, at planes winking their way to China, Moscow, London. She'd never replaced the blind.

'I think getting the rhythm is more important.' It might help her headache. 'Let's practice rhythm so that you sound as convincing as possible when you give a presentation. It's a

212

question of highlighting certain words.' She wrote up on the board:

*There are **two** points I'd like to make about the **bus** service in Aberdeen. **Firstly** there aren't **enough** buses. And **secondly** the fares are **much too high**.*

He read out the sentences like someone trying to cross a river on slithery stepping stones. He'd probably never been on a bus since he'd arrived in Aberdeen.

'Again,' she said. 'Take it more slowly and say it with authority.'

'And now stand up and say it once more as if you were addressing a meeting –

*There are **two** points I'd like to make about the **bus** service in Aberdeen. **Firstly** there aren't **enough** buses. And **secondly** the fares are **much too high***

'You can apply the same framework to any amount of situations,' she told him.

*There are **two** points I'd like to make about **company policy**. **Firstly**, we need to **cut down** on **staff**. And **secondly**, the **remaining** staff will need to work **much harder**.*

*There are **two** points I'd like to make about **living alone**.*
What were they?

'It has been anything but a pleasure learning English with you,' he said with a smile as he shook hands with her half an hour later and said goodbye for the last time.

She assumed he'd meant 'nothing – nothing but a pleasure.' Nothing

Driving in from Kineldie to face another day, wondering what on earth she was going to do with Laurent, the idea of a dictation came to her. She would give him a dictation, and Denis too, if he turned up. Thierry had phoned again the evening before. Was she sure? Was there anything he could do to make her change her mind? Did she need more time to think? He could offer her so much.

Dictation had been the other great standby when she'd arrive breathless at the Language Centre to face the young girls from Passy. *The road to my favourite haunt was impassable that winter,* Tess would read out, knowing that at least ten of the manicured hands would be busy writing *The road to my favourite aunt was impossible that winter.*

She got out the recipe for Shepherd's Pie that she'd started making up the evening of the midnight visitation. She'd been unable to find a recipe for Shepherd's Pie in Mrs Beeton - either in the lamb/mutton or the beef section - only instructions on how to dress a sheep's head or a bullock's heart or palate. Other books she'd consulted just said you could use any sort of minced meat. They would do the recipe as a dictation, with Laurent writing it up on the board.

500 grams of any sort of minced meat, she read out slowly

'Mince meat,' Laurent wrote up.

'Minced meat,' said Tess, exaggerating the *-ed.* Should she explain the difference between that and mincemeat? She'd once had a student who'd set out with some friends from France to cross Scotland on foot at its narrowest point - north of Inverness. It was one July when it had actually snowed and they'd spent the day stumbling round in the bog in the snow with Etienne encouraging them with the prospect of a good meal of spaghetti bolognaise that evening.

'By the time you've got the tents up it will be ready - quick cook pasta and a jar of heated up mincemeat emptied over it.'

It wasn't until they were actually eating it that they discovered the mistake and then they were so hungry ...

She decided Laurent could find out for himself the difference between mincemeat and minced meat, or she could tell him to ask someone in his office. Easier than explaining a word like *freedom.* Freedom - what she had now, what she'd chosen.

Denis, when he eventually turned up in his Fair Isle pullover, was resistant to the idea of a dictation. It's true, she'd promised to practise hearing the difference between *sh* and *ch* with him. French only had the sound *sh.*

'To pronounce English *ch* you have to put a *t* in front of the *sh* - *ttttsheep* gives you *cheap.*'

214

He was looking at her as if he knew - had Thierry phoned him?

'I helped you out with Barbara, Denis. Now it's your turn to help me out. Talk to Tess.'

'Only first you have to hear the difference between *ch* and *sh*.'

'Tess, Thierry is very upset ....he doesn't understand ...' Denis would begin. She wrote up pairs of sentences on the board. 'Point to the sentence I'm saying.'

That's my share/that's my chair
He loves ships/He loves chips;
She dropped the sherry/She dropped the cherry;
The story was about 3 wishes/The story was about 3 witches

He was staring at her. How could she be so heartless as to go on teaching like this as if everything was normal. *'That's my chair,'* she read out. 'Point, Denis, point to the sentence I'm saying: *That's my chair'* He pointed to *share.*

'Tttshshshair,' she repeated.

'What is a wish?' he asked. A wish? A wish was if only Thierry was less...more ... If only she was less ....more.... If only Fergus ....

Or did he mean *witch*?

'It's s*orcière* in French,' she said.

'Ah, sorcière!' He laughed.

'They come into a play by Shakespeare.' (Ah Shakspeerrr!) '*Macbeth*. It's set in Scotland. Macbeth lived in a castle called Cawdor Castle not far from Aberdeen.' She could have taken Thierry to visit it. 'And there's a butcher's shop in the main street of the nearby town called Macbeth.'

Not knowing the play how could she expect him to appreciate a butcher called Macbeth? Thierry was surely coming back into his mind.

'Tess, why don't you ... ' he's about to say.

Before he could open his mouth she jumped to her feet, rubbed out the pairs of sentences and in their place wrote up: *So fair and foul a day I have not seen.* The opening line of *Macbeth* and definitive proof of Shakespeare having visited

Aberdeen. How else could he have described the weather here so aptly?

She had succeeded. Denis was very taken by the sentence. He was no longer thinking of Thierry. He copied it down.

'Yes, I will tell that to the people I will meet down in London tomorrow. How is the weather like in Scotland? they will ask to me and I will tell them 'So fair and fool a day I 'ave not see.'

He was almost through the door when he turned as if suddenly remembering. Thierry was going to be in Aberdeen next week on business, he told her.

Chapter 34

Pete's had an idea to save the Institute,' said Kirsty as they drove in to Aberdeen. It was the first night in weeks that Kirsty had not spent with Pete in Footdee. 'He'll tell you about it.'

'Yes,' said Pete as they looked out over the seagulls nesting. He was holding a pale green leaflet. 'Look at this brochure. *Why not come and learn English through bread making? Last year 30 students between them turned out 900 rolls and 400 loaves as well as perfecting their English in a friendly and lively environment.*'

'What do you think?' asked Pete. 'We could do the same. here. We could turn the Institute into a *Learn a Language through Cooking* Centre. Kirsty could teach French cookery and Quentin - with a bit of help from Emilio - could do Spanish. and Maggie could do Italian. And you could do puddings, Tess, like Dead Baby and Laundry Pudding and Treacle Tart and Summer Pudding and Trifle.'

Yes, she wouldn't mind doing puddings. She hardly ever ate them, let alone made them, but she liked the idea of them.

She found herself discussing the subject with Laurent an hour later to take her mind off Thierry who she was seeing at one o'clock. He'd phoned, inviting her to have lunch with him and she'd said Yes. But she was not looking forward to it. She'd done her best to explain to him in the letter she'd written and she couldn't think of anything else to say, except that her heart wasn't in it.

. Was Summer Pudding like Christmas pudding only eaten in the summer? Laurent asked. No, it was made with fresh fruit. Like trifle? What was the difference between summer pudding and trifle? He was a geologist in pursuit of exact definitions.

Summer pudding: a large garden with bushes heavy with blackcurrants and redcurrants and plump raspberries on canes and a lady in a straw hat and a flowery dress filling baskets with the red and purple fruit. She wanders up a path towards the house, brushing the purple nepata and lavender as she goes, dead-heading a rose, stooping to pick tarragon and chives for the salad at midday. Then in the kitchen, which has a copper berry pan hanging from the wall and a heavy wooden table in the middle of the floor, she lines an earthenware bowl with wholesome slices of bread and fills it to the brim with the soft fruit, makes a lid with another bit of bread, puts a saucer over it and then takes copper weights from the iron weighing scales and places them on top. And then the next day when the juices from the fruit have soaked into the bread she turns the whole thing out onto a pretty plate and serves it with thick cream.

Trifle, on the other hand, altogether more democratic. You rush to the shop, buy trifle sponges, jelly, custard powder, milk, a tin of mango oranges maybe or fruit cocktail and a tub of Hundreds and Thousands and a carton of Dream Topping to decorate. It is made in the time it takes for the jelly to set, for the milk for the custard to boil, and then for the custard to cool. Should she go into all this?

'Summer pudding's made with bread and fresh soft fruit. Trifle's made with sponge cake and custard - and usually tinned fruit,' she said.

They'd arranged to meet at *The Silver Darling*. 'The silver darling' was the local name for the herring which in days gone by had brought riches to Aberdeen. It was one of Aberdeen's smartest restaurants. On Saturday evenings sometimes, as she and Kirsty sat eating a pizza or a pie they'd imagine themselves dining at *The Silver Darling* with two beaux. 'How about a glass of *Vouvray* to start with? And I believe the *scallops à la provençale* are particularly good ...'.

A square grey building – the old Customs House - right by the sea, next to the old lighthouse and inside not unlike how she imagined a *manoir* in Burgundy to be. The entrance paved with flagstones and a round table in the corner covered with a coarse woven cloth and an earthenware jug filled with red tulips in the centre of it. Thierry was sitting there waiting for her. Together they went up the curved staircase to the restaurant.

218

'We've chosen the right day,' she said as they unfolded the large white napkins. Outside a storm was raging - waves two metres high leaping up and breaking into surging white foam and sunlight flashing down like a clutch of swords through the chaos. Thierry was sitting with his back to the window but there was a large mirror on the wall facing him so he would still be able to see the havoc the wind was creating. Only his gaze was on Tess. What would she like to eat?

'I believe the *scallops à la provençale* are particularly good,' he suggested

They were alone, the only people in the restaurant, others put off by the weather so the tables round about neatly set and undisturbed, a pleasing colour scheme of white linen and shining glasses and pale yellow daffodils.

'It's lovely being here with you,' she was stopping herself from saying.

'It's lovely being here with you,' he said.

But her heart wasn't in it. 'I could never live among people not able to appreciate the difference between summer pudding and trifle,' she tried joking to herself.

Desire hovering between them - she'd only to catch hold of his hand or he of hers. Why couldn't she settle for this, for him? She kept them carefully in her lap, asked him about Odile.

The handsome blonde waiter set before them glasses of Muscadet and recommended the *sole meunière*. He was called Yves and he was from the Auvergne.

'Ah, the south west. My father was from a leetle village near Clermont Ferrand but I am from Bourgogne,' Thierry told him, his way of pronouncing Bourgogne conjuring up an image of deep red Burgundy wine.

What if he came back to work in Aberdeen? They could live together out at Kineldie, no? And spend the summers in the manoir. No, it couldn't be..

'He's going to start talking about 'us',' she thought as she squeezed lemon onto her sole. She must find something to say, she'd tell him about Pete's crazy idea to turn the institute into a cookery school.

Before she could begin he was telling her about an interesting article he'd been reading about genetic engineering. He'd gone into French and she was having a problem following what he was saying.

And then another article – about free trade.

But what does 'free' mean? Free to get rich while the rest of the world gets poorer?

Why was she taking him as a symbol, why was she holding him responsible for what was wrong with the world? What was she doing anyway to change things?

A Greek student during the time of the colonels - 'We can do nothing, we are powerless - but at least we *know* what's going on, at least we *know*.'

And all the time as she met his eyes they were saying something different. She was glad when Yves reappeared. What was the name of the village Thierry's grandfather had come from, he wanted to know.

Tess looked out at the sea, still behaving outrageously.

'Look at those fantastic waves!' she interrupted them.

But they were talking about the woman, famous in the region, who'd died from pricking her finger on a thorn from a rose bush. Thierry's grandfather had actually known her.

Maybe that was it. What she loved was the wild. While Thierry was at home here in this peaceful place, among the beautifully laid tables.

Creme brulée? Or sorbet? - fraise, cassis, citron ....

No, they'd just have coffee.

Outside they stood for a moment looking out at the sea, at the giant waves still hurling themselves against the beach.

Chapter 35

Where was the kettle? Who'd gone and taken it? A large room crowded with people finishing having breakfast. Tables full of packets of muesli and cornflakes and empty jugs and pots, and the debris of crumbs and half eaten slices of toast, bacon rind and smeared yolk of egg and dirty cups. Where in all this was the kettle? She went from table to table hunting for it, nobody taking any notice of her, all smoking and talking and laughing. They'd had their breakfast and she hadn't. She'd arrived late and all she wanted was a cup of tea but where was the kettle? She couldn't talk to them, she couldn't ask. She got down on her hands and knees to search. Maybe someone had put it under one of the tables.

She opened her eyes. Light was coming into the room. She'd overslept. She was going to be late for the meeting in Emilio's restaurant.

Even Franck had turned up and Emilio was already in the kitchen making empanadillas for them to eat as an early lunch before the restaurant opened at midday.

'But it would take ages to get a place like the Institute ready,' Maggie began. 'We'd have to get a licence. And before that we'd have to re-organise all the rooms and buy masses of equipment. And there'd be all sorts of health and safety requirements we'd have to meet. And we're none of us qualified to teach cookery anyway.'

Maggie could really be tedious, you could see Pete thinking. He was twitching his flowery tie impatiently. But of course she was right. She was dressed casually this morning in a smart denim jacket and new red T shirt, with matching lipstick, making the rest of them look like scruffs.

'Is not a problem,' Emilio kept shouting through the open door. Good old Emilio. He had been through all the red tape when setting up his restaurant. And there *was* Quentin's money that he seemed enthusiastic enough about spending. And it was only March. Plenty of time to get organised before the summer.

Kirsty, loyal to Pete, kept saying she thought it was a

great idea.

'At last I will be able to show the people here what they can do with all the lovely lobster and venison that we leave to the French to eat. Not to speak of the mushrooms. I will take them to find mushrooms and teach them which ones are poisonous and which ones they can eat.' Kirsty had learnt a lot during her stays in France.

'I'll come with you. You can teach me too what's venomous and what isn't,' said Pete with a mock leer.

'And I could teach them words like *merde* and *cette putain de mixer.*'

'*Putain*, doesn't that mean *prostitute?*' asked Franck, opening his mouth for the first time. Everybody turned to look at him. Could he be a dark horse?

'What do *you* think about the idea, Franck?' Tess asked. He liked it. He was an expert maker of stollen. But they mustn't neglect the grammar all the same.

'There's that thing with grated fried potatoes that I ate once in Germany,' said Tess. He didn't seem to know about that, but stollen, yes, he was an expert maker of stollen.

'You could teach them some typical Scottish dishes, Tess.'

'But you do not discuss about this sort of thing in your lessons. Why do you not discuss about this sort of thing if you are attaching so much importance to language?'

'Maybe not Scottish dishes.' After all these years she still wasn't sure what went into stovies or how to cook the oatmeal stuffing they put in chickens - *oat cuisine,* as Annie called it. 'What about you, Hilary?'

How would Hilary fit in? Hilary had difficulty making a pot of tea.

'She could do poems with food in them,' said Quentin. You know that one by William Carlos Williams - *This is just to say ... I have eaten the plums that were in the ice box ...* And there are lots of novels with things about food in them - Pip stealing the pie for the convict in *Great Expectations.* And what was the name of that book by Iris Murdoch where the hero was always cooking himself up refined little dishes?

222

You remember? He was scheming to win back a lost love and then, when he found her right at the end of the book, she'd turned into a plump, grey-haired old woman in a flowery dress?'

Had he still gone on loving her?

'I like the idea of Japanese businessmen in their suits making brackbelly clumble,' said Hilary.

'And losing sleep about their sauces being too rumpy,' said Kirsty.

'Pete, your Japanese don't need to cook Scottish food,' said Quentin. 'You could take them round the fish market in the early morning to buy really fresh fish and then they could make sushi and that sort of thing.'

'And we could get them to talk about their childhood memories of eating the sushi their grandmothers made them when they were children,' said Pete.

'Oh please, no! The whole place would stink of fish.' Maggie shuddered.

'I wonder how much it would cost, converting the place.' Quentin, who never normally talked about money, was looking suddenly doubtful. How much had he actually inherited from his crystal gazing mum?

Emilio emerged from the kitchen and joined Quentin at the end of the table, their shoulders just touching.

'You could give up this restaurant and run the restaurant in the Institute, Emilio,' said Hilary, happy to give the idea all her support, just as long as she didn't have to get involved in the actual cooking. 'You could serve them up all the things they've been cooking during the classes.' Like burnt onions and doughy pizzas. Emilio wasn't so sure about that.

'No, I am muy contento here. But I will come once a week, I will come each Monday and I will learn the students how to do gazpacho, paella, calamares, sangria, empan ....Ah los empan......!' He ran into the kitchen and was back a few minutes later with a plateful of little golden pies in one hand and a carafe of vino tinto in the other.

'I'll pick up a few recipes while I'm in Rome, just in case the thing does get off the ground,' said Maggie after a large glass of wine. 'And Judith's got quite friendly with a guy who makes the pizzas where's she's working.' Her daughter, Judith, worked at *Pizza Place* at the weekends. 'I'm sure Luigi could come and demonstrate so they'd have a chance to hear Italian spoken by a real Italian as well.'

'Yes, but we must bear in the mind that the shtudents are here languages to learn and not the cooking,' said Franck.

Quite right. What they were planning was all the same still a language school run by language teachers, not a cookery school with eccentric cooks brandishing their frying pans and spilling sauces and gravies all over the place.

Hilary was thumbing through the Collected Works of Keats. 'How about this?' she said, reading aloud in her rich, smoker's voice:

> *... he from forth the closet brought a heap*
> *of candied apple, quince, and plum and gourd;*
> *With jellies soother than the creamy curd,*
> *and lucent syrups, tinct with cinnamon;*
> *Manna and dates, in argosy transferred*
> *From Fez; and spiced dainties, every one,*
> *From silken Samarcand to cedared Lebanon.*

There was a silence. Emilio sat nodding and smiling.

'is lovely' he said. 'Is like music.'

'Yes,' said Tess. It would certainly be a change from the subjunctive.

They emerged into the grey of Golden Square. Off Golden Square were Silver Street and Diamond Street and Ruby Lane and Ruby Place. All just as grey in spite of their names but this morning for Tess the buildings had a pleasing harmony. Everything was becoming brighter; like Emilio she was thinking 'Is lovely, is like music.'

'Maggie is probably right, though - it's a crazy idea,' she thought as she drove back to Kineldie. But maybe they didn't need to do any cooking at all. They could just *tell* the students about how to make things like sticky toffee pudding and bubble and squeak. After all, that's what happened most of the time. People bought cookery books and watched cookery programmes on television and then went out and bought readymade dishes, or ordered carry outs.

Wild daffodils appearing along the roadside. They were early this year. She passed the woods where she'd once walked with Fergus and where she'd planned to go with Thierry. The silver birches were just coming into leaf. Bob had always seemed all wrong in the country. Urban, civilised, cautious, it would have been unimaginable for him to have stumbled through undergrowth in search of a sunny glade where they could lie down together on a floor of moss and pine needles with birch trees forming an arch above their heads. No need to, he'd have said - what was wrong with the bedroom? Overhead a skein of geese. The winter was over. They were heading back to Iceland.

And Fergus would be heading home. He'd return accompanied, no doubt, by some glamorous Polish girl or by a soulful Russian with liquid eyes or by a saucy Hungarian. The look he had sometimes of a lost child, his vibrant chords on the cello, he was bound to have stirred them, won their hearts.

'I have fallen in love with you utterly. Carry me away from here. Take me back to your country,' Tess could hear them commanding him. He would have been spoilt for choice.

'But I have no money, I would not be able to afford to keep you,' he'd have said.

'We will live on love,' they'd have breathed in his ear.

But she could live without Thierry, without Fergus. Bennachie in the distance. She remembered suddenly the dream she'd had a few nights ago. She was driving to the airport to catch a plane to she didn't know where. A lake in the distance, dark and shimmering, half hidden by a clump of beech trees. She'd felt compelled to stop the car. Surely there would be time to reach it and stand for a moment beside it before getting on the plane. She'd made off over the rough ground, dodging gorse bushes and pine seedlings and jumping the stream. It was further than she'd thought but no, there would be time, if she hurried.

Once home she put on a CD of *Bob Marley*, got down Mrs Beeton from the shelf and installed herself at the table by the window, just in time to see a deer coming into the garden - she'd given up on the idea of a seven foot fence. She felt tender towards the deer. *This is all there is, this moment here and I'm happy.*

She looked up Aunt Nellie's Pudding in the contents - the pudding she'd discovered one winter day when Annie was off school recovering from chicken pox. She'd made it for her. *Half a pound of flour. Half a pound of suet. Half a pound of treacle ...... Treacle is of great use as an article of domestic economy ... and it is accounted wholesome.* Maybe she and Hilary could get together and produce a book for learners of English - a collection of poems and recipes about food.

Chapter 36

Kirsty and Pete were going to see the latest James Bond film at the cinema down by the beach. Did Tess want to join them? She didn't but they could all go for a walk along the sea front before it started if they liked. A great site for a cinema where you could have a walk along a beach, or even a paddle on a good day, before becoming engulfed in the dark. Only a slight breeze coming from the east but enough to get them walking briskly, Pete huddled inside his green corduroy jacket, his hair falling into his eyes. 'Here, you can have my hat,' said Kirsty stretching up and plonking her grey woollen cap on top of his head. 'I have enough hair to keep me warm.'

Meaning Pete didn't, but he didn't seem to mind the implication, maybe hadn't even noticed it, so happy was he to be walking beside Kirsty, his arm around her shoulders. Would they even notice if I just disappeared? Tess wondered. The tide was coming in and there was someone out there in a wet suit wrestling with the curve of the waves before they broke. That's me out there, the lone surfer, thought Tess. She drew in a great gulp of the sea air.

'But Pete, I wonder if *Termoil* are going to want to pay out good money for their engineers to come and learn how to make tapioca pudding,' she said.

'Well, a geophysicist making predictions about where there might be oil, it's all more or less the same language, isn't it? *First you pour milk into a saucepan/First you make your map ..... . And next ...... and then ..... and last but not least ..... . And as long as you don't stop stirring/as long as you interpret your seismic map correctly, you will certainly/probably/possibly/you should/ ought to/ may/ might/ could ...'* Pete was by now addressing a seagull *'end up with a delicious tapioca pudding/lots of lovely oil.'*

'Well, *you* can be the one to go to Termoil and talk to the head of Human Resources about tapioca pudding.'

'And then there'd be agreeing and disagreeing and challenging and asking questions and expressing opinions. *You say that this is the only way to cook rice but in*

Indonesia/Japan/Thailand we do it like this.' Pete was now standing on the parapet, waving his arms around. *'Would you not agree that Mars bars fried in batter are .....? Do you really think it's a good idea to serve sausages with trifle ....?'*

'And it wouldn't just be *Termoil* employees anyway,' said Kirsty. 'We could publicise the school via the British Council which would mean we'd get people from all over - South America, Thailand, Greece, Egypt .... .'

'All learning how to cook Scottish dishes?' asked Pete, jumping down from the parapet, as if an incoming wave had sloshed over him. 'Then we'd go off to Crete or Cairo for our holidays and find Scotch Broth and Skirlie and Cullen Skink on the menu.' The awful possibility was just dawning on him.

'What's wrong with Scotch Broth and Skirlie and Cullen Skink as long as they're made properly?' asked Kirsty. 'My Nan used to make Clootie Dumpling every Christmas. It was delicious. But people don't make it anymore, or they don't do it properly.'

'Clootie Dumpling?' shouted Pete. 'My Nan made it once and it was the vilest, the ... the .... the most disgusting cannonball of suet sitting in evil brown liquid that you ever saw. No wonder my mum walked out on us that Christmas and never came back. I hate Clootie Dumpling. I loathe it. I abominate it. The only place for Clootie Dumpling is the sea.'

He'd come to a standstill and was shouting out, addressing the waves, with Kirsty's hat perched on top of his head. A couple passed. 'Fit's adee wi' 'em?' the woman was muttering, giving him a wide berth.

'Okay, okay' said Kirsty. 'Maybe Clootie Dumpling is not to everybody's taste. But Scotch Broth.'

'Scotch Broth?' roared Pete, louder than the sea now. 'You boil up some nasty-looking bones with scraggy bits of meat hanging from them and then you throw carrots and neeps and those things that look like babies' teeth into the greasy liquid and then you have the smell of it all round the house for hours. You can't possibly like it.'

Kirsty had started to laugh but then stopped, noticing his eyes.

228

'Maybe we should be getting back,' said Tess. 'What's happened to that surfer? I can't see him any more. We'd better hurry or we'll be expected to mount a rescue operation.'

They walked back towards the cinema, Pete's arm no longer round Kirsty's shoulder.

'Okay, well maybe French cooking is better than Scottish,' said Kirsty breaking the silence. 'How about if I made us an *entrecote au poivre* for this evening?' Pete gave her a hug and Tess watched as they disappeared hand in hand into the cinema.

'And now I'll go home and eat my way through two packets of oatcakes with a tumbler or three of wine while I watch *Fargo* with Trotsky on my lap.'

Trotsky had caught a bird. It was lying inert at the foot of the stairs. Feathers all over the place. She picked it up - a thrush, its body still warm. She wrapped it gently in newspaper. She'd bury it in the garden.

She was just on her way out when the telephone rang. 'Hello. Tess? This is Fergus. I just got back last night.' She stood listening to his voice, holding on to the phone, holding on to the moment. In a few seconds she was going to hear him saying 'And Tess, I don't know how to say this, but I've fallen in love - with Agnieska, Tanya, Katia.'

'How are you?' he asked.

'Just fine.' Silence.

'It's been a fantastic tour - Prague, Budapest, Pécs, Bucharest ... . You got my cards?' She waited for him to go on.

'The really interesting place was Transylvania.' Ah, a Transylvanian. Not Agnieska nor Tanya nor Katia but a young Transylvanian woman. 'Their folk music is amazing. We met a group of dancers and musicians we sort of combined with. We did a concert together and they may be coming over to Britain. We're going to try and see if we can get funding for them.'

'Oh really? What sort of instruments do they play?' Tess asked, looking out at the deer and wondering how long this conversation was going to go on for. What sort of instrument did the young Transylvanian woman play? Or was she a wild dancer? More likely - her eyes flashing, her skirt twirling, her shiny boots skimming the floor.

He started out on a description of outlandish instruments with funny names. And lots of drinking, of course, some funny alcohol they produced there, very strong, a bit like - what was that stuff they'd drunk that time in the Dolomites?

'Grappa,' said Tess. 'You remember, we drank a whole bottle of it practically, after coming down from climbing that mountain - what was it called? The Cima de something or other.' Fergus couldn't remember, he wasn't even making an effort to remember. His whole being in thrall to the strange music played by Transylvanian Roma.

'Anyway, it was good. And if they do come over here we'll do some concerts together probably and you'll get a chance to hear them.'

Lesson 16: Making polite responses:

'That will be nice,' she said.

'But ... ' He seemed to be searching for words. What was he wanting to tell her? 'I'm sorry you couldn't make it for Christmas,' he said at last.

'But you didn't try very hard at inviting me?' she wanted to say.

'Tess, when are we going to meet? I don't have much time for the next week or so. We're making a recording of some of the music we were playing on the tour.' Silence. 'But, I don't know ...'

What didn't he know? Didn't know what to say? Out of the window she could see the geese, high up in the sky.

'Would you like to come down all the same? It would be great to see you,' he said then. Did he really mean that? Why couldn't he say that he'd missed her, that he loved her, that he couldn't live without her, that there was no Agnieska, no Tanya, no Katia, no wild Transylvanian woman that would ever supplant her?

'I'm not sure when I'll be free,' she said, 'I think there's something happening this week end and maybe next.' I

230

haven't been twiddling my thumbs and staring into the fire for the last six months while you've been away. 'Look, I'll phone you back.'

She went out into the garden, just in time to see the deer departing up the hillside. Where were all the tulip and cianadox bulbs she'd laboured to plant last October? Surely there should be signs of them emerging from their winter sleep, or had the deer eaten them all? Thierry had had no difficulty in saying that he loved her. He'd been ready to devote his life to her. As long as she fitted in with the rest of it, with his work and his friends, of course.

But was it fair to be expecting Fergus to say *I love you* when she'd never actually ever used the words herself to him? She remembered the thrush and started to dig a hole for it, with Trotsky lying on the grass looking on.

She'd all the same shown in many other ways that she cared for him. Surely he knew that she cared for him, so why had he gone off like that without a by-your-leave? She remembered her decision after he'd gone, to close the door on their relationship. And that's what she'd done, more or less, sort of, by encouraging Thierry.

So why had she started opening the door again? It should be kept closed. They were no longer the piece of music in two part harmony, coming together, parting, then coming together again. They'd become two separate pieces and it was better like that, she was better on her own. She went inside to get the thrush. Later on she would phone him back.

'Fergus, I think now is the time to end this.'

That evening as she poured herself a glass of wine and moved slowly round the room to the sounds of *Massive Attack* the phone rang again.

'Hi, Tess.'

'Oh Fergus, I was going to phone you.'

'Were you?' He sounded pleased. 'I meant to tell you when I phoned you this afternoon, while we were away, during the day we had quite a lot of time to ourselves when we weren't rehearsing. So I started composing this thing - quite a long piece actually - for solo cello. I don't know what you'll think of it but it's for you, I mean it's about you and I composed it for you. It's sort of finished except maybe the end bit I'm not very happy about. But I'll play it for you when you come down.' Pause. 'Do you know when that will be yet? Tess, are you still there?'

'Yes, I'm here.'

'You're really not free this coming week end?'

'Well maybe I could be. Yes, maybe I could be...'

She put down the phone. A piece of music especially for her, and she, what had she done for him while he'd been away? She pushed aside the recipe for Aunt Nellie's pudding, took a blank sheet of paper and at the top, in large letters, wrote *Recipe for Love*. Or should that be *Lust*?

Lightning Source UK Ltd.
Milton Keynes UK
24 March 2010

9 781849 237840